SCHOOL OF SLEUTHS

Happy Sleuthing!

Happy
Sledding!

SCHOOL OF SLEUTHS

MATT J. AIKEN

BOOKLOGIX®
Alpharetta, Georgia

ISBN: 978-1-6653-0646-1 - Paperback
eISBN: 978-1-6653-0647-8 - ePub

Library of Congress Control Number: 2023916086

☉This paper meets the requirements of ANSI/NISO Z39.48-1992 (Permanence of Paper)

090623

For the kids who think they're weird
and the kids who think they're alone.
Good news: You are weird.
Better news: You are not alone.

PROLOGUE
(If you guys allow that sort of thing.)

BRIGHAM

It all started with a broken nose.

Or, technically, a deviated septum.

And that septum belonged to my best friend, Marshall Fairbanks.

Really, I feel bad writing this, but his septum deviation was pretty much the best thing that ever happened to us.

It was a real game-changer. I mean that literally, because after the attack, we stopped spending every waking hour playing Founders of Framptonworth, an awesomely time-consuming table-top role-playing adventure board game and focused our full brain powers on something better.

Something worthwhile.

Something real.

Something that allowed me to actually get a tan at some point.

I mean, a farmer's tan. But still a tan.

And that was solving the mystery of Marshall's poor broken face.

Yes, it was because of that poor broken face, and that poor deviated septum, that we became . . . **BrainForce**.

Copyright pending.

MALCOLM

BrainForce?

Did Brigham call us BrainForce?

That is the dorkiest name for a high school-based detective unit I can think of.

It sounds like our superpower is the ability to withstand atomic wedgies in a single bound.

We can't, by the way. Wedgies still hurt.

They hurt so much, I once went to urgent care for one.

But Brigham is right about one thing.

Marshall's face getting broken was an ultimately wondrous event.

Marshall doesn't like it when we say that but c'mon. He knows it. We know it.

We went from spending all our weekends in my mom's basement to fighting actual crime!

Catching the crooks!

Hunting down the bad guys!

I mean, still mostly in my mom's basement. But it was at least a lot cooler than anything having to do with Framptonworth.

It is the best of table-top RPGs, and it is the worst of table-top RPGs.

Did Brigham tell you that the lead jester of Framptonworth is required to wear a velvet cape and shiny buckle shoes for the duration of a game? Did he tell you that a standard game lasts ten to seventeen *days*? With breaks for meals, sleep, school, and religious holidays? Did he tell you that because of that rule, I went to gym class wearing shiny buckle shoes from mid-September to early October?

People at James E. Carter High School still call me Buckle Shoes Boy.

People at James E. Carter High School are not very creative.

But that was life pre-mugging. Post-mugging, you can switch out the wizard capes and buckle shoes and replace them with crime-fighting tools. Blueprints of buildings. Police sketches. A dry-erase board with the names of our top suspects, like we're New York City cops or something.

And a stakeout.

Yes.

A real-life stakeout.

Somebody even brought donuts to it.

Marshall's poor smashed face made all that possible.

Because Marshall's poor smashed face gave birth to, are you ready for it? . . . The Academics.

We are a highly educated, super brain-powered team of deep thinkers and modern-day scholars.

We are . . . **The Academics.**

BRIGHAM

We are not The Academics.

That completely sounds like a group of forty-year-olds smoking pipes, wearing jackets with patches on their elbows, and discussing James Joyce in a room full of ceiling-to-floor bookshelves.

Also, I would think one of us would have to wear a monocle.

Malcolm's brother Martin used to have a lazy eye that sometimes required a patch but no . . . no monocle.

And not all of us are all-brains-and-no-brawn. Some of us actually know karate, you know?

Self-taught. YouTube.

If backed into a corner, we can fight.

So, if BrainForce is too nerdy, how about this?

From now on, we shall be known as . . . **Hero Squad.**

TM.

QUINN

Hero Squad? BrainForce?

We can't live up to that.

Brigham says he knows karate, right? Did he tell you he's self-taught? YouTube?

The only black belts he owns are the ones his mom bought for him at Costco in a three-pack.

You know what my greatest superpower is?

Cross-stitching.

It's my thing.

But not in an ironic hipster kind of way.

I really, really like it.

Heroes do not cross-stitch.

Heroes are popular.

We are not popular.

Heroes are cool.
We are not cool.
We stay out of the spotlight; we remain in the shadows.
We are . . . **the Shadow Guild**.
That's the name.

THE SHADOW GUILD

BY QUINN CARSWELL & FRIENDS

QUINN

See?

MARSHALL

Um, Shadow Guild is not the name. I see how you could be confused there. I know we're not supposed to look at each other's notebooks right now, but I could spot that title-page forgery from across the room.

Though, really, I wouldn't be too surprised if we do eventually go with it anyways.

Why?

Because Quinn came up with it.

And what Quinn says goes.

Because Quinn . . . is a girl.

Not just a girl, but a girl who hangs out with, um . . . us.

Completely voluntarily.

That's the equivalent of Hermione completely voluntarily hanging out with a bunch of Hobbits. Or house elves, so I'm not mixing my nerd-lore.

It's like she has magical powers.

Magical powers of not being a boy.

She's also beautiful.

Even if she wasn't, we'd still all love her.

But she is. And that's almost not fair.

She isn't going to read this, right?

She also smells like mint and strawberries.

Really, honestly, she is not to read this.

Anyways, since this is all about me, shouldn't I be the one to name this project?

After all, it's about my face.

My sad, broken face that changed the world, right?

I just had to be at the wrong place, at the wrong time.

And, man, I was.

So, I suppose I should take it from here.

Because it all starts with my face.

CHAPTER ONE

TROUBLE ON C-WING

MARSHALL

My mom has always said I have a nice face. But that's what moms are supposed to say, right?

She seemed sincere though and I never really had a problem with it. Besides the occasional acne breakout, it seems to be pretty symmetrical, and does all the functional jobs of a face.

Or, I mean, it *was* symmetrical.

Now my nose bends slightly to the left at the bottom and slightly to the right at the top. It's kind of . . . smashed looking. Think Owen Wilson without the good hair and the Wes Anderson-indie-cred.

The other guys, Malcolm, Brigham, and Quinn, think they know what it was like, but they don't.

They don't know the fear.

The terror.

The numb pain.

The much-less-numb pain that came after that.

They don't know . . . the mucus.

There was a lot of it.

Oh man, the mucus.

So. Much. Mucus.

Tell me if this is too much information, but for some reason, it was bright neon-green. And I'm not sure where that came from.

Have I been storing a deposit of bright neon-green mucus in my nasal cavities for years for just such an emergency?

I'm sure that's not scientifically sound but that exact thought actually flashed through my head as I stared at a smear of it on the linoleum floor of C-Wing that night.

The night began mucus free.

It was just after nine p.m., and I was at school by myself. At this point, my face was unbroken.

Most kids don't go to school at nine p.m. but then most kids aren't junior star students.

Maybe they aren't on purpose.

But it's a little-known fact that when you're named junior star student, you get a key to the school for after-hours research projects.

Absolutely no one's jealous of this at all. Unless they're the type of student that would actually *want* to be the junior star student. At Carter High, that's me and maybe seven people. You've already met three of them.

But, believe it or not, it's usually pretty great.

For starters, I know all the janitors.

There's Doug. He's juggling two jobs and two girlfriends.

There's Ms. Moreland. She smokes like a chimney and is so addicted to nicotine that I once saw her smoke a cigarette while she was already smoking another cigarette.

And there's Winky Jeff.

Also known as Creepy Jeff.

I think Winky Jeff is misunderstood. He's less of a creepy pervert and more of a friendly pervert.

He just really needs to stop winking whenever he's near the girls' locker room and/or volleyball practice.

Anyways, I wasn't working on anything specific at school that night. Just tooling around in the lab and fixing a broken cell phone for what the cool kids would probably call a "side hustle."

I was done pretty quickly so I started to mess around with a Bunsen burner and I kind of went into a zone. That nice, relaxing, no-thought zone that I can't exactly achieve at home.

I remember staring at the flame and holding a yellow number two pencil directly over it. It was turning brownish, then greenish, then a strange combination of both, when Ms. Moreland stuck her head in the door.

"You cure cancer yet?" she said.

I jumped.

"Wha? No. Not yet. I might have a shot at polio, but they've already cured that."

She let out a raspy laugh.

"Don't worry, hon. You'll get there."

She gave me a friendly gap-toothed smile.

"I'm gonna pop outside and have a smoke. Yell if you need anything, okay?"

She disappeared and I added another pencil to the fire.

So, why was I at school during prime non-learning hours on a Thursday night?

Three words.

Mom's new boyfriend.

Three cliched words, I know, but the guy is awful. His name is Ted. He has a tribal arm-band tattoo and he's from Tampa. What tribes are there in Tampa?

Mom works late on Thursdays. The gang—um, the fine people you know as The Shadow Guild or Nerd Force or whatever—were all busy.

So it was school or Tribal Ted.

It was a no-brainer.

I didn't mind really.

There's something soothing about the still silence of school at night. The old, sprawling building.

It's cool and calm and echoey.

During the day, it's a stress-ball-in-my-stomach-inducing place.

But at night, the building is my friend.

Or was.

Until I heard the clatter.

It was something metallic bouncing off the linoleum floor, sounding just unusual enough to require investigation.

I wish I hadn't investigated.

I think about that a lot.

What if I had just stayed in the lab and kept staring into the flame?

My nose would probably be straight and completely un-smashed.

But Ms. Moreland had slipped on her own mop water a few weeks back and I thought we might be facing another fallen-and-I-can't-get-up situation.

I shouted her name as I walked down the dimly lit corridor of C-Wing.

She didn't answer.

Then I heard the soft squeaky sounds of sneakers on linoleum.

I stopped.

The fluorescents were flickering frantically.

Of all the school wings, C-Wing is definitely the most, um, "old-school."

Think Hogwarts. But with more dirty words written in permanent marker on the walls.

And without the wonderful witchcraft and wizardry.

And an increased chance of tetanus.

I heard another clatter and turned the corner, and there he was.

He was at the end of the hallway.

The stillness of him is what I remember most.

I didn't catch him midstride or walking away.

He was just standing and looking at me.

As if he'd always known I'd be there.

Silent.

Perfectly silhouetted in the dead center of the hallway.

My first thought, and this is a stupid thought, was that he was some sort of department store mannequin.

I stared.

He stared.

I stared some more.

He stared some more.

I felt like I should say something. Sure, he was giving off a distinct Michael Myers vibe, but I didn't want to be rude.

"Hey!" I said.

My voice echoed off the walls and I jumped.

No reply.

"School's closed," I continued. I'm not sure why I said that. I'm not on the payroll at this place. It just seemed as though I should relay the message. Being helpful, you know?

Still nothing.

And then he ran.

Directly at me.

He ran fast.

One moment he was cardboard-cutout still, the next he was in a dead sprint. It happened so fast, it was like frames were missing from an old movie.

I'm not sure exactly how long it took my legs to run in the other direction but, thinking back, it seems comically delayed. Like one of those cartoon characters that runs off a cliff and looks around before plummeting to the ground.

By the time my brain told my legs to run, he was within striking distance.

And, man, did he strike.

BRIGHAM

I know it was bad.

All nose jokes aside, I know it.

And I know because Marshall has never said it was bad.

My buddy Marsh is quick to complain.

He complains about girls. He complains about slow Wi-Fi. He complains about the line at Taco Bell. He complains about the nonsensical series finale of *Battlestar Galactica*. Which is valid.

But not this.

He has never complained about this.

It's as though, by admitting how bad it was, he'd unlock some kind of reservoir of fear he's keeping locked inside.

I know the feeling.

I've taken a couple of blows before.

Remember, I know karate.

And I have five brothers.

And my dad, before he left, was not a good guy.

But this was different.

Something happened to Marshall that night that made him want to scream. And he still hasn't let that scream out.

MARSHALL

No, I didn't scream.

There was no time for screaming really.

Only time to get caught.

It was run.

Get caught.

Take the hits.

Hit.

Hit.

Hit.

Hard fists hit soft cartilage. *My* soft cartilage.

My face bent in ways I never thought it would or should.

I fell to the ground.

And I bled.

Man, did I bleed.

Mostly all from my nose.

As well as the aforementioned neon-green mucus.

Then the man was gone.

For a while, I didn't move. Not one bit. I didn't want to get up and face the reality of what had just happened to me. So, I just blinked and stared and looked at a locker with my head pressed against the cool floor.

It was locker 178.

Ms. Moreland found me in a big, bloody mess and let out a scream that sounded like a froggy croak.

She wrapped me in a stanky towel and sat with me until the

police came. Then Tribal Ted showed up and took me to urgent care.

He seemed really excited about it all.

He kept talking about the time he broke his nose during football practice and the coach told him to shove some Arby's napkins "all up in there."

Like I said, Mom was at work. My options were limited.

Speaking of football, my nose swelled up to the size of one.

And now, I'm a poor man's Owen Wilson.

So, yeah, everybody's right.

It was great.

It was wondrous.

It was the best thing that ever happened to anyone.

Except, of course, me.

QUINN

Poor Marshall.

When I heard about his face I started cross-stitching.

Feverishly.

This is what I do when I'm upset.

Or when I'm happy.

Or when I'm sad.

Or hungry.

Or anything, really. I like to cross-stitch, okay?

But in this case, I was cross-stitching with a purpose.

I was cross-stitching for poor Marshall and his broken face.

And so, by the time he was back in school, I was able to present him with a framed 8 x 12 stitching of Luke Skywalker from *Empire Strikes Back*.

He was staring up in horror at Darth Vader and screaming, "Sorry about your nooooooose!"

It was a masterpiece.

My Mona Lisa.

Poor Marshall.

He started to tear up when he saw it.

MARSHALL

I started to tear up when I saw it.

Not because I was moved to tears, but because my tear ducts were leaking. That's not me trying to be macho. My face had been constantly physically leaking since the face attack.

Not that I wasn't moved either. It was an awesome cross-stitch and even more awesome considering who it came from.

She's just so great, right?

And so pretty.

I think I mentioned before she smells like strawberries, but now I think it may be more like raspberries. Again, she is not to read this.

Agreed?

So, in the days that followed the big face attack of Carter High, we hit the RPG streets of Framptonworth hard.

It was our instinct in a time of crisis.

Quinn. Malcolm. Brigham. Even Malcolm's too-cool-for-Hyrule older brother Martin.

We huddled around the chipped wooden coffee table in Malcolm's mom's basement as though it was our only source of warmth in this cruel, cold world.

It was obvious we were all slightly traumatized.

Except for Martin.

"You guys are such losers," he said just before he rolled a perfect fifty-seven on the Crown Dice.

"Then why are you hanging out with us?" said Malcolm nonchalantly. We were all used to this kind of treatment from his brother.

"Because I'm grounded. No cell. No tablet. No laptop. No . . . anything with a USB port. And you losers and your lame game are just one step above reading an actual paper book with paper pages and words in it."

Then the dice roll.

"FIFTY-SEVEN ON THE CROWN DICE! SUCK ON THAT LOSERS!"

"Son of a . . ." Brigham trailed off and began to scribble furiously on his notepad. "That gives you Jasper Manor and Fielddale Foundry. How can someone who cares so little for life in Framptonworth be so good at this?"

"Because I am, chumps," Martin grinned, leaned back, and counted his shillings. "I just am."

"And also, because you spend half the night watching online Frampton tutorials," said Malcolm.

"Well, only because it's so fun to beat your face!" said Martin.

I must have flinched.

"Oh, um, sorry, Marshall," he said. "You know I know karate, right? I can teach you something called Lightning Strike. Nobody will mess with you after that, bro."

"Wait," said Brigham. "You subscribe to Master Kensei's YouTube Channel too?"

This was the night that I tried to thank Quinn for her cross-stitching.

Technically I already had thanked her at school. But it wasn't *thankful* enough, you know?

When she gave me her awesome Lucasfilm-inspired artwork I sniffed out something that sounded like, "thankssnortsniff."

That's a direct quote.

Then my nose bled.

Not a lot. But enough where I had to run to find the nearest tissue.

By the time I made my way back, study hall was over, and she hurried on to AP calculus.

When everybody had cleared out of the basement, I motioned to her. It was a goofy gesture that made me feel like a beckoning yard gnome. So, I waved both of my arms and now I felt as though I was helping someone park a moving van.

"What are you doing?" asked Quinn from the other side of the room. "Waving in a jetliner?"

"No," I said. "Just . . . you."

I looked into her eyes. It's hard to look into her eyes but also too easy.

I'm afraid if I do, she'll see too much. My hopes. My dreams. My plans to one day propose to her on top of the Eiffel Tower and ride to our own Hobbit hole for a life of bliss and second breakfasts. That. All that.

"I wanted to say thank you."

"You're welcome," she said. "For what."

"You know," I said. "The cross-stitch."

"Ah, shucks, you already thanked me." She tucked a blondish strand of hair behind her ear and gave me a playful kick on the shin, not knowing that was the best thing that had ever happened to me.

I swallowed much too loudly.

"I know, but I didn't really *thank-you* thank you."

"What's a *thank-you* thank you?

"You know, like a . . . double thank you."

"Ah," she said. "Well, you're welcome, you're welcome."

We both snort-laughed. It's a thing we do, which made us laugh some more. Forget the Eiffel Tower, if I had a ring on hand I would have proposed at that moment. International flights are expensive anyway, right?

"I mean," I said. "I just wanted you to know that it was awesome. It was just what I needed. Besides a new septum."

She was staring at me now.

Oh, man. She was staring.

Her eyes honed in on me like beautiful deadly lasers.

Was she seeing too much? Did she know? I began to babble.

"This whole thing has been pretty tough, and it was, it was just perfect. And when I look at it—it just kind of warms my, well, my—"

"Blood," said Quinn.

"Um, I was gonna say heart, but sure, blood too. Always good to have warm blood in your—"

"No, blood! Nose!"

I reached for my face and sure enough . . . blood.

Nose.

"Anywaythankssnortsniff!" I yelled as I fled the room and dove for the nearest tissue box.

From the upstairs, I heard Martin cackling and saying something about shoving some Taco Bell napkins "all up in there."

MARSHALL

That night I had The Nightmare.

Yes, I capitalize it now.

It's pretty much the same thing every night.

I'm in C-Wing.

It's bright and bustling and Quinn is there.

So are Malcolm and Brigham.

Then everyone disappears.

And I'm alone. I look down the hallway and my attacker is there.

Standing.

Staring.

Waiting.

Except this attacker is different.

Because this attacker has a horse's head.

No, not just a horse's head.

A unicorn's head.

Not a magical-looking unicorn either. A dead-looking one. Like a zombie, with glassy eyes and a frothy foaming mouth.

I try to scream but can't make a sound.

He puts his head down and charges.

Naturally, I turn to run, but nothing happens. I go nowhere. My legs are rooted to the ground.

I look down at my feet. I look up. And he's there, breathing on me with horsey breath, staring right through me with dead, giant horse eyes. And then he lowers his head and that's when I know . . . he's about to shove his horn straight through my stomach. And there's nothing I can do about it.

That's when I wake up.

Sometimes screaming.

Sometimes not.

Okay, all the time screaming.

QUINN

I could tell something was bugging Marshall when he trudged into Coach Craig's study hall alongside a chattering Malcolm that October morning.

Whatever it was, it was about to get worse.

"Hey, nerds," said Coach Craig as they filed in.

"Hey, Teacher," said Malcolm, throwing up air quotes around "teacher."

Coach Craig responded with a gesture that wasn't air quotes.

"Inspiring," said Malcolm. "You're really my favorite educator."

"Thank you, Buckle Shoes," said Coach.

It feels strange to call Coach Craig . . . "Coach Craig," because one year ago he was just Craig.

Craig Connerly.

Otherwise known as Craig the Concusser: star defensive back or tight end or wide receiver or whatever for the Carter Cougars.

Phssh.

Sports games.

Whatever.

Color me not impressed.

And neither were the community colleges or trade schools of nearby greater Atlanta, because once Craig the Concusser graduated, he did not pass go, he did not collect $200—he just grabbed his diploma and headed right back in line to start the next school year, this time as a coaching assistant for the Carter Cougars football team.

Which means he went from giving wedgies to the underclassman to inspiring the young minds of those same underclassman.

Ha ha. Just kidding.

Our minds remained uninspired and I'm pretty sure he'd still give all of us wedgies if he had the chance.

"Hey, Marshall," said Craig. "Does your face still hurt, kiddo?"

We simultaneously froze before taking our seats in the front row.

Was Coach Craig actually concerned? Was that a sense of actual humanness I detected in his voice?

Marshall seemed equally puzzled. His brow furrowed and tendrils of curly hair fell across his forehead. It was exceedingly cute.

Don't tell him I said that.

"Um, it feels better actually," he replied. "Thanks for asking."

"Are you sure?" Coach Craig grimaced. "Because it hurts to look at!"

Marshall shook his head and sunk into his seat.

Malcolm slow-clapped.

"And to think, my stepdad wants to send me to a private school."

He leaned toward Marshall.

"C'mon, man, you have to step livelier than that. Coach Craig is king of the dad jokes."

Coach Craig snorted. "That's because I am your dad, Buckle Shoes." He shifted his gaze to Marshall. "No, really though. While you were off getting your nose job, I've been waiting for a certain something that I have already paid you straight cash for."

Marshall sat up in his desk chair. "Your phone! I completely forgot! It's still in the chem lab."

"Well," said Craig. "What are you waiting for?"

"Can I get a hall pass?"

"Hall pass away," said Coach Craig as he handed Marshall a toilet seat with a wooden block attached to it.

It was his idea of a hilarious joke.

"Enjoy your dookie!" he said with a guffaw.

Coach Craig really is the worst.

MARSHALL

Coach Craig really is the worst.

But he pays well. And he's always dropping his cell phone. Which means he's a steady stream of revenue for my side business.

It's child's play, really.

The thing is iPhones are easy to fix once you have the right tool. That's the trick. Steve Jobs didn't want just anybody cracking open his creation, so one must possess a hard-to-find Five-Point Pentalobe Screwdriver to get inside.

I have three.

And so, for the low, low price of seventy-five dollars, I will fix up your smashed cell in twenty-four hours or your money back.

It usually takes all of five minutes.

But in this case, it had taken two weeks of face recovery.

And it looked like I was out seventy-five dollars.

Mrs. Ricardo's chem class was in session when I knocked as softly as possible on the door of Room 126. When I opened it, she raised her painted-on eyebrows.

"Coach Craig sent me to get something out of the storage lockers," I said.

"Go then," she said.

I went.

Mrs. Ricardo is not one of those I'm-Your-Teacher-But-Also-Your-Friend teachers. She's old school. And old.

I think you might even call her a "School Marm."

Everyone seemed to be preoccupied with a pop quiz, which was good because Greg Garland was in that class and he likes to call me by my more popular name, Nerd Pants.

Why?

Because I'm a nerd, I guess? And I wear pants, I guess?

I think that's the whole backstory on that one.

Really, I'm telling you, most of the kids at this school need a creative writing course or something.

Anyway, there's a wall full of puke-ish green lockers at the back of the chem lab that no one uses, and that's where I stored Coach Craig's cell phone right before I ventured down the hall and directly into my face beating.

Except, only, it wasn't there.

I opened the locker, and the cell was gone.

But there was something else.

A smear of dark dried blood on the metal.

And mixed with it, a dried streak of mucus.

Noticeably neon.

BRIGHAM

Of course we heard about Marshall and the snot.

Everybody did.

It traveled via text messages, TikTok, and audible laughter straight from Mrs. Ricardo's room to our study hall before he even returned with the toilet seat.

Better let him tell you how it went.

MARSHALL

"That's my snot!" I yelled.

I actually yelled that.

That's. My. Snot.

That's what I said in the middle of Mrs. Ricardo's calm, quiet chem class.

And then . . . uproar.

The laughter was loud and long and came from all directions.

"You keep your snot in a locker?!" yelled professional jock Caleb Poole.

"What kind of experiments you got going on back there?" shouted semi-professional hipster Marisa Carson.

And then there was Greg Garland.

Oh, Greg Garland.

He dropped his quiz, stood up, and wound up for what I could tell was going to be a master class in insult comedy.

"Maybe your Nerd Pants left the snot in there!"

See?

That made absolutely no sense. But I was too stunned to tell him.

The bag was gone.

The blood and dried snot were there.

My blood.

My snot.

No phone.

So, the mugger attacked me and then went for my stuff with his blood/snot-covered hands?

That was terrifying. And also . . . *ew*, nasty.

I felt dizzy and I crouched down on the floor.

The laughter died down a bit as it appeared my fellow class-mates were concerned for my well-being. Maybe there is some good in the world.

Then, Greg Garland made a giant fart noise and the laughter shot to record levels.

Okay, maybe not.

As I sunk to the ground, a fellow underclassman I didn't really know leaned in from his chair. I think his name is Barrett. He has an abnormal amount of freckles on his face.

"Why do you keep your snot in a locker?" he asked, quieter than the others. "Is that healthy?"

I just shook my head.

"No, man," I said. "No, it's not."

Mrs. Ricardo was viciously shushing left and right. The line between silence and pure pandemonium is a thin one in high school and I had just given Chemistry 101 a firm push in the wrong direction.

"Mr. Fairbanks! Get your toilet seat! Get your snot! And get out of my class!"

I got out of there fast.

CHAPTER TWO

THE EMERGENCY FLARE

MARSHALL

I took my toilet seat.

I left my snot.

I kind of wandered back to class. One foot in front of the other.

I studied a bulletin board without really seeing it.

Hey, look, it's time to sign up for the pep rally banner committee . . .

I looked out the window at the gray wintery day. Well, technically it was a warm October day, but at that point, it sure didn't feel like it.

Then I stopped and stared at the water fountain for a while, gazing into the dull metal basin as though it held some hidden answers.

"You know how one of those works don't you?"

Kimberly Boyd from AV club was standing right over my shoulder.

We usually joke around but I wasn't up to it.

"Yep," I said and wandered off.

I think I offended her.

"I was being quippy!" she shouted after me. "That was a perfectly good quip, jerkface!"

"I'm quipless right now," I muttered, though I don't think she heard me.

Back in class, I walked past Coach Craig and said something about needing more time to fix his phone. He was messing around with a new Samsung-something so he didn't seem too concerned.

"Whatever," he snuffed. "Saves me seventy-five bucks."

"What's wrong?" said Quinn as I slid into my seat next to her. "You look like Haley Joel Osment."

I stared at her.

"What?"

"*Sixth Sense*? You see dead people?"

I shook my head.

"No dead people."

"Then what?" whispered Malcolm from a few seats over. "You constipated?

"No," I said. "Well, maybe a little, but no. We need to talk."

"About being constipated?" said Quinn.

"No, I can handle that on my own."

I looked at Malcolm.

"I'm calling an emergency meeting."

Malcolm literally licked his chops.

He knew what that meant.

We hadn't called one since eighth grade when it became apparent not a single one of us would be going to the Winterfest Snowball Dance.

We called the meeting. We plotted. We planned. It made no difference. No one went to the dance except for Malcolm.

He went with his mom.

Hopefully, this meeting will be more productive.

"I'll send up an emergency flare," he said. By that, he meant a group text message.

MARSHALL

"That. is. Awesome," said Malcolm.

We were in the basement, and I was breaking the news to them about my snot smear.

"What's awesome?"

"Your snot smear!"

"My snot smear is awesome?"

"Are you kidding me?! Of course your snot smear is awesome!"

Malcolm jumped up from one of the three battered recliners that count for furniture in his basement.

"It's a clue! The mugger targeted you for a reason and then left a clue! This is a mystery! A freaking *Murder, She Wrote* mystery!"

I did not share his enthusiasm.

I sunk into another recliner and started peeling off the faux leather.

"So, I was . . . *targeted*."

Quinn put a hand on my shoulder and a mild volt of electricity shot through my arm.

"Sorry, man. Looks like it."

"But why?" said Brigham. "For a crummy busted cell phone?"

"It was crummy. We're talking about an iPhone 5."

"A five?" said Malcolm. "Coach Carl might as well have been using a rotary telephone."

"Or one of those old-timey phones you had to crank" snorted Quinn.

"Like in Andy Griffith?" said Brigham.

I leaned forward and put my head against the back of a hard plastic chair that Martin had stolen from the school storage closet for some reason. It pushed against my forehead and helped dull my throbbing headache.

"Well, what was on the iPhone?" said Brigham. He was half studying his physics because he's always worried about the next test.

I can tell he's worried about me too.

"I'm not supposed to say. Code of the business. Anything I see is confidential."

Malcolm smirked. Quinn arched an eyebrow. Brigham went back to his physics.

"Eh? Did you snoop through the pics?" said Malcolm. "Something incriminating in there?"

I actually had. Now, don't look at me like that. Or, um, *the page* like that. It was more of a natural nosey thing, like looking through the medicine cabinet in a relative's bathroom. Nothing creepy about it.

"Um, yes," I said. "Nothing that interesting."

"You little cyber stalker!" said Quinn. "Remind me to delete my hidden pics if you ever fix my phone."

Brigham broke his pencil point.

I slowly pivoted in my plastic chair.

"What?" said Malcolm.

"Oh yeah, I've got tons of them," she grinned conspiratorially. "They're all handsome photos of Mark Hamill, but they're really artistic. I'll send you a few later today."

Malcolm looked ready to faint.

Quinn winked at me.

Some say this was when BrainForce/Nerd Squad/The Academics was born.

Brigham

And that was when BrainForce was born.

I wish I'd been paying more attention, really, but I was cramming for a physics exam.

Yes, it wasn't for three more weeks but a guy can't be too prepared, right?

For me, a test isn't just a test. It's one more step to graduation, which means one more step to a scholarship, which means one more step to a real job. Which means one more step to money. Which means one more step to not wearing clothes that didn't previously belong to one of my five older brothers.

Oh yeah.

I dream big.

A life of no hand-me-downs, no shared mattresses and all you can eat . . . food.

Don't get me wrong, we're not exactly dirt-poor. More like clean-poor.

My mom runs too tight of a ship for us Weaver kids to get dirty.

But she also juggles three jobs at last count.

My dad helps out too with a semiannual grocery check mailed from wherever he happens to be living that year.

Mom promptly burns it in a pot on the stove.

"If we're gonna make it, it's not going to be because of that man," she says.

I get it. It's the principle of the thing. But principles won't pay for a pair of pants that hasn't previously housed a total of five Weaver butts.

Also, I know I said I had five brothers, but actually, it's six.

Marshall is my brother too.

From another mother.

Sounds cheesy, but it's true.

We met in first grade.

I was wearing oversized hand-me-down overalls that made me look like a child farmer. He nobly refrained from pointing and laughing at me.

Marshall had a stutter that I ignored because I really didn't care.

I just wanted to play *Star Wars* and so did Marshall.

It was buds at first sight.

Together we formed a protective shield against the slings and arrows of our public school peers. During the years, as the arrows became pointier, our shield became stronger.

We expanded to include Malcolm in middle school when he moved from Cincinnati after his parents' divorce. He was the smallest kid in class and impatiently waiting on his growth spurt. Technically, I think he's still waiting. But soon after his arrival, the RPG years began. A heavy rotation of D&D and we were also knee-deep in Middle Earth for a while.

And then the impossible happened.

A girl.

Quinn arrived from Chicago about a year ago, during freshman year, and fell into our group like an angel descending from heaven.

She's like that really pretty girl in every teen '80s movie with glasses and a baggy sweater who would be obviously beautiful in real life but nobody notices for some reason until the end when she shows up with no glasses and a prom dress.

Except since this is real life, everybody notices right away.

She doesn't need a prom dress either.

I can see how Marshall fell in love with her.

I could too, of course.

On account of she's a girl.

And she has strong feelings about *Star Trek*. But I am betrothed to Katherine Underwood who doesn't quite know I exist. That's another story.

But the truth is I wouldn't want to mess up anything with me and my best buddy.

I need him a lot more than he needs me.

His stutter cleared up with speech therapy by fourth grade.

My poorness doesn't seem to be going anywhere anytime soon.

But hey, even if I was rich and he lived in a cardboard box we'd still be best buds.

We were BFFs before that was a thing people said.

MARSHALL

Did he call me his BFF?

Aw, the big sap.

But it's true.

He's the brother I never had. Especially when compared to my actual brother who I do have.

He's also valiantly refrained from going after Quinn in my honor.

He thinks I don't know this. He also thinks he doesn't stand a chance because of something about his clothes being too big.

That's ridiculous.

It pains me to say this, but Brigham is very handsome.

Yeah, that felt weird to say. But it's true. He's the only one in the group that doesn't seem to have noticed that his ridiculously square jawline distracts from the fact that he's wearing hand-me-down Wranglers.

Meanwhile, I've valiantly refrained from going after Quinn too because I'm terrified of messing everything up.

That's another story.

Anyway, it was after our basement meeting that I began to realize that my face-beating was popularly considered less of a disturbing act of violence and more of an exciting Encyclopedia Brown caper.

And no one was more excitable than Malcolm.

MALCOLM

It was so exciting.

I mean really, really exciting.

C'mon! A real-life mystery?

It was about time!

When I was in elementary school, I used to watch *Murder, She Wrote* with my Nana every day after school. And I'll say it, because I'm not afraid to say it. Angela Lansbury is a real American hero.

Her practical cleverness.

Her bravery in the face of danger.

Her sly wit.

Her . . . old-school typewriting skills.

Naturally, when I was eight years old, I assumed adulthood was just like her show. And as I grew older I expected that the mysteries would come rolling in much like they did for Angela's street-savvy character, Jessica Fletcher.

A jewel thief here.

A poisoning at a dinner party there.

A stabbing of a cruise director while I was vacationing in the Caribbean also there.

No, sir. No such luck.

In my sixteen years of life, the closest I've come to a real "caper" is the time somebody left a flaming bag of poo on our doorstep.

Spoiler alert. It was Martin. An inside job.

(I have no idea why he did that because my mom made him clean it up.)

But then this happens.

That dried snot smear launched us into a tailor-made caper for our crew.

Finally, we had an actual adventure as opposed to the made-up ones in Framptonworth.

So, of course it was exciting! The gang didn't see it that way at first.

With no suspects to go on, I started with our one and only witness. Marshall.

The game was afoot.

I know that's a Sherlock thing and not a *Murder, She Wrote* thing, but still.

It's afoot.

MARSHALL

Malcolm really thinks he's Angela Lansbury.

I don't know, maybe he is.

Add a string of pearls, a nice quilted shawl and maybe he could pull it off.

On Monday, he was mainly wearing an air of forced casualness as he slid in next to me at an extra credit study hall in the cafeteria.

"Hey, Marshall, whasuuup?" he said.

I said nothing because I was mid-decimal point.

"I said . . . whasuuuuuup."

"Trig," I said. "All trig, all the time."

"Yeah, I know."

He glanced at my paper.

"Did you carry the three?"

"What three?"

"I don't know—anyway, it's crazy about that phone isn't it?"

I said nothing.

"Crazy, crazy, cray-zeee."

My pencil point broke on problem fifteen.

"Yep, crazy," I searched through my book bag for another pencil. "There's no three here by the way, so I have nowhere to carry it to."

"Must have been a six, you have sloppy handwriting."

I scanned the problem. There was no six.

"So, when you were snooping on Coach Craig's phone, what exactly did you see?"

I shot him a back-off look and he threw up his hands.

"Not judging! Not judging! I mean, you have to familiarize yourself with the software right?"

"Sure, right."

"So what kind of pics? What kind of apps? What kind of contacts?"

I cursed and put down my pencil. I could tell he wasn't going anywhere. I hadn't seen him this excited since he acquired the master wand from a Roaming Framptonworth Troll Dragon.

"I don't know. The usual. Uber. Insta. Yelp. Facebook. Nothing strange."

He didn't like that answer.

"Pretty standard. Boring even."

"How about pics?"

Actually, there were some pics. But nothing special. Mostly sad. It looked like Coach Craig had been hanging out at Johnny B's a lot lately by himself. Lots of selfies with IPAs but no one in the bar with him. I think most of his friends left town after they graduated. It kind of made me feel sorry for him. I told Malcolm that.

"Never feel sorry for a grown man who still gives wedgies," he said. "Any other apps?"

"Well. It's probably nothing but . . ."

Malcolm leaned in.

"What?" he said. "What's nothing?"

"I mean, really nothing, but . . ."

"What's really nothing?!"

I shushed him.

"Quiet man, this is study hall!"

"Well we're studying unsolved crimes," whispered Malcolm.

"It's probably nothing . . . but . . . he had two calculator apps. The usual Apple app and then another one. I remember thinking that was strange because why would he need two calculators? Does he even know that math is a thing?"

A wide Grinch-like grin slid across Malcolm's face.

"Jackpot."

"Jackwhat?"

Malcolm held up a finger, pulled out his own phone, and began to scroll. He paused for effect and then stuck the screen directly in my face.

"Did it look like this?"

He pointed to an icon that said "Digital Calculator."

It actually did.

I remember it looking kind of cheaply designed and spam-ish.

I nodded.

He silently fist-pumped and put his hand up for a high five.

I left him hanging.

"Maybe Coach Craig just really likes math," I said, knowing full well how dumb that sounded.

Malcolm let out a sharp donkey laugh that earned us a shushing from Mrs. Barton. She was looking at us now. We were about to get in trouble. Did I mention I don't like to get in trouble?

I hunched low over my homework.

"Okay, but what does a back-up calculator app have to do with my face beating?"

"Well . . . this."

In a blur of tapping, Malcolm typed 19+77 and then hit the equal sign.

The phone emitted a gong-like *bong* and the calculator app screen split into two like a curtain.

Behind that curtain was a familiar space princess wearing a metal bikini.

"I give you Slave Leia," he said proudly.

I looked at Leia. Then I looked at him. Then I looked at Leia again.

"From Episode VI??"

Of course I knew this. But . . . why?

"It's a trick calculator! A spy calculator! A password-protected app designed to hide secret pictures and videos and all that stuff."

I had to admit, it was kind of cool.

"And you hide Slave Princess Leia on yours?"

"Slave Princess. Empire Princess. Cinnamon Bun Princess. Hot stuff."

"Um, but you know about the internet right? There's . . . hotter stuff there."

Malcolm stiffened.

"Please. I'm a man of standards. I prefer the classics. And also, my mom would kill me if she ever found anything dirtier than a Victoria's Secret catalog in my browser history."

Understood.

"So, why is this such a big deal, Mrs. Lansbury?"

He beamed.

"You act like that's an insult . . . It's a big deal because Coach Craig has something to hide on his cell phone."

"Maybe he doesn't want his mom to find his Princess Leia pictures," I said.

Malcolm ignored this.

"That cell phone was stolen. In fact, someone wanted that cell phone so badly, they were willing to smash your poor face to get it . . ."

Visions of neon snot flashed before my eyes.

Malcolm seemed to notice.

He patted me on the back.

"Sorry, bud."

Then he launched ahead undeterred.

"Sooo, if it's a cell phone worth stealing, whatever is hidden on that cell phone must be worth stealing too."

I stared at the desk for a moment while Malcolm fiddled with his princess pics.

"Didn't you say the attacker was just standing there?" said Malcolm. "Almost as if he was waiting for you?"

I nodded. Not liking one bit where this was going.

"Well, maybe he was. Maybe he was waiting for you. Personally."

My body gave an involuntary shudder.

"Man, I hope not."

And I really, really hoped not. Because I still hadn't told them about the worst part.

The strangest part. The most terrifying part.

It was the reason why I still slept with the lights on. Heck, it was the reason I hadn't slept more than thirty minutes straight since the attack.

I hadn't told them about the unicorn.

Malcolm cheerfully blabbed on for the remainder of study hall.

Something about how all we needed to do now was access the Cloud, hack into Coach Craig's backup accounts, and other things that sounded highly illegal and likely to land us in a juvenile detention center.

I barely heard a word of it.

I just thought about the silhouette on C-Wing.

And how monsters are real.

QUINN

Shadow Guild Meeting Number Two marked the big debut of The Board. (Later dubbed The Crazy Board by Brigham.)

Introduced by a so-excited-it-was-apparent-he-was-going-to-pass-out-on-the-floor Malcolm, it was a floor-to-ceiling scrap of drywall with a bunch of tacks in it.

"Friends, family, countrymen . . ." He looked at me. "And country woman, I give you: The Board. Capitol T, Capital B. The Board."

He beamed proudly at us as though he expected the group to break out into a standing ovation.

"Speaking of bored," said Martin. He popped up from a bean-bag chair, made an unnecessary obscene gesture mixed with a fart noise, and headed up the stairs.

No one noticed. This is how he leaves the room all the time. Every room.

"Awesome," said Brigham as he nodded to the drywall. "So, you planning on doing some renovations?"

"Oooh, good idea," said Marshall. "This wood paneling is in need of a little updating. Maybe throw in a few curtains and throw pillows . . ."

Malcolm shook his head seriously.

"This has nothing to do with home decor. It's about crime fighting. And also wood paneling never goes out of style."

He struggled to secure the board to the wall as we looked on.

"This is an essential crime-fighting tool for us at Academics HQ," he said with a grunt.

"Shadow Guild HQ," I said.

"Whatever," said Malcolm. "Whatever we are. We are awesome."

He turned and looked at the blank board as though he had just hung the Mona Lisa.

"Every good mystery-solving team needs a board," he said. "One with tacks, mug shots, lists of things, maps, personality profiles, papers with coffee stains on them, all preferably connected by strands of bright red yarn."

"Ohh, I've got the yarn!" I said.

Marshall smirked and gave me a *you too?* kind of look.

I shrugged.

"Well, I do."

And I do. I have all kinds of yarn. For times when the cross-stitching is just too intense, I like to calm down with a nice round of knitting.

Did I mention I'm a dork?

Well, I am.

CHAPTER THREE

THE CRAZY BOARD

QUINN

Malcolm repeated the details that he'd already repeated once in the lunchroom and twice after school. Except this time, he had props.

"This . . ." he said as he held up a printed copy of Coach Craig's staff photo, "is Coach Craig Connerly."

"Oh," said Brigham. "I thought he looked familiar."

"Coach Craig Connerly is what we in the sleuthing business call *a person of interest.*"

Malcolm pulled out a red Sharpie and scribbled "A Person of Interest" across Coach Craig's forehead and then pinned it in the center of the board.

"Should I be taking notes here?" said Brigham.

"Probably," said Malcolm.

Brigham nodded and pretended to scribble on his Trig homework.

"Is that Connerly with a *Y* or two *E*'s . . . or a silent *Q*?"

"It's Connerly with a 'please shut your face,'" said Malcolm calmly.

Brigham slapped a hand over his mouth and gasped.

Marshall leaned over and pointed to his notebook. "That's 'shut your face' with a S-H-U-T . . ."

They laughed. We laughed. This went on for a while. Malcolm persevered.

"And this person of interest is a person of interest . . . because of Exhibit A . . ."

He pulled out another printed picture of an iPhone and held it aloft like Simba on Pride Rock.

"Since his cell phone was stolen, Coach Craig must have some kind of connection to the crook. Do you have that yarn now?"

"Yeah, I'm looking," I said as I rummaged through my cross-stitch bag.

Yes, I travel with a cross-stitch bag. It's big and wonderful and I call it my Magic Bag.

I know. Dork. We've been over this.

And, really, I had to admit that I was becoming supremely intrigued by Malcolm's presentation.

"He does have a point," I said as I dug past a spare collapsible knitting needle and into the bowels of the bag.

Marshall and Brigham looked my way all incredulous-like.

"Well, I mean who would break into a school? There's no money there. Nothing worth that much. Maybe some old, janky, broken-down iMacs in the computer lab? But he or she didn't take that. Just one specific cell phone, hidden in a very specific spot. So, they had to know Coach Craig had given it to you. How?"

"Whoa, hold up, hold up now," Marshall raised his hand. "Did you say 'she'?" As in girl-she?"

"Um, yeah, I was trying to be all-inclusive."

"Yeah, it could have been a girl," said Malcolm judiciously. "A big strong girl."

"No, no," said Marshall. "If we're going to play detective games we have to establish one thing. The dude who broke my face was a dude. A big dude."

He looked from Malcolm to Brigham to me.

"Big dude. Can we write that on the board?"

Malcolm uncorked the Sharpie again and wrote "A Big Dude" on a white piece of paper. He slapped it on the board.

Marshall leaned back in his chair and crossed his arms looking equal parts ruffled and equal parts satisfied.

It was cute.

"Ahem, sorry about that," I said. "So, when this *big dude* broke into the school he was looking for Coach Craig's cell phone. And he was roughly the size of Dwayne "The Rock" Johnson. Good?"

"Yes, good."

Brigham chimed in.

"And this hulking manly man knew Marshall had his phone how?"

"How indeed!" said Malcolm and I couldn't help but imagine him in a shawl.

"I suggest that the answer lies on the phone itself!"

He turned to me.

"Find that yarn yet?!"

I jumped back into the bag, grabbed the nearest spool, and pulled it out.

"Will purple do?"

"Purple?!" Malcolm sighed. "Yeah, it'll do but it should really be red."

I tossed it to him and he got to work connecting Coach Craig's face to the cell phone.

"And so that means one thing," he said as he jabbed a new tack into Coach Craig's forehead. "It means we need to hack into his computer, access his account, and get our hands on those hidden files. And we need to do all of that in study hall."

This is where he lost everybody.

MALCOLM

That's where I lost everybody.

I kind of figured.

It sounds a lot worse than it is.

When you use the word "hack" it makes you sound like "a hacker" or something.

But I'm not talking about breaking into the dark web and hooking wires into the school mainframe and remotely accessing security footage from a moving van. Though that would be completely awesome.

I'm talking about information that's from the Cloud. Can you really hack a cloud?

"Yes," said Brigham. "Yes, you can definitely hack a cloud."

"Okay, but it's floating around in the air so it's not as bad," I assured him. "And it will be so easy! And it's a smart plan!"

He didn't look assured.

"So anyway, remember when Creepy Jeff the janitor AirDropped a selfie of himself wearing a kilt onto Courtney Carlyle's phone in gym class?"

"That's Winky Jeff," said Marshall defensively. "And he said that pic was from the Renaissance Fair."

Quinn nodded.

"Good point. A Renaissance selfie. Not at all creepy, go on."

"Well, it gave me an idea. Coach Craig had to have backed up his phone to his iTunes account. And we all know that he has his music on the class computer because we have to occasionally listen to early 2000s white-boy rock, right?"

Marshall shuddered.

"If I have to hear that Limp Bizkit song one more time."

Brigham looked queasy.

"Does this mean you're adding a picture of Fred Durst to The Board?" he said.

"Good suggestion, but no," I said. "But I like where your head's at."

"Ah," said Quinn. "So, if he's backed up his iTunes, he's also backed up his apps, so they should be sitting on his desktop right now."

"Poor Caveman Craig probably doesn't even know it," I said.

Marshall, ever skeptical, crossed his arms tightly and leaned back in his plastic chair.

"So, you think we should hack into his computer and AirDrop his files onto one of our own cell phones?"

"But his computer is password protected," said Brigham. "How do we get around that?"

"We don't get around it," I said. "Because he'll invite us in."

As I laid out the plan, entitled Operation AirDrop, I began to feel a little dizzy. First off because my blood sugar levels were low. I needed a sugar cookie. But more than that, because it was so darn exciting. The team. The plan. The mission. The Crazy Board. This was actually happening.

MARSHALL

"I can't believe this is actually happening," I said to Brigham as we hurried to third-period study hall. It was the period I've been dreading since that fateful meeting.

Brigham nodded grimly.

"I'm not sure how I got talked into this," I said as I stopped by his locker.

"I do," said Brigham. "It was the Katherine Underwood speech."

Of course.

"That really was a low blow."

When we balked at Malcolm's crazy plan that night, he brought up the name of Brigham's unrequited love since sixth grade. The beautiful Katherine Underwood. (Thankfully, he waited until Quinn left for this.)

"Remember that time you asked her out and she shot you down?" he said.

"No," said Brigham with as much dignity as he could muster. "She has never shot me down."

"Of course she didn't shoot you down! Because you never asked her out! You never took a chance!"

Ouch, man.

"Hey, take it easy tiger," I said.

Malcolm turned to me.

"Take it easy? Like you did with Amy Zellinger?"

"What?" I said. "That was in sixth grade!"

I kind of wanted to punch his face a little.

"I'm sorry," said Malcolm, perhaps sensing this. "But we all know that if you would have asked her to the Valentine's Dance, she would have said yes!"

"I was busy that night," I muttered.

"We played seven hours of Magic that night," said Malcolm.

"And it was fun," added Brigham.

"You're right, it was fun," said Malcolm. "It was fun because it was safe. And we like safe. And we always play it safe. Just like Marshall's playing it safe with the cross-stitching dream-girl goddess who hangs out with us in the basement every day! If you're not gonna ask her out, can I at least try?"

"Dude!"

I stood up and my plastic chair went clattering to the ground.

"It's true though!" said Malcolm.

"I'm . . . getting around to it," I said.

"I know you are. But it's scary. And I get that. We don't do anything that scares us. And so, we don't do anything. We are the most responsible teenagers of all time."

I couldn't argue there. I had a literal key to the school and no one was checking up on me to make sure I wasn't throwing keggers in the gymnasium on weekends.

"Brigham, what's your curfew?" said Malcolm.

"I don't have one," he said.

"I know you don't have one. Because you don't need one. Because everybody knows you're never going to do anything that will get you into trouble."

"Ugh, will you stop asking me rhetorical questions," he mumbled.

"Sorry again," said Malcolm. "But I'm trying to make a point here."

I raised my hand.

"Is the point that you're obnoxious?"

"No, that's just a footnote," said Malcolm.

We laughed.

"The point is somehow we missed the memo that being a teenager is doing stupid things! Things that we'll laugh about later on and write inside jokes about in our senior yearbooks. Being a teenager is supposed to be an adventure. All of our adventures are imaginary. All of our adventures are in our minds. Well, let's start adventuring out there! It's not like we're dealing drugs or smoking meth like the other kids are doing!"

"You think the other kids are smoking meth?" I said.

"Well, you know. The really bad ones are . . . But not us! We're just trying to solve a good ol' fashioned mystery. We're actually doing good here!"

"You seem really proud that we're not smoking meth," said Brigham.

Malcolm sighed.

He plopped down onto the thrift store sofa in front of us.

He looked at Brigham. He looked at me. We looked at him.

I hated it. But he was making sense.

"C'mon, guys. You're my best friends. If I ever convince a girl to marry me, you'll be in my wedding."

"Who's the best man?" I said.

"Both of you," said Malcolm. "It'll be a tie."

"That seems fair," said Brigham.

"And you can work all this into your toast at the reception. It'll be great material," said Malcolm. "So, let's get out there and make some yearbook memories, have some adventures, and do something stupid for once."

"I thought you said your plan was smart," said Brigham.

"Well, it is," he said earnestly, "in the stupidest way possible."

And somehow that worked.

He was right, in a weird way.

Our entire adolescence had been one long, safe, cozy board game in Malcolm's basement.

It was pleasant, sure, but I was beginning to have a hard time differentiating one night from the other. They were all blurring together.

Time to do something different.

Time to do something adventurous.

Time to do something stupid.

And, man, was this stupid.

Brigham

Marshall and I might have been a hard sell, but Quinn was surprisingly easy to convince.

We met her after school and Malcolm was winding up for an edited version of his basement Katherine Underwood speech, but she cut him off before he could really get going.

"I'm in!" she said.

"You are?" said Malcolm, stunned.

"Yeah, I never have anything cool to write in the yearbook."

"Do you think they have yearbooks in prison?" I said.

Quinn snickered. Malcolm shook his head.

"Just kidding, just kidding," I said. "Kind of."

Marshall

Operation AirDrop took all kinds of planning.

Which meant many tacks and much yarn for Malcolm.

"Your tack-and-yarn budget must be off the chain!" said Quinn.

It didn't stop there.

Somehow, he'd also acquired a giant blueprint of the entire school campus.

He cleared a spot on the gaming table and unfurled it with ease.

"Um, hold up," said Quinn. "Did you just roll out a big blueprint of a facility that we plan to infiltrate?"

"I did," said Malcolm with a self-satisfied nod.

"Have you been practicing that?" I asked. "That was a really good unfurl."

"I have," he said.

"I kind of got chills," said Quinn.

"Yep. Goose bumps," said Brigham as he pointed to his forearm.

Then he patted me on the back in a *sorry, I'm excited about this* kind of way.

I didn't blame him.

Looking back, that was the moment we went all in.

After the map-rolling, there was no going back.

And, to be honest, I don't think anybody wanted to.

Even me.

MARSHALL

It was the final night before Operation AirDrop and The Crazy Board was looking truly crazy.

There was the picture of Coach Craig connected via yarn to the picture of the cell phone to a scaled-down blueprint of the school to our classroom schedules to a makeshift classroom seating chart to a printed group photo of all of us taken by Malcolm just for this occasion.

And Malcolm had more to add. He moved to the front of the room with a Sharpie and paper in hand.

"If all goes wrong," he said, "your momma jokes are the key."

"Um, what?" I asked.

"Your momma jokes," said Malcolm. "Well, not *your momma* personally."

He swiveled to the gaming table and began to write on the sheet of paper.

"It's the perfect diversion," he said. "We all know that Coach Craig's weakness is your momma jokes. He cannot and will not ever resist them."

We must not have looked convinced enough so Malcolm pressed on.

"Marshall," he said. "Remember when we were working on our statistics assignment last week and you said we needed to 'drop the two from the top line?'"

I nodded. I knew where he was going with this.

"What did Coach Craig say?"

"He said, and I quote, '*Your momma* likes to drop a two from the top line.'"

Brigham chuckled.

"That's actually a good one."

Malcolm shifted his teacherly gaze to Quinn.

"And Quinn, remember when you said you needed to go to the

water fountain for a drink of water the other day? What was Coach Craig's response?"

Quinn stood up and cleared her throat.

"His official response was, '*Your momma* wants to go to the water fountain for a drink of water too.'"

"Correct," said Malcolm.

Brigham frowned.

"That one just doesn't make sense."

"No not at all," said Malcolm. "But that doesn't really matter."

He tacked a paper that said YOUR MOMMA to the board.

"Your momma jokes," he said rapping on the poster board with a pointer that appeared from nowhere. "Don't you forget them!"

BRIGHAM

So, it all led up to that third period.

The meticulous planning.

The unnecessarily long Malcolm lectures.

The Board work.

The your momma joke memorization.

The tater tots and pizza rolls. (His mom brought us snacks.)

For all the tacks and yarn, the plan was pretty simple.

"We rely on our greatest strength," said Malcolm. "Nerd power."

"That does play into our strong suit," said Quinn.

CHAPTER FOUR

OPERATION AIRDROP

MARSHALL

"Hey, nerds!" barked Coach Craig midway through third-period study hall. (And right on schedule.) "The Wi-Fi's out."

Cue the taunting cackles from my classmates like a canned laugh track.

Coach Craig's regular berating of the less-than-cool students of Carter High is always a source of high entertainment for the more-than-cool ones. No one seems to enjoy it more than perpetual homecoming queen contender, Kim Kirkland, and her gaggle of hot friends.

"Get to work, Geek Squad," she purred.

Malcolm turned in his seat and gave her a wink.

"As you wish, madam."

She made a dramatic gagging face.

Malcolm's wide grin only grew wider.

"Geek Squad's not a bad name either, you know," he said as we moved to the front of the class.

"Probably copyrighted," I said.

"And it's no BrainForce," whispered Brigham.

"Exactly," countered Malcolm. "Because BrainForce is awful."

In this particular class, everyone knew the "Geek Squad" members were officially defined as Brigham, Malcolm, and myself. Not

Quinn. For some reason, she's not traditionally classified as one of the group. Probably because she's pretty and no one seems to believe that she actually hangs out with us by choice. But c'mon she carries a cross-stitch bag!

In this case, we were counting on exactly that kind of gender-based nerd-bias.

Quinn's segregation from the Dork Side was crucial to the plan. Ha! Dork Side! That's a good name too. Don't tell Malcolm about it.

Anyway, a few minutes earlier, Quinn had not-so-discreetly moved to the back of the room.

"Oh, darn!" she said loudly. "My pencil broke."

She gave a much too obvious nod and headed in the direction of the pencil sharpener. It was a pencil sharpener that was within arm's reach of the wireless router.

Coach Craig is a notorious fantasy football addict and we knew he couldn't handle a minute without refreshing his sports-ball stats.

Quinn pulled the plug and the reaction was instantaneous.

"C'mon, computer brains!" Coach yelled. "You know what to do!"

We did know what to do.

Brigham sat down at the keyboard. I blocked his left side. Malcolm blocked his right.

"Do your thing, Poindexters," said Coach Craig. "Just stay off the nudie sites."

More cackling from the class.

He grinned, eating up the attention, and plopped down in his desk chair near the door, propping up his giant white Nikes.

"Looks like you've got network problems," I said as nonchalantly as possible. "A quick reboot should help."

"Whatever," he said. "Just make it work. You guys are twice as fast as the IT guy."

That probably isn't true. But we all knew Coach Craig and Micah the IT Guy were former classmates and apparently have a tumultuous past. Most recently, he turned in a browser history report that led to a written warning from Principal Chang.

Micah had seen too much. And Coach Craig was eager to avoid any other entanglements with the administration.

This is why our "computer brains" were frequently called into action.

Brigham worked fast. He went to recent history and then typed "digital calculator" in the search bar. And there it was. Sure enough, Coach Craig had backed up his entire phone to the school computer.

Malcolm let out a gasp.

I shushed him.

He shushed me.

Brigham shushed both of us.

Coach Craig looked at us.

We froze until he looked away.

Brigham highlighted AirDrop on the file and an upload bar appeared in the center of the screen.

"Hackers," muttered Brigham as he leaned toward the screen and double-clicked. "No turning back now."

I felt kind of woozy.

On the other side of the room, Quinn was slowly turning the crank on the pencil sharpener, staring at us as though she was watching a slow-motion car crash.

For some reason, I winked at her.

Nothing I planned on.

She grinned, winked back, and pulled a strand of blondish hair behind her ear. And then, maybe, was it—was she blushing? She was blushing! She looked down and concentrated harder than needed on her pencil sharpening. The strand of hair spilled back out across her forehead.

Her hair always looks so pretty. And smells so good. What was the scent again? Maybe not raspberries. Strawberries mixed with Fruity Pebbles maybe?

Brigham let out a cough and looked my way as if reading my mind.

"Focus, Romeo," he said.

"Sorry," I said.

Now Quinn was looking at her cell phone, eyebrows raised, watching with obvious excitement as the mysterious files appeared in her hand.

She had already replugged the router, but Coach Craig didn't know that. He was spinning a plastic ruler on the end of a pen.

The upload was slow.

It reached 19 percent.

Then 20 percent.

Then 21 percent.

This was actually going to work! The classroom was quiet. Peaceful. We just needed it to stay that way. As long as no one paid any attention to us we would actually get away with this and—"Hey guys!" said friendly Sam Hammond from the second row. "What are you doing?!"

I couldn't have jumped higher if he'd fired a shotgun directly into the ceiling tiles.

Friendly Sam was peering from behind the tattered cover of *Prisoner of Azkaban*.

"You copying the hard drive or something?"

Coach Craig's ruler clacked to the ground.

"What's that, Dork Squad? You guys doing some cybercrimes over there?"

27 percent.

Malcolm let out a high-pitched squeal-laugh that sounded like a gerbil in distress.

Coach Craig leaned forward in his rolling chair.

35 percent.

"Oh, yessir," said Brigham brightly.

Cool as a cucumber.

He glanced back at coach.

"We just hacked into the Pentagon mainframe. There's some great stuff here about Area 51. Wanna see?"

36 percent.

Malcolm let out another gerbil squeak and I joined him with something that sounded like a seal bark.

"Hey, looks like there's a file on Bigfoot here!" I said cackling much too loudly.

An entire bead of sweat rolled down my forehead. Where did that come from?!

Coach leaned back into his chair.

"You wish," he said. "Pentagon. Pssh. We'd have black choppers on the building by the time you guys could wipe your butts. Just make it quick. I got papers to grade and stuff."

"Right away, Coach," said Brigham with a mock salute.

He clacked a few more fake commands on the keyboard.

"But why would we be wiping our butts in class?"

Another giggle-squeak from Malcolm.

We were at 57 percent and slowing.

The fake calculator definitely had some solid data on it.

58.

59.

61.

We were getting somewhere. Most of my fellow classmates were either texting, napping, or talking amongst themselves. This was good. We just needed the focus to stay elsewhere.

"Why would you need to reboot?" asked Friendly Sam.

I almost pitched backward, directly onto the floor.

He has moved on from *Azkaban* and was focused completely on us now.

"It was probably just a blip in the Wi-Fi," he offered helpfully. "All you have to do is restart the router. Did you check it out?"

He gestured to the back of the room where a frozen-smiled Quinn was grinding her pencil down to a nub.

Sam looked at Quinn and grinned.

"You got any more pencil left to sharpen there, Carswell?"

Stupid Sam!

Why was he being so helpful and observant?!

Couldn't he just stare at his phone like the rest of the class and Instagram his life away?!

Coach Craig was leaning forward again.

74 percent.

He rose from his chair.

75 percent.

76 percent.

He began to walk toward us.

77 percent.

78 percent.

"No, I'm all out of pencil," said Quinn, her voice quavering. "But YOUR MOM still has some pencil for everybody!"

The room went silent for two solid seconds.

And then pandemonium.

Cheers and jeers erupted.

"OOOOH," said the cheerleaders in the mid rows. "BUUURRN!" shouted some jocks in the back. Coach Craig turned from us to Sam Hammond and let out a steady heh-heh-heh.

"Burned by the Quilting Bee," grinned Kim Kirkland.

Quinn looked immediately apologetic.

"Sorry, Sam," she said. "Was that a burn? I actually didn't think it made sense."

Sam scratched his head.

"Well, it didn't," he said. "But that's okay I guess."

The classroom was in a tumult but Coach Craig still seemed much too interested in our progress. He turned his attention back to the computer and Brigham's hunched shoulders.

81 percent.

82 percent.

He took a few more steps forward.

84 percent.

He stood behind us and peered over my shoulder.

85 percent.

I tried my best to block his view while also not passing out.

86 percent.

He grabbed my shoulder and shifted me to the side.

The jig was up!

"WELL, YOUR MOM'S JUST OKAY I GUESS TOO!" yelled Quinn.

More howling from the crowd.

Coach Craig turned toward Sam and let out a loud Beavis chortle.

Meanwhile, poor Sam seemed more confused than anything.

"What? Why?! You like my mom, Quinn! Doesn't she lend you cross-stitch patterns sometimes?'

"Ooooh! Buuurn!" shouted someone indistinct.

"That's not a burn!" yelled Sam. "They're literally on the same cross-stitching Facebook page! They DM all the time!"

"That's actually true," said Quinn, still slowly cranking the pencil sharpener. "She has amazing needle control . . ."

92 percent.

Quinn trailed off and Coach Craig turned back toward us.

93 percent.

He was super close.

94 percent.

I could feel his hot breath on my neck. It smelled like Fritos.

95 percent.

"BUT SHE'S STILL YOUR MOM!" shouted Quinn.

Total uproar.

"WHAT?!" said Sam. "Now you're just stating facts, Carswell!"

"Your mom is a stated fact!" shouted Caleb.

"What does that even mean?!" yelled Sam.

"What does your mom even mean?" shouted someone from the back.

Even more total uproar.

Coach Craig pivoted to the front of the room.

"Ms. Carswell! That's enough!" he bellowed. "Your trash talk is awful!"

She flushed red.

"So awful," he said, shaking his head. "Just really, really bad."

He wasn't one bit upset about the classroom chaos, just disappointed in the subpar stream of your momma jokes, which weren't up to his standards.

"Sorry, Coach," said a visibly ashamed Quinn as she headed back to her seat. Then she beamed widely and flashed us a thumbs up.

Coach Craig was right. It was quite possibly the lamest set of your momma jokes in the history of your momma jokes.

But also the most brilliant.

Because the upload reached 100 percent, Brigham deleted the transfer history and swiveled around in his chair.

"All done," he said. He held an open hand in coach's direction. "That'll be one hundred dollars."

"How about a big pile of jack squat?" said Coach Craig and slapped his palm.

"Um, I'll pass," said Brigham as the bell rang.

Malcolm giggle-squeaked and we were out the door.

Mission accomplished.

Score one for The Academic/Shadow Guild/Hero Squad.

And also Sam Hammond's mother.

CHAPTER FIVE

THE VIEWING

MALCOLM

The rest of the day crawled by.

Calculus.

AP history.

Even glorious trigonometry.

I couldn't enjoy it.

I could only think of the file sitting on Quinn's iPhone.

She sent one maddeningly tantalizing group text message before shutting down for "safety purposes."

It's a video file. One big video file.

Followed by a winky face.

"Whaat?!" I blurted in the middle of Mrs. Conner's American History lecture.

"Yes, Mr. Ringold," she said. "The Teapot Dome Scandal was the turning point in the Taft Presidency, thank you for your enthusiasm."

When the hour finally came, we gathered in my basement.

It was slightly exciting.

BRIGHAM

"I've never been this excited about anything ever in my life," said Malcolm.

He hugged me. Hugged Quinn. Hugged Marshall. Hugged his mom when she came down to offer up Hot Pockets.

We declined.

We didn't want anything to interfere with The Viewing.

That's what Malcolm called it.

He'd written it in bold letters on a sheet of paper and tacked it to the "Timeline" section of The Crazy Board.

"Listen," said Quinn as she plopped down on the orange sofa. "You should know I am the best person in the world. I really, really wanted to watch this all day but I saved it for you guys. Because you know why? This is official Shadow Guild business."

Malcolm looked love-struck.

"It's official," he said. "You *are* the best person in the world. Also, it's pronounced *The Academics*."

Quinn snort-giggled.

"Ah, no, no," said Quinn. "I see how you could be confused. 'The Academics' part is silent . . . and then replaced with completely different words."

They laughed and cackled and I gave Marshall a side-eye.

He was grinning vacantly at them in an awful, plastic-faced kind of way. I could tell his brain was somewhere else. Somewhere . . . haunted.

He'd been doing that a lot lately.

With all the late-night crime-solving sessions, I hadn't been able to check up on how my best buddy was really handling all this.

Sure, he put on a brave face. But there was a girl watching. If Quinn was in the room, he'd probably put on a brave face if he was bitten in the face by a king cobra.

I leaned toward him.

"You okay, man?"

He nodded too quickly.

"Oh, yeah," he said. "Yeah, just . . . excited."

Excited was one word for it.

He swallowed, fake-smiled, and cleared his throat.

"Well, then," he said. "Let's do this thing."

Quinn nodded and we all piled around her on the orange sofa. She pulled out her phone and held a finger over the play button. "Drumroll please."

We made appropriate drumroll noises.

She elbowed Marshall.

"See you on the other side, Ray."

Marshall let out a legitimate laugh and leaned into Quinn.

"Nice working with you, Dr. Venkman."

He was real-smiling now.

It wouldn't last.

MARSHALL

It began with a toilet.

One seriously dirty toilet.

"Oh no," said Malcolm. "Is this a weird internet toilet video?"

"What's a weird internet toilet video?" said an understandably alarmed Brigham.

"You don't want to know!" said Malcolm. "Get ready to shut it off!"

I clapped my hands over my eyes instinctively. Then peeked. There were a few more seconds of toilet, then the camera swiveled upward and we were looking at Coach Craig's sweaty face.

Bright red. Perspiring. He was not on the toilet thankfully.

He was looking into a mirror.

"Okay, so not a weird toilet video," said Brigham. "But remind me to ask you how you know about all that later on."

Quinn snickered.

"Some things we don't want to know."

The mirror image of Coach Craig carefully held his phone and then placed it into the front pocket of his bright green polo shirt. For a moment everything went dark as he fiddled with the camera. There were a few muffled curses and then we were back, but with a frayed ring around the edges of the screen. We realized Coach had positioned his phone so the lens was lined up with a small discreet hole in his shirt pocket.

"Whoa," said Malcolm. "Hidden surveillance."

"Homemade hidden surveillance," said Brigham. "MacGyver-style."

"Testing, testing, one, two, three," said Coach Craig, looking directly into the camera. "Testing, one, two, three."

Coach Craig took a deep shaky breath and then another. He was obviously nervous. I'd never seen him nervous.

He took another deep breath.

Then he turned away from the mirror and opened the bathroom door. And then it was all noise and thumping bass and flashing lights.

"It's a party!" said Malcolm.

It was a party. But a party like no party the likes of us had ever seen.

First off, it glowed. Somewhere, some unseen blacklight was turning the entire room neon.

Second off, many of the females appeared to be, um, scantily clad—if clad at all.

"Does that girl have a shirt on?!" said Quinn, as a possibly topless blur passed through the frame.

"Wait, wait, go back!" shouted Malcolm. "Let's see!"

Quinn slapped his hand away from the phone.

"Control yourself! This is detective work!"

The party was packed. Wall to wall. Face to face.

Coach Craig worked his way through the blurry, bouncy crowded room as the hyped-up voice of Lil Jon shouted from a nearby speaker.

"Maaan, they're turning-down-for-what up in theeere," said Quinn raising her hands to the ceiling. We looked at her blankly.

"No?" she asked. "Okay."

Coach Craig stopped and lingered near a couch and checked his watch where a girl with blue hair appeared to be talking to herself. Next to her, an enthusiastic couple was apparently rounding second and headed for third.

For the first time, I began to fear that we were going to see more of Coach Craig than we'd bargained for.

"Um, what kind of party is this?" I said.

"I don't know," said Malcolm. "Is this what parties are like? The ones we don't get invited to?"

"That would be all parties," said Brigham.

"Yeah, where do they even set up the Framptonworth castle?" cracked Quinn.

"Poor planning," I said.

Then someone in a big stuffed bear costume walked by the frame.

"Bear!" shouted Malcolm.

Then someone in a chicken suit.

"Chicken!" said Brigham.

Coach Craig stopped and loudly asked the chicken for directions.

"HEY, CHICKEN," he yelled. "IS THERE BEER AROUND HERE?"

The big chicken didn't respond.

"BEER?" he said. We could see his right hand make the universal cup-tipping motion for beer.

The chicken pointed a wing somewhere to the right and moved on.

Eventually, coach made his way into a kitchen with 1970s-looking yellow decor that put off a radioactive glow beneath the blacklights.

He found his way to a keg and filled up a glowing Solo cup.

And that's when a girl appeared in his face. Or his chest pocket at least.

She had pink hair, a nose ring, and was pretty. Her eyes were also abnormally wide and glowing.

"Heeey," she slurred.

"Uh, hey," said Coach Craig. He sloshed some frothy foam on the floor.

"You wanna party?" she asked.

Coach Craig said that he did.

A bass beat dropped somewhere nearby, and you couldn't hear much for the next few minutes. The wide-eyed, pink-headed girl looked entranced by Coach Craig. And maybe a little hopeful?

"Well, that's redundant," muttered Malcolm. "She asked him if he wants to party and they're obviously already *at* a party."

"Um, I think she means something more than a party," said Quinn.

"Oh," said Malcolm as it slowly dawned on him. "Ohhhh."

The pink-haired girl leaned toward the camera and we were now staring directly at, um, her cleavage.

Quinn covered my eyes.

"I need the dust," she said. "Then we can party however you want."

More beer spilling from Coach Craig.

"Umm, where do I get the dust?" said coach.

"From one of Mister Happy's men, of course," she giggled. "Is this your first Hell Party?"

"Mister Happy?" said Quinn.

"Hell Party?" said Brigham.

"The plot thickens," said Malcolm as he stroked his chin.

The pink-haired girl grabbed Coach Craig by the hand and led him through the crowd. They took a turn down a less crowded hallway and it was here that the vibe of the party changed completely. It was quieter, and passed-out partiers lined the wall. From the looks of it, they were either comatose or just silently staring into space.

At the end of the hall was a glowing, bright purple door that looked like it was floating in the darkness.

Pink-haired girl rapped on it and then stepped aside.

"You got money, right?" she said.

Coach Craig didn't have time to answer before the door flew open and he was greeted by a wall of a man.

Crossed arms. Menacing frown. Unnecessary sunglasses.

"Arms up," rumbled the man.

There was some kind of patting down and searching going on. Would he find the phone? Apparently, he was looking for something more substantial.

Coach Craig walked into a cramped room that was strewn with plastic barrels and cardboard boxes.

At the center of it all was a strung-out-looking dude with wild hair and bulging eyes. He was leaning over a coffee table that was loaded down with money on one side and small plastic baggies of green powder on the other.

"Yeah?" said the man, barely acknowledging Coach Craig's presence as he counted a stack of what looked like hundred-dollar bills.

Coach Craig cleared his throat.

"Heya, um, hello, um . . . can I get some of those drugs?"

We gasped in unison.

The man stopped mid-count and looked up.

His eyes seemed to bulge out further. Coach Craig now had his attention.

"Some of those what?"

"Um, drugs?"

"You a cop?"

"No, man," Coach said, his voice rising one too many octaves.

"Why'd you call them drugs? Like this is a D.A.R.E. class or something?"

"That's just what they call it where I come from."

"Where you come from?"

"Canada."

"Where in Canada?"

"The coast."

"Which coast?"

"The east one."

"I don't think Coach Craig is from Canada," said Malcolm in a whispered hush.

The man gave coach one long crazy stare and broke into a jagged grin.

"Well, then . . . wanna throw another shrimp on the barbie?"

Coach Craig let out a nervous donkey laugh.

"Sure," he said.

"Geez," said Quinn. "That's not even the right continent."

The man laughed wildly and then stopped.

"Because if you are a cop . . ." He pulled out a gun. "Then you need to tell me."

We all gasped in unison again.

The frame jumped as Craig stumbled backward.

The wild-eyed man placed the gun casually on his knee. It was shiny and seemed much bigger than it needed to be. Like something Dirty Harry might carry.

"How about you tell me a little more about yourself first, mate," he said. "And then I'll decide whether or not to let you leave here with or without a hole in your kneecap."

Coach Craig made a noise that sounded like a lamb's bleat.

"Hey, man, I don't want trouble!" he said. "I just want dust!"

"Ah, he knows the name now! If you're not a cop, what do you do for a living with that fancy shirt?" He looked directly into the lens of Coach Craig's pocket.

Did he know we were in there?

"I'm a teacher," said coach. "At the high school."

Wild Eyes let out a wilder laugh. A string of greasy hair fell in his face, but he didn't bother to move it.

"A teacher and a dust head?!" he said. "We could probably use a guy like you, help spread the product to the younger demographic, right?"

"I mostly just teach study hall," said Craig.

"That was my favorite class," said Wild Eyes.

He looked at his security guy who was now looming at the edge of the frame.

"I like this guy."

"Oh," said a relieved-sounding coach. "Thanks."

"Still thinking about putting a hole in your kneecap though. But in a friendly way."

"Oh," said Craig, much less relieved.

And then there was sudden and sharp gunfire. Not from Wild Eyes, but from somewhere else in the party.

A *pop-pop-pop* and the room turned upside down.

Wild Eyes jumped up, gun in hand.

"Annnd, that'll have to wait!"

He pushed Craig out the door and plunged into a pack of panicked partiers.

"Remember, I owe you a friendly bullet!" he yelled.

There was another *pop-pop-pop* and a stampede of neon bodies. Craig was knocked to the side and his phone went spinning into the air. We were now looking straight up at the ceiling as a riot of glowing shadows passed overhead and one big heel stepped directly on the screen.

There was another crack and then Coach Craig's giant panicked face appeared as he loomed over the screen and froze.

The video came to a sudden end, with the shocking realization that Coach Craig was nearly gunned down by a drug dealer.

And he was also possibly Canadian.

QUINN

"What. Just. Happened?" said Malcolm.

He sprung from the couch.

"Was that some kind of undercover sting?!" said Brigham. "Like *The Wire*?"

"I don't know, I've never seen *The Wire*!" said Marshall.

"Well, it's like that!" said Brigham. "Except this was with a cell phone and no wire!"

Malcolm was pacing back and forth with his hands to his temples.

"Or maybe this is some kind of *21 Jump Street* situation!" he said. "Coach Craig is a narcotics officer who works undercover at the high school. He's not really a jerk in real life but he just acts like one so he can infiltrate drug gangs and—I'm sorry I can't finish saying that with a straight face."

"And who is Mister Happy?" said Marshall.

"And what is the Hell Party?" I said.

"And why was there a chicken at the party?" said Marshall.

"And a bear?" said Brigham.

As Malcolm was frantically scribbling *Mister Happy, Hell Party, chicken,* and *bear* onto a dry-erase board, I realized there was something else on my phone.

A single JPEG right next to the video file.

It was the JPEG that changed everything.

MARSHALL

"Wait!" said Quinn. "There's an image here too!"

We jumped back on the orange couch.

"It's not toilets, is it?!" said Malcolm.

"Man, what has the internet done to you?" said Brigham.

There was no toilet. That actually would have been better.

There was only one picture, but one was enough.

It was a blurry screenshot taken of the video we had just watched.

A still photo of someone or something standing in the crowd of partygoers.

Its silhouette loomed taller than the others. Slanted. Abnormal. Unnatural.

At this point, Brigham said something to Malcolm.

And then Malcolm said something to Quinn.

And they all laughed.

But I didn't hear it.

I didn't hear any of it.

All I saw was the photo.

All I saw was the still, stark, deathly-pale image of a man with the head of a unicorn.

CHAPTER SIX

THE NIGHTMARE

MARSHALL

I never knew what a panic attack was until right then.

Turns out it's when your brain thinks you can't breathe even though you can.

That doesn't seem like much of a difference when you're in the middle of one.

Because, man, I couldn't breathe.

I opened my mouth and let out a croak.

Malcolm and Brigham began to say things to me that I couldn't really hear.

It was all faint and faraway and muffled.

There was a ringing in my ears, and I could feel myself being dragged down into some dark hole of panic and fear inside myself.

Then Quinn put her hands on my shoulders and guided me to the ground.

Somehow, her words cut through the ringing.

"Sit on the floor," she said. "Head between your knees."

I made a horrible retching noise and then Brigham was at my side patting my back.

"Are you gonna puke?" said Malcolm. "Do you need a puke bucket? Get him a puke bucket!"

"It's okay, give him some space, guys," said Quinn. "He's not gonna puke. This is a panic attack. I used to get these all the time when we lived in Chicago. They suck."

She crossed her legs and sat down on the floor next to me as I gagged and gulped like a goldfish out of water.

"I can't breathe," I gasped.

"You can breathe," she said. "You're breathing right now. You wouldn't be able to talk if you couldn't breathe."

I gagged some more, and it felt like my eyes were bulging out of my skull *Total Recall*-style.

"Look at me."

I looked at her.

"Look into my eyes."

I looked into her eyes.

Straight into her eyes.

I knew they were green, but I never noticed there were flecks of gold in them. Beautiful, but I couldn't quite appreciate that at the moment on account I was dying.

"You're not dying," she said, reading my mind.

She put a hand on my chest.

It did nothing to help my skyrocketing heart rate.

"Feel your chest rising."

I felt my chest rising.

"Feel it falling."

I felt it falling.

"Are you with me?"

I was.

I nodded.

My breathing slowed. The gasping stopped.

"Here's what's happening. Your lungs are working. But your brain is playing a practical joke on you right now. He's a real jerk that way."

I let out an involuntary horse-cough laugh.

Quinn laughed with me.

"Close your eyes," she said. "Imagine a field and take a deep breath."

I did that.

"Imagine faraway lands and take a deep breath."

I did that too.

"Imagine the forest moon of Endor and take a deep breath."

I opened my eyes a crack and she shrugged.

"It's one of the more tranquil *Star Wars* planets, right?"

"Better . . . than . . . Mustafar," I gagged.

"Ah, geez," Quinn rolled her eyes. "Don't go all prequel on me."

I shrugged.

She hugged me.

And I cried.

Oh no, not a manly cry either. This was full-on body-shaking crying.

It felt like a core workout.

When it was done, "sorry" was the only word I could muster.

"Sorry for what?" said Quinn.

"Sorry for lying," I said.

And I had been.

Lying to them.

Lying to myself.

Lying to you, even.

It seemed easier that way. It still does sometimes.

Brigham plopped down in front of me.

"Don't apologize," he said. "If you need to talk, we can talk."

I nodded.

We did need to talk.

I needed to tell them about the monster.

MARSHALL

"I haven't slept since the beating," I said.

I noticed they flinched when I said that word.

Like, they had thought of it less as a violent crime and more like bloodless fisticuffs. Kind of like how cowboys fought in old black-and-white movies.

No, this was in pure, living, violent color.

Neon green color.

And it sure felt like a beating.

But that wasn't the scariest part.

That wasn't the part that kept me wide awake at night.

The part that haunted the back of my brain all day like a shadow I couldn't shake.

The part that made me dig out my old *Power Ranger* night light and plug it back into the wall next to my bed.

That part was the mask.

My assailant wore a freaky, horrible, nightmarish Halloween mask.

And it frightened me so much that I didn't tell anyone about it.

Not my mom.

Not my best friends.

Not even the cops.

I'm not sure why.

Maybe because to say so would make it seem real?

And if it was real then that meant there were monsters in the world.

Real monsters.

But I guess there is.

"The man who beat me," I said, "was wearing a unicorn mask . . ."

I pointed to Quinn's phone and the image that might as well have been a screenshot of my nightmares.

"Just like that."

QUINN

"Whut?" said Malcolm.

"A unicorn mask," said Marshall.

He shivered and sniffed through his poor dented septum.

"Like a fluffy unicorn mask?" I asked.

I was hoping for fluffy. Somehow, I thought fluffy would seem less creepy.

Marshall shook his head and lost his breath again.

He pointed to my cell phone.

I put a hand on his arm.

He breathed a little harder.

I took my hand off.

"It was that rubber mask. Big rubber eyes. Big floppy horn. And it was . . ."

He trailed off again.

"It was what?" asked Brigham.

He looked pale.

"It was severed . . . looking."

Malcolm let out an actual scream.

"What do you mean?" he blurted.

"It was a severed unicorn head."

I cursed loudly, startling everyone.

"How?!"

"I mean it was bloody around the edges of the mask, like it was supposed to be chopped off or something. It was all decapitated and dead looking."

Brigham sunk into the sofa.

"Sick," he said.

"That's deranged," said Malcolm. "Why didn't you tell us?"

Marshall shook his head.

"I didn't tell anybody," he said. "Not even the cops. I just . . . I just didn't want to deal with it. I figured it was bad enough getting my face destroyed. I just kind of pushed it all down."

Marshall trailed off and drew in a ragged breath.

"But that doesn't work. He's there all the time. I see him every night in my messed-up nightmares. And now he's on that cell phone."

We were quiet for a moment.

"Dude," said Malcolm. "You were attacked by a man in a zombie unicorn mask. How are you functioning right now?"

"I'm not really," said Marshall. "I'm just good at faking it. Or I was."

We all wanted to simultaneously hug our friend.

Brigham beat us to it.

He walked over to Marshall and wrapped his arms around his buddy.

I noticed there was a hole in the armpit of his long sleeve shirt.

He noticed that I noticed and looked away quickly.

I could have cried.

"I know what a beating is," said Brigham. "Not a unicorn beating. But a beating."

Marshall sniffed and nodded.

"And I know you," he said. "And you're stronger than this. You're stronger than all this."

Marshall didn't say anything. He just hugged his best buddy.

Malcolm and I looked at each other. It was a hug that made me feel both happy and alone. I've never had a buddy like Brigham.

Brigham seemed to sense this.

"Bring it in," he said.

We encircled Marshall, our arms wrapped around him and each other.

It wasn't just a hug. It was us holding him together. Us holding each other together.

We stayed like that for a while. Not talking. Listening to Marshall's wheezy nose.

It was Malcolm who finally spoke.

"Man," he said. "I wish it'd been an Internet toilet video."

MARSHALL

Malcolm was the first to leave the hug.

Or . . . "The Hug That Saved Me," as I like to call it.

He stood and stared at The Crazy Board. And then he started to pull out tacks and yarn.

"What are you doing?" I said.

"Sorry, man," he said. "This isn't cool."

"What isn't cool?"

"I'm sorry that I'm so excited about this. I'm sorry I'm making this into a game. Like we're still playing Framptonworth or something. Like the most disturbing thing to ever happen to you is . . . is . . ."

"Fun," said Brigham.

Malcolm nodded quickly.

"Right," said Malcolm. "Fun."

"It's not fun," said Brigham. "It sucks. It's awful. I hate it. I wish we could find the guy who did this to you and . . . and . . ."

"Murder him," said Quinn coldly.

"Whoa!" said Brigham. "I mean, I was gonna say 'break his nose' or something but that's another way to go."

We all laughed and I felt something loosen inside of me. It was a strange feeling that replaced the gnawing fear that had been gripping my stomach for so long. For the first time in weeks, I felt something like, what was that? Relief? Relief tinged with . . . bravery?

I know. It surprised me too.

But seeing the fear and total freaked-outness in the eyes of my friends somehow made things less scary for me. They were scared too. They were here to share in the scariness.

I walked over to Malcolm and took the tacks out of his hand.

"Listen," I said. "This is exactly what I need."

I replaced the pins on the board and rehung the photos.

"If you all weren't joking around and planning and acting like the Scooby Gang on a very special episode of *Stranger Things* . . . I don't think I could have kept it together this long. I don't think I'd have even left the house. Or gotten out of bed."

I stepped back from The Board and began to study it, really study it, for the first time.

"I don't need more fear," I said. "I've had enough of that. And I don't need more seriousness. I need you guys. And I need you guys to be you. There's no escaping all this for me. I see it every time I close my eyes. So, keep doing your thing, Ms. Lansbury."

Malcolm snorted.

It's a funny thing confronting your fears.

It's scary, yes. But it's not as scary as *not* confronting them.

Running from them is much more terrifying.

Even if you're running from a beheaded zombie unicorn man.

MARSHALL

That night, my nightmares changed a bit.

They were still nightmarish.

But, this time, I wasn't alone.

I was back in C-Wing.

The Unicorn Man was there.

Waiting. All drooling and dripping. He leaned down to charge at me and I turned to run. Like usual, I was rooted to the ground. As I braced myself for my nightly unicorn impaling, all the old green lockers in the hallway flung open simultaneously. The Unicorn Man, for the first time, paused.

Brigham jumped out of one in full white martial arts gear, looking like *The Karate Kid*.

"HIIIIIYA!" he screamed.

Then Quinn glided out looking like Galadriel, the elf queen from *Lord of the Rings*. All flowing robes and fire and fury.

And then Malcolm sprung out in a chicken suit. He seemed cool with it.

"I got your back, Jack," he said with a wink.

One by one, they fought the Unicorn Man as I watched from the orange couch—which had suddenly appeared in the hallway.

They all lost. Unicorn Man broke their noses with a single punch and then he went on to impale me.

But still, I appreciated the effort.

QUINN

"First off . . ." said Malcolm at lunch the next day. "That's highly insulting."

We were all laughing except for him.

"What?" said Marshall innocently.

"Why do I have to be in a chicken suit?! Brigham gets to be a ninja. Quinn is a warrior princess. I'm the San Diego Chicken?!"

Now people at the next table were starting to laugh even though they had no idea what Malcolm was ranting about.

"Hey, at least you had a good catchphrase!" said Marshall.

Malcolm seemed to consider this.

"'I got your back, Jack' is pretty sweet," he said.

"Yeah, I didn't even get a speaking role," I said.

"You didn't need it," said Malcolm. "You were the elf queen. Your powers speak for themself."

He turned to Marshall.

"Can you put in something more awesome next time? Maybe like a mech suit? Or could I be a Jedi with a lightsaber?"

"Yeah," said Brigham. "And I'd like a Cobra Kai *gi* next time. Miyagi-Do is a little played out."

Marshall shrugged.

"Sorry, man, I don't do requests."

CHAPTER SEVEN

THE OTHER CARSWELL

BRIGHAM

It was about this time that our investigation hit a bit of a wall.

Surprisingly, a Google search for "severed unicorn head mask" wasn't as fruitful as you'd expect.

It turned up plenty of results. Just the wrong kind of results.

"There are some sick and twisted art majors out there," said Quinn as we browsed the images.

"How about just 'unicorn mask'?" I said. "Maybe it's actually supposed to be a non-decapitated unicorn head and the sicko painted it to look severed."

"Makes sense," said Malcolm. "Seems like there'd be more of a market for non-dead unicorn head masks, right?"

We typed in "Unicorn" and "Mask" and there it was.

Bright pink mane. Large black eyes. Gaping horse mouth. Floppy unicorn horn.

"Well, that's the creepiest thing I've ever seen," said Quinn.

"Yes," said Malcolm. "But it's also the creepiest *clue* you've ever seen."

He clapped his hands together.

"So," he said. "We need a plan."

MALCOLM

We all knew it was coming to this.

From the first time we joined together and unanimously agreed that The Academics would be our official name. (Just go with it.)

It was only a matter of time.

I stood in front of my group of brothers and sister in arms and uttered the word everyone had been waiting to hear.

"Stakeout."

"Stake what?" said Marshall.

Silly Marshall, always being silly.

"You know it has to happen."

"I do?"

"Of course you do. All of you do."

"We do?" said Brigham.

Quinn smiled and arched a perfect eyebrow.

"Yep," she said. "It's stakeout time, baby."

One day, I will marry Quinn. And she and I will have beautiful, mystery-solving babies together. I mean—assuming Marshall doesn't do that first.

I laid it all out there for them with several large color copies and thumbtacks. That's right. I upgraded to a color printer and that ink is not cheap.

"We've reached a dead end," I said. "It's time to move to real live boots-on-the-ground intel."

"Boots?" said Brigham. "I don't have boots."

Silly Brigham, always being silly.

"We don't have intel either," I said. "That's why we need a stakeout."

"And who are we staking out?" said Marshall.

"Coach Craig of course," said Quinn.

I smiled at her and nodded. So many babies we will have.

"Okay, how are we going to have a stakeout? We don't even have a car?" said Brigham.

"Valid point," I said. "But Quinn's sister does."

Quinn's perfect eyebrow un-arched and lay flat across her perfect forehead.

"Um, what?" she said. "Um, no."

I expected this.

If you haven't heard yet, the perfect and beautiful Quinn has a perfect and beautiful big sister.

Some people might say she's even more beautiful and more perfect. I wouldn't say that. Just some people.

But, as luck would have it, she has a car.

"C'mon, she drives the perfect stakeout vehicle!"

"It's a busted-up Astrovan," she said. "And no."

"But it's ideal for a stakeout. It's got three rows! It's got plenty of room for donuts and coffee and binoculars and stakeout things. Plus, it's nondescript!"

"Really, no," said Quinn flatly.

"We can't very well park our own cars in front of Coach Craig's house. He'll know we're on to him."

"We don't have cars," said Brigham.

"Exactly! That's why we need Quinn's sister's car! We'll just need it for a few hours and then we'll return it to her. Or if she doesn't trust us, she can come along with us and—"

"NO!"

Marshall flipped back in his plastic chair and spilled orange drink all over his face. Normally, this would have been the height of hilarity, but we were too startled to laugh.

The normally smiling, amiable, quick-to-hug, and/or cross-stitch a throw-pillow Quinn Carswell rose from her own plastic chair like an indignant elf queen.

"You keep my sister out of this!" she hissed. "My sister is not to be trusted. And my sister will never, EVER, set foot in this basement! DO YOU HEAR ME!"

I tried to talk but it came out like a croak.

There was silence as Quinn fixed all of us with an ice-dagger stare. All of us. At the same time. How was she doing that?!

Then there was a creak at the stairwell. Another creak.

"Who's that?" she snapped. There was a look of wildness in her eyes that made me want to run and dig a hole and hide.

Another creak.

"Um," I was finding it hard to speak.

One last creak.

"It's your—"

My throat closed. Sometimes I think my asthma is coming back, you know?

"It's your sister," said Sloan Carswell.

BRIGHAM

She entered the basement legs first. I know that's how most people enter a basement. But nobody enters a basement like Sloan Carswell enters a basement.

She entered in this order:

Beat up black Converse Chucks.

Perfect calves.

Eagle tattoo.

Criminally short shorts.

And then Sloan.

The Sloan Carswell.

In all her glory.

"'Sup, losers," she said. "I brought donuts."

MARSHY

Sloan Carswell brought donuts.

And not the cheap kind you get at the gas station.

We're talking real donut-store donuts.

Quinn took a step in her direction.

"You can stuff your donuts up your—"

"Heeey!" I blurted, somehow I was standing between them and kind of wanted to jump under the sofa. "Hey-hey there, Sloan! How you doing?!"

Sloan's perfect red lips parted into a smile, and she looked directly at me.

It was like staring into the sun.

I think my face did something resembling a smile back.

"Hey, Marshy," she purred.

My name's not Marshy.

I don't care.

BRIGHAM

How can you describe Sloan Carswell?

Well, how can you describe a five-alarm fire?

How can you describe an F5 tornado?

How can you describe an F5 tornado that just ran over a five-alarm fire?

Just like that, I guess. A firenado.

She graduated last year but her presence is still felt at CHS. And people still speak of her as though she's some kind of urban legend. She was a varsity cheerleader, but she has a visible eagle tattoo on her thigh. I think I mentioned that.

She was a National Honors Society Student but had her own personal reserved VIP desk in the in-school suspension room.

She won homecoming queen but then she punched the homecoming king in the face a few minutes later when he got "handsy" on the dance floor.

They say her crown didn't even move an inch on her perfect head.

Sloan Carswell is brilliant.

Sloan Carswell is mythical.

Sloan Carswell is terrifying.

And for a moment I thought Quinn was going to throw Sloan Carswell through the wood paneling.

MARSHALL

"What are you doing here!" spat Quinn, spitting sparks into the electrically charged room.

Brigham, who had been half-heartedly studying, texting, and cracking jokes quickly scrambled onto the sofa and sat there, mouth slightly agape. Give him a bucket of popcorn and he'd be a Michael Jackson meme.

"You need to go," said Quinn in a feral tone that I hadn't heard before. It gave me the shivers.

Sloan, for her part, didn't seem fazed.

"Well, that's rude," she said. "I'm a guest in the Ringold home. Isn't that right, Malcolm?"

Malcolm froze.

Deer in the headlights.

Deer in the beautiful bewitching headlights.

He eventually nodded slowly, up and down, as if a puppeteer was pulling a string attached to his forehead.

"Yes, I, um," he swallowed. "Yes, I, um . . ."

He swallowed some more.

"I . . . just thought it'd be nice if she joined us."

Brigham settled deeper into the sofa.

"You thought wrong, bro."

MALCOLM

Um, I'm just going to go over the events as I remember them.

First off, there were two girls here.

One was Quinn. One was Sloan.

Both were beautiful.

I don't care if they read that.

Actually, can you let Sloan read that?

Do you think there's a chance she'll read that?

Never mind.

I invited Sloan over because of her car, but also because I felt she could get us into places we wouldn't be able to get into by ourselves.

I just didn't expect her to say yes. Really I didn't even expect her to respond to me with verbal acknowledgment.

At first, she didn't.

When I approached her in the senior parking lot, she looked through me as though I was wearing an invisibility cloak. She was there to pick up Quinn, but it still seemed as though she never left high school the way people talk of her.

"Hey, Sloan." It felt weird calling her by her first name, like calling the dearly departed Queen of England by the name of Liz.

She stared directly through my head.

I figured I should make some small talk first. Maybe point out the weather.

"There's weather today," I managed.

And indeed, there was. This was going great. Then I figured I could talk about school.

"Also, there's school."

She scrolled through her Instagram. She has 40k followers. I have nineteen, including my mom.

But then I mentioned Quinn and Marshall and Coach Craig and the Unicorn Man and she turned to me as though I had activated something in her sexy-cyborg brain.

"Keep saying things," she said.

And so, I said things.

I said everything.

I told her about the beating.

I told her about The Academics.

I told her about The Board.

I told her about the cell phone.

I told her about the snot.

And most importantly, I told her about the stakeout.

"Oh," she leaned in and I almost fainted. "Well, that sounds like fun."

I couldn't tell if she was being sincere or sarcastic.

In fact, every sentence I've ever heard Sloan say sounds both sincere and sarcastic.

I can see how that might drive Quinn crazy.

And crazy is exactly what happened in my basement.

"OUT!" screamed Quinn. "Or I'll kick you out!"

It was wild.

If we had been in a dive bar I could see Quinn smashing a beer bottle over her sister's head and tossing her out a window. And that might have actually happened, if my mom hadn't walked in at the worst possible time.

Or, honestly, maybe it was the best.

"Everything all right, sweeties?" she said.

She calls everybody sweetie. Even if they're about to throw down in her basement.

"You kids getting upset about your board games?"

She shot a darting glance at Sloan, and, for a minute, I wondered if she wasn't as oblivious as she was letting on. Of course she wasn't.

The sound of my mom's voice snapped Quinn back to reality like a bucket of ice-cold water on her head.

Her cheeks turned red, and she headed for the stairs.

"We're fine, Mrs. Ringold. I was just going."

And she was gone.

MARSHALL

Normally, the hasty departure of Quinn would have been a pure unadulterated catastrophe for the group.

What if she was gone for good?!

We wouldn't have a girl anymore!

We needed a girl!

No one ran after her.

And we were left with Sloan Carswell sitting between us, alone in Malcolm's basement.

"So," she said as she slipped next to Brigham and draped an arm around him. "Guess there's an opening for a girl on the Dork Squad. What do you little maniacs want to do first?"

BRIGHAM

Malcolm isn't right about a lot of things. But he's right about this.

Sloan Carswell is a cyborg.

A strawberry-blondish-haired cyborg from the Planet Sexytron.

After the door had slammed at the top of the stairs, she put an arm around me. I'm thinking of having my shirt bronzed.

"So," she said. "Is the stakeout still on?"

"Yes!" blurted Malcolm.

She looked at me. I'm not proud to say it, but I slowly nodded yes. It was as though I was under her mind control.

Quinn is great. But Quinn who?

She looked at Marshall and only he appeared to be immune to her powers.

He cleared his throat.

"I don't think," he cleared his throat again. "I don't think we can do it without Quinn."

Sloan grinned like a cat toying with a half-dead canary.

"Why not, lover boy?"

He gulped.

"We're a team," he said. "We have to stay a team."

Sloan sighed dramatically and stood up from the sofa. As she did, her bare leg brushed up against mine. I may have my leg bronzed.

She strolled over to The Crazy Board, studied it, and then turned and cocked a hip out like some kind of runway fashion model.

"Well, good," she said.

"Good?" said Marshall.

"That's how a boyfriend is supposed to act when his girlfriend's older, much more awesomer big sister insults his true love."

"Girlfriend?" said Marshall.

"I'm taking the donuts though," she said.

Then she was gone.

We listened as she moved up the creaky stairs, into the living room, and then out of Malcolm's house.

There was a good thirty seconds of silence before anyone spoke.

"Do you think Quinn's ever going to come back?" said Marshall.

"Probably not," I said.

"Do you think Sloan will ever come back?" said Malcolm.

No one answered.

"I really hope not," I said. "And I really hope so."

MALCOLM

I understood perfectly.

Of course, we wanted Sloan to stay in our basement.

We would be her hostages. Under her spell of awesomeness until the world literally ended in fire and fury. We would remain by her side.

But Quinn was the true friend of the group.

And we knew the two could not exist in the same space at the same time.

Sadly, it's against the laws of hot sibling physics.

MARSHALL

The next day was awful.

Awful for so many reasons.

First off, Tribal Ted passed out on the couch in his underwear the night before. And I can't be too sure, but it really looks like Tribal Ted sleeps in an electric blue Speedo. Sorry for the mental image but it's what I was greeted with over my off-brand Chocolate Frosted O's that morning.

Second off, I completely forgot about our chem test since I was too busy studying up on online retail outlets that provide dead unicorn masks into the wee hours of the night.

And third off, this is by far the worst of it, even worse than Speedo Tribal Ted . . . Quinn walked completely by me during first period. She looked right through me as I stood there with my hand up and a goofy smile.

In study hall, she sat with Lily Murphy.

At lunch, she sat with Sam Hammond. The same Sam Hammond who nearly, single-handedly blew the cover off Operation AirDrop!

Sam Hammond looked like he had won the lottery.

I felt like crying into my school lunch mashed potatoes as I pushed them around on my plate.

"Maaan," I said as I watched Sam excitedly chat with a nodding Quinn from across the lunchroom. "We really, really messed up."

"Did we?" said Malcolm as he stuffed a Fruit Roll-Up in its entirety into his mouth.

"Well, yeah," I motioned across the lunchroom. "Look! We lost Quinn! To Sam Hammond!"

Brigham snickered.

"Are they a power couple now?"

"Yeah, probably," said Malcolm.

"What?" I said.

"Just kidding," said Malcolm grinning.

"How can you be so nonchalant about this?"

"I don't know." He shrugged and dipped a Cheeto into some applesauce. Gross.

"Should I be more . . . chalant?"

He leaned back in his chair.

"Ha! More chalant!" laughed Brigham. "That's good."

They chortled and chuckled and I wanted to knock their heads together *Three Stooges* style.

"Well, yes," I said. "You should be all the way *chalant*. We lost Quinn! We lost our girl! Without a girl, what are we?!"

"Just some dudes," said Brigham.

"Just some dudes who like to solve mysteries and play awesome board games in the basement," added Malcolm, still unfazed.

"Right," I said. "So that's why this is bad."

"Um, I hate to break it to you buddy," said Malcolm. "But Brigham and I haven't 'lost' Quinn."

He threw up some air quotes.

"We both apologized this morning," he said. "She accepted. We're good. No harm, no foul."

"Yeah, right," I said.

"You don't believe me?"

"Nope."

"Watch this," he said.

"Hey, Quinn!" he yelled and waved across the lunchroom.

Quinn looked up, gave him a sunny smile, and waved back.

"Hey, Malcolm!" she said. "Hey, Brigham!"

She was forgetting me somehow. Maybe she didn't see me?

"Hey, Quinn!" I said, reminding her I was there.

Her sunny expression turned stormy, and she stared hate-lasers directly through my skull.

Then she turned back to Sam Hammond with a friendly grin.

I would have preferred another swift punch to the face from the Unicorn Man.

I put my head on the table and groaned.

"Well . . . she hates me now, right?"

Malcolm snickered.

"Marshy, Marshy, Marshy."

I was hoping that nickname wouldn't stick. Did I mention this day was awful?

"Dude," said Brigham. "You don't see it do you?"

"See what?!"

Brigham and Malcolm smiled, looked at each other, and shook their heads. Now I was thinking the *Three Stooges* eye-gouge would be more appropriate.

"Let me explain," said Malcolm. "Brigham and I had friend trouble. That's much easier to resolve. You, my good buddy, have girl trouble. It's more complicated."

Girl trouble.

The phrase took me by surprise.

"Girl trouble?" I said as I lifted my head from the table.

It was as if the sky parted slightly, and a thin ray of light shot through the clouds.

"Yep," said Brigham.

"But don't people who have *girl trouble* have . . . girlfriends?"

They nodded in unison.

"Exactly," said Malcolm. "Quinn is mad at you because she likes you."

"Likes me?"

"She expects more from you," said Brigham. "She doesn't care as much about the behavior of me and Malcolm because we have been friend-zoned. But you still have a chance, you lucky son of a gun."

The sky parted completely, and the warm sun shone down upon me. As I looked at Quinn, frowning in my direction, there were harps playing and choirs singing above my almost-maybe-someday-soon-to-be girlfriend.

This was quite a turn.

"I have girl troubles," I said.

Malcolm shook his head.

"Like he said . . . lucky son of a gun."

I've never had girl troubles before. Because there's never been a girl to have troubles with.

"So, what do I do now?"

"Beats me," said Brigham with a shrug. "You're in uncharted waters. But I think you have to find a way to solve the troubles now."

"Oh," I said. I looked at Quinn and smiled at the back of her head. "Well, I guess I'm going to the Carswell residence."

Malcolm nodded.

"Godspeed, my friend."

MALCOLM

At first, I thought there was a mistake.

I was walking out of Mrs. Ricardo's chem class at the end of the day on Friday when she handed me a paper with strange markings on it.

C-

That's what it said.

"What is this?"

Mrs. Ricardo was scribbling the next classes' assignments on the dry-erase board.

"That is your grade, Mr. Ringold," she said and continued to scribble.

"I know that, but why is this letter on it? What does it mean?"

"It's a C-," she said, "which means you performed slightly below average on this test."

I nearly passed out.

I would have preferred it if nice, sweet Mrs. Ricardo had delivered a roundhouse kick directly to my temple.

"What?! But no! I know all these things!"

Mrs. Ricardo stopped scribbling and finally looked my way.

"I know you know those things," she said. "It surprised me too."

She folded her arms.

"Are you perhaps distracted by non-school activities? Sports? Girls?"

"Ha! I wish!"

"Well, whatever it is, you made some pretty obvious mistakes. Take a look. You put the answer for question two on the answer line for question three. And then you skipped questions six and seven altogether."

"Ohhh," I said. I took out my pencil, hunched over her desk, moved answer two to its proper place, and quickly solved answers six and seven. Then I handed the paper back to her.

"Is that right?"

Mrs. Ricardo put on her reading glasses and examined my work.

"Yes, it is," she said. "Perfect."

"So, what's my grade now?"

She took out her red pen and added a single line to the paper.

C+

"Congratulations," she said. "You're now slightly above average."

Remember when I said Mrs. Ricardo is nice and sweet? I take that back.

As I wandered out of the classroom, I had to balance myself for a bit on the doorway.

This was my first C.

Ever.

But I knew what was happening. I *was* distracted, but not by sports and/or girls.

I couldn't stop thinking about the case. Every day. Every night. All the time. My mind itself was becoming a Crazy Board.

I suppose these are the dangers of being a high school-aged detective.

Honor's student by day. Master sleuth by night.

The clues were all there.

Marshall's face.

Coach Craig's phone.

The Hell Party.

Unicorn Man.

Mister Happy.

It just didn't make sense.

We needed more info. I had said it before, and I would say it again.

It was time to take this investigation up a notch.

It was time . . . for a stakeout.

For real this time.

CHAPTER EIGHT

ESCAPE TO WINDHAM WOODS

MARSHALL

I've never been to the Carswell residence.

But on Saturday afternoon I showed up on their doorstep.

No phone calls. No text warnings. No DMs.

Just biked over on the ol' ten-speed and knocked on the door like it was the 1950s or something.

A large man with a walrus mustache answered the door. I recognized him from the school carpool line as Quinn's father.

His bushy eyebrows were lying flat against his forehead.

"Go away," he growled.

Welp, so much for that!

I turned to go away.

Mr. Carswell's face broke into a wide grin and his mustache rippled.

"Just kidding! Come back!"

I turned to come back.

"Sorry about that!" he said. "Just some joking for you."

His eyebrows were high on his forehead and now that he was smiling, he kind of reminded me of a younger Santa without the beard.

"So, you must be one of my daughters' many suitors!"

He added that last part with a regal bow.

"Um, yes sir."

His eyebrows dropped.

"So, you're saying my daughters get around then?"

"Wait, what?"

His mustache rippled.

"Kidding again!"

He leaned in conspiringly.

"Between you and me, no one wants to date them anyway after they murdered their ex-boyfriends."

His eyebrows activated and his mustache danced.

"Kidding! They were acquitted anyway! KIDDING!"

Man, this guy was a kidder. And it was terrifying.

I was contemplating backing away, hopping back on my bike, and riding home. We could talk in study hall on Monday right?

Then I heard a familiar beautiful voice echo down the stairwell.

"Hey, Dad," said the beautiful voice. "Is this man bothering you?"

"Of course he is," said Mr. Carswell. "We should probably call the cops right?"

Quinn stepped into the door frame.

"Nah," she said. "I'll take care of him."

"Oh, hoho," said Mr. Carswell as he receded into the doorway. "I know that tone of voice. I'll keep you in my thoughts and prayers, buddy."

He crossed himself like a priest, did a little more eyebrow dancing, and then he was gone, leaving me and Quinn alone on her front doorstep.

She crossed her arms and looked at me.

"Um, hey," I said.

"Um, hey to you," she said.

She was wearing a green hoodie and her hair was in a no-nonsense ponytail.

Magical.

"Your dad is funny, right?" I said. "And also kind of scary."

"Well, somebody has to keep the riffraff away," she said as she casually scanned the lawn behind me. "So, what's up?"

She stared at me with her green eyes that were only intensified by her magical hoodie.

"I was just wondering . . ." I looked down the street and then back at her. "If you wanted to go on a walk?"

She arched an eyebrow.

"What is this, the 1950s?"

MARSHALL

We went on a walk.

Though I wasn't really sure where we were walking to.

"Where are we walking to?" asked Quinn flatly.

"Um, I'm not sure."

We headed down the weedy sidewalk in the direction of the old bike trails that Brigham and I carved out of the woods during simpler times.

"I figured since it's the 1950s and all, we could go to the soda fountain and maybe stop over at the sock hop?"

No reaction.

I stopped in the middle of her next-door neighbor's driveway.

"I'm sorry."

Quinn kept walking.

"Sorry for what?" she said without looking back.

I scrambled to catch up.

I wasn't really sure. But I felt as though I had betrayed her in some way by sticking around in the basement with sexy Sloan.

"I'm sorry about the thing with your sister."

She crossed her arms and kept walking.

"I'm sorry that your sister isn't nearly as interesting and engaging as you."

At this, she slowed her pace. I figured I should continue.

"Or as appealing."

She slowed a little more.

"Or as attractive."

She turned around and scowled.

Too far.

I caught up with her again.

"C'mon now," she said. "She's basically an Instagram model. She's got like 100K followers."

"Pssh," I scoffed. "Who isn't an Instagram model these days? Anybody could be an Instagram model."

She rolled her eyes and frowned but the frown was less frowny now.

"Anybody?"

I nodded. "Yes. Malcolm could be an Instagram model with the right angles and lighting."

She tried to hide a smirk.

"Your dad could be too!"

She let out a snorting laugh in spite of herself. Success!

"You're right," she said as she pulled a strand of hair behind her ear. "He would look good in a sepia filter."

"Except your sister wouldn't," I said. "She's no Mr. Carswell."

She shoved me.

It was a playful shove, but I almost wound up in a hedge of rose bushes.

"Okay, okay," I said. "She's a . . . she's semi-attractive."

She shoved me again and I wound up in a butterfly bush.

"BUT . . . I could see that she'd be a lot to deal with . . . as a sibling."

"Right?"

"And maybe kind of exhausting to hang out with . . ."

"Right?!"

"And everything's kind of all about her."

"RIGHT! Like she's the only one in the room at all times and no one else matters and we're all just extras on the latest episode of *The Sloan Show*?!"

"Um, right," I said.

I didn't want to add that *The Sloan Show* was edge-of-the-seat, can't-look-away entertainment . . . so I didn't.

Quinn got quiet again and I could tell I touched a nerve there.

We turned the corner on Warwick Street and a chittering squirrel scrambled up a tree.

"I know the feeling," I said. "I've got this cousin named Monty. He was the runner-up to the runner-up on *The Bachelorette*. He's got Superman's pecs and arms and Batman's jawline. His Instagram looks like a sexy fireman's calendar. Everybody makes a big deal about him and, if he's in the room, Monty is the only topic of conversation. Monty got a new promotion. Monty got a new Mercedes. Monty's dating a Brazilian supermodel. Blah blah Monty blah—I'm glad we only see him on the holidays. You could get lost in those eyes."

Quinn arched an eyebrow and stroked her chin.

"Hmm, what did you say his name was again?"

"Hey!" I said. "Please don't date Monty!"

She laughed more naturally.

"Okay, I won't. Just as a personal favor to you."

She hopped over a fallen branch on the sidewalk.

"Well, imagine living with Cousin Monty and his jawline and his beautiful eyes. I live in *The Sloan Show*. It dominates my life and all family topics of conversation. So, when she brought that show into the Ringold basement, I guess I kind of flipped out."

"Yes," I said. "Yes, you did."

She grinned.

"Well, that's sacred holy ground," she said. "You guys are my refuge from the show."

"I get that you wouldn't want her messing up the vibe," I said.

"Well, yeah, but it was kind of stupid. It's just when I saw her strut in the basement with her short shorts and donuts, all I wanted was to throwdown WWE style."

I snickered.

"What?"

"Um, I'm just imagining Malcolm's reaction to an all-girl wrestling match in his basement. It would be the greatest day of his life."

Quinn laughed. A real laugh this time.

"I have a feeling Mrs. Ringold would have clotheslined us and put us both in a sleeper hold before it got out of hand anyway." We walked a little farther and took a turn onto North Grove Street. It was warm for October and the streetlight started to flicker on. As we walked, we brushed hands, and I got the feeling she didn't mind.

"So, uh, will you join us for lunch again on Monday?" I said.

"Suuure," she said sweetly. "As long as you don't ever cross me again."

She stared at me with her eyebrows lying flat across her forehead and I got the strange feeling I was looking at a lady Mr. Carswell.

Then she laughed. I laughed. It was a joke. I think.

We headed down the road and passed a couple of kids shooting baskets in the driveway.

"Do you remember the first time I sat with you guys in the lunchroom?" she asked.

Did I? *Did I??* This was like asking me if I remembered the first time I opened up the Scribe's Instructional Book of the Founders of Framptonworth. That means yes by the way.

It was a monumental moment for Brigham, Malcolm, and myself. Like Beyonce casually plopping down beside you in a Denny's.

I said yes, but didn't tell her all that.

"So, I was sitting at the popular girl table between Gwen Harris and Sydney Carroll. It was my first day and they were showing me around."

"Well, that was nice of the popular girls," I said.

"I guess, but 'showing me around' meant that they just talked trash about everyone within visual distance."

"Well, that seems about right."

"Yep. They were even talking about you and Malcolm and Brigham."

"Me?" I felt honored. Really, I didn't think we were significant enough to be worthy of mention at the popular girl table.

"Yep. Gwen said you guys were tragically dorky. And Sydney said you snorted when you laughed."

At this, I snorted and laughed. "Yeah, but you're the real snort laugher!"

"I know! And I almost told her that but then I didn't. And I'm not sure why. And so, the whole time I was sitting there making sure I didn't accidentally snort-laugh. But it was actually pretty easy because those girls are terrifying. So, I'm eating my carrot sticks and suppressing my snort laughter . . . and then I look at you . . ."

She blushed when she said this, in the most glorious way.

"Um, and at Malcolm and Brigham," she added quickly. "And you had pudding on your nose, and you were acting like you didn't notice."

"Ah, yeah," I snapped my fingers. "I told them I was a fancy gentleman on his way to a gala and was asking directions!"

"Ha! Right, the fancy gentleman bit!"

"A classic."

"And then you all started cracking up and Malcolm fell out of his chair and Brigham spit out his chocolate milk and you guys looked like the least cool people I'd ever seen."

Quinn hopped up on the curb and balanced for a minute.

"That tracks," I said.

She hopped down, her ponytail swinging back and forth, and she looked at me with her emerald eyes.

"But you also looked like the coolest."

I had to catch my breath for a moment, but Quinn didn't seem to notice.

"Anyway, Gwen said that I needed to avoid your table at all costs if I cared about my reputation." She looked at the ground. "And that's what got me. Because I did care about my reputation in Chicago. And it's a lot of work caring about a reputation. I had friends. And technically I was popular. But it always felt tenuous. I always had this tightness in my chest. Like if I ever messed up, it would all go away."

"What would go away?"

"My friends." She let out a rueful laugh. "That's not how friends are supposed to work, right? They shouldn't leave you if you mess up. There shouldn't be a test. You shouldn't have to prove yourself over and over again. It shouldn't be like a job interview every single day. But it was. And the thought of doing all that again with another set of uptight girls made me feel . . . tired."

She kicked a pinecone and it skittered off a trash can.

"So, when I saw the fancy gentleman routine, I couldn't help it. I let out this gigantic carrot-stick-spraying snort-laugh. It went all over the table. And all the popular girls looked like I'd grown another head."

"What?!" I laughed. Brigham, Malcolm, and I had dissected this scene many times over and over, but I actually didn't know this part of the story.

"Gwen looked at me and said, 'Oh, so you're one of them?' And I said, 'No. I'm just me.'"

"Whoa, good one." I wanted to break into applause. "So, you walked over to our table and asked me if I recommended the pudding, right?"

"Yep, and you said, in your fanciest gentleman's voice 'Yes, it pairs quite nicely with the school's finest chocolate milk.'"

I nodded seriously. "It's true."

Quinn laughed.

"You weren't wrong," she said. "And so that's why I officially moved from the popular girl table to the unpopular-but-much-more-fun-guy table."

"Yesss," I said pumping my fist. "All part of my plan!"

She slugged me on the arm.

"Okay, not really," I said.

"Well, it worked," she said. "Now I've got friends in low places."

"Glad to have you, Garth Brooks."

She laughed. I laughed. And we walked some more, now in warm friendly silence.

This was turning into a pretty good date.

Wait, was this a date?

If it was a date did that mean we were going to kiss?

If we kissed, did that mean my nose would bleed?

I began to sweat.

I touched my nose.

What if we make out and I bleed all over her face?

And that's when it happened.

Not the nosebleed.

Believe it or not, that would have been much better.

That's when Quinn stopped talking and pointed to the far end of Waycross Street.

The streetlights had come on. The night was still nice and warm, but ice water shot through my veins when I saw it.

Underneath the farthest light, standing in the center of the road.

The Unicorn Man.

MARSHALL

Okay, maybe that's still up for debate.

Because this man had no unicorn mask on.

But there was something about his posture. His broad shoulders and stiff arms-to-the-side stance that was the actual spitting image of the silhouette from C-Wing.

"Um, I think we're being watched," I said.

Quinn squinted and looked down the street.

He was about one hundred yards away.

"Well, that's creepy AF," she said.

The man stood stock-still and rigid. Then he started to run our way.

"Is he . . . just jogging?" asked Quinn.

"Um, he's not wearing jogging clothes," I said.

"An improperly dressed jogger maybe?" said Quinn.

He was picking up speed and I started to back away.

It was all happening again. And now it wasn't just me in danger. Quinn was too.

Last time I did nothing. I just stood there like a stupid tackling dummy and waited for my beating. Not this time.

I turned to Quinn and said one word.

"Run."

QUINN

"Run," said Marshall.

And so, we ran.

I felt kind of silly at first.

Surely this was just some weirdly dressed jogger out exercising in the nice autumn air, right?

"Why are we running again?" I panted.

"Just a precaution," said Marshall brightly. He was trying to stay calm, but it was obvious he was about to lose it.

I glanced over my shoulder and the man was still headed in our direction. He was pumping his arms back and forth and gaining on us.

"He's getting closer!" I said, panic starting to set in.

Marshall grabbed my hand and sped up and we both stumbled.

Chivalrous but ineffective.

"Holding hands and running doesn't work!" I yelled. "Where are we going?"

The running man was about four driveways back and closing the gap.

"Just stay with me!" he said. "I've got an idea!"

We were now in a dead sprint. Our footsteps echoed off the asphalt. But the running man seemed to be moving silently.

I was wearing my Converse low tops and one of the laces had come untied.

I managed another quick glance over my shoulder long enough to see the jogger actually hurtle a small hedge and keep coming at us like a Terminator.

"He jumped a bush!"

"Keep going!" said Marshall. "I know where we can lose him!"

We turned a corner around a parked Suburban and skidded into the backyard of a ranch house.

We ducked past a swing set, dodged a tool shed, and ran right into the woods.

And then the lights went out.

MARSHALL

It was nearly pitch-black dark in Windham Woods.

It's old growth forest.

Middle Earth-type stuff.

It gets dark in there at three p.m.

But these aren't just any woods.

These are my woods.

Brigham and I grew up in these woods.

We built the trails that wind through them for miles. We camped here. We fished here. We built tree forts on every limb possible.

That's right. We were free-range kids. The last of our kind. Blessed with single, overworked mothers who cared enough not to care too much. Technically, we were trespassing on this land, but the owner lived somewhere in Florida and had thankfully resisted the lure of the strip mall developers.

If we were to lose the unmasked Unicorn Man, it would be in these woods.

And I knew just where to go.

I turned right at the old oak with a board nailed to it and took another left at the bunch of privet that used to stand in for Jabba's prison.

It was here that my feet found hard dirt.

Sidewinder Trail.

Rated a Triple Black Diamond in the Brigham/Marshall BMX Forest Guide.

I knew every dip and dive on the quarter-mile stretch.

I assumed the Unicorn Man didn't.

And that was our one chance at making it out of there without spilling more blood.

QUINN

It was dark. But Marshall didn't seem to notice.

Forget what I said about handholding.

It wasn't just chivalrous. It was necessary.

I held tight to Marshall's sweaty palm as he dragged me through a Mr. Toad's Wild Ride of banks, bends, and hairpin turns.

We never hit a branch.

From the sound of it, Running Man was hitting everything.

He was as loud as a bull crashing through the woods and, for one crazy moment, I imagined him as a mad minotaur. Crossbow and all.

Though we were moving fast, he still seemed to be gaining. And then the invisible trail stopped. There was nowhere to go.

We stopped at a wall of briars and brushes that might as well have been made of stone.

Running Man let out a loud grunt.

He wasn't far away.

And I realized we had just made the classic horror movie blunder of running from one terrifying situation into an even more terrifying situation. We were the people who went into the basement to investigate creepy ghost children. We were the summer campers that went for a skinny dip during a machete murder spree.

We . . . were idiots.

Marshall dropped low and began to feel the trees.

I wondered for a moment if he'd lost his mind.

He ran his hands over a cluster of roots. Then another one. Then another.

"What are you—"

He put a finger to his lips.

"There it is," he whispered and motioned to a skinny pine.

Marshall squeezed my hand and through the gloom of the woods, I could still make out a white smile.

"Now, we go up," he said.

MARSHALL

Imagine the Ewok Village.

Now imagine that village if it was built by two ten-year-olds with minimal construction skills, supplies, and building knowledge.

None of the rope lines and platforms that crisscross the sprawling acres of Windham Woods are up to code.

Not even close.

But what Brigham and I lacked in quality, we made up for in quantity, as we spent the better part of third to fifth grade nailing every board or plank we could find to the branches of the forest.

Calling them treehouses is much too generous. They were pretty much boards nailed to trees.

And that's what we clung to as we made our way up an old skinny pine.

I knew exactly where I was.

Terror Tree.

And it was fitting.

Brigham and I named it that years ago because, one day, he lost his balance on the platform and barely avoided a thirty-foot fall by grabbing hold of a creaky vine.

We shakily climbed down from the Terror Tree and never climbed it again.

Until now.

QUINN

Marshall's butt was six inches from my face as we shimmied our way up questionable wooden planks up an even more questionable skinny pine tree.

He moved fast.

It was like he was born in these woods.

Raised by the Tree People.

We made our way to a rickety platform that was really just a few old two-by-fours nailed to the upper-most limbs.

Marshall silently motioned for me to sit next to him as we crouched up against the slender tree.

We said nothing.

All I could hear was the distant *caw, caw, caw* of birds and our heavy breathing.

We were swaying ever so slightly, back and forth.

At first, I thought we'd lost him.

Then I heard the snap of a twig.

A muffled cough.

The flick of a lighter.

Running Man was right below us.

MARSHALL

He stopped right at the base of the tree, stood, and lit a cigarette.

I wished I had a paint can with a string to toss at his head.

Kevin McCallister would have been disappointed in my lack of planning.

He huffed and puffed and stood in the darkness of the woods.

I heard the distinct vibration of a cell phone and then he spoke.

"Yeah," he muttered. His voice was higher than I expected.

"Just going for a run . . . near the kid's house . . . you know what I mean . . . in the forest . . . Well, it's fun."

I looked at Quinn and her eyes widened.

He took another drag of his cigarette and made a noise that sounded like a chuckle.

"Are you serious? Does he think I'm the kind of guy who messes around? . . . Yeah, I can head that way . . . Yeah, I know where it is. Looks like a pool hall . . . No, I just got distracted. I'm on it. He's not a problem . . . Tell him I'll take care of it . . . Don't worry about it . . . I know. I know. Keep Mister Happy happy. That's the job. That's what I'll do."

My stomach plummeted and the icy water returned to my veins.

The phone went to silence and the man sat down on a fallen log next to the trunk of Terror Tree.

He finished his cigarette, flicked it in the brush, and let out a long loud sigh like he was a harried factory worker on the night shift. Then he turned and headed into the forest.

We could hear him crunching and cracking through the woods, until we were eventually left with darkness, silence, and the realization that we had nearly come face-to-face with Mister Happy's hitman.

MARSHALL

We waited a full ten minutes before we spoke again.

"Okay," whispered Quinn. "We've got a lot to add to The Crazy Board now."

I laughed despite my terror.

"Yeah, you're gonna need to buy some more yarn."

Quinn was shaking.

I was too.

"Do you think he's gone?" she said.

"I think so. But we should probably wait here a little bit longer before we head back to civilization."

Quinn nodded.

"And where is here?"

"Terror Tree."

"That seems appropriate."

"Yeah, it's one of the tree forts Brigham and I built back in third grade. This is probably our most rickety craftsmanship."

As if on cue the wind began to shift and Terror Tree swayed a few inches.

Quinn wrapped her arms around the skinny pine. I did too.

"So, we're relying on the engineering of ten-year-old you and Brigham?"

I nodded. Her face was a couple of inches from mine.

"Um, that's even scarier than the forest jogger."

We sat and listened to the woods.

The forest was alive with creaks and cracks and croaks.

Our shoulders were touching now.

She leaned into me.

I leaned into her.

"It's weird," she said. "I feel like I should be more scared. That was terrifying. But also kind of . . . exhilarating?"

I laughed and nodded.

"Yeah, I know what you mean. It's much more fun when you don't get caught."

She grinned.

"Yeah, another broken nose would have put a damper on our date—"

She said date! She said it!

It was dark but I detected blushing.

"I mean . . . if it is a date. I mean, you know, getting chased through the Forbidden Forest of Hogwarts is more creative than, like, dinner and a movie if you know what I mean . . . if it's a date."

I swallowed, completely forgetting that we were possibly being hunted by the Unicorn Man at that moment.

"I'd like it to be a date," I said.

"Me too," she said.

"So, then," I said. "We declare it a date, right?"

She nodded.

"The date has been declared. Do we have to get it notarized now?"

Her face was moving closer to mine.

"I think so."

My face was moving closer to hers.

"We'll need to go to the courthouse for that?"

I looked into her eyes.

She brushed the hair from my forehead.

She was still shaking.

I was too.

For different reasons now.

"No," she said. "My uncle is a certified notary."

"How convenient," I said.

Then I leaned in, just an inch.

She was there to meet me.

Her lips parted. Then . . . she leaned back.

"Oh," said Quinn.

"Oh, what?"

"Oh, blood."

I grabbed my nose.

Oh. Of course. Blood.

QUINN

You can't make out with a bloody nose.

It's just a proven scientific fact.

Which is a shame, because in the aftermath of danger and in the rush of adrenaline, I was ready to do some hardcore making out.

Instead, I talked Marshall through one massive bloodletting as he pulled out a wad of tissues from his back pocket.

Once we hit the ground the potential for romance had ended.

We were in survival mode again.

Marshall crouched low and led me through another looping, swooping trail until we somehow came out of the forest in the backyard of my across-the-street neighbors.

"Um, how did you do that?" I said.

"The forbidden forest holds many mysteries, young student," Marshall said, doing his best old Dumbledore.

We checked that the coast was clear of creepy smoking joggers and then scrambled to the door.

Marshall's nose had pretty much dried up now. And I knew what I was going to do.

I was going to take him upstairs, sneak him into my room, give him the proper amount of emergency tissues, and then . . . make-out time!

"Speaking of forbidden," I whispered. "Want to come up to my room?"

Marshall froze for a moment, as though a million different responses were processing through his brain.

"Yes," he said simply.

I grabbed his hand, turned the doorknob, and walked right into my dad.

He was in a bathrobe and beaming.

"So! Did he pop the question yet?!"

Marshall turned beet red and clapped his hands to his nose.

The blood had returned.

"Can I borrow some tissues, sir?"

"Sure, sonny!" said Dad. "As long as I can walk her down the aisle on the big day!"

I groaned.

Make-out session canceled. Called off on account of a deviated septum and a dad who was too good at playing dumb.

MARSHALL

That night the Unicorn Man was waiting for me in C-Wing again.

Except this time, he had a nosebleed.

I tried to warn him, but he didn't listen.

He charged. He lowered his head. He stabbed. All the while, his big gross nostrils were bleeding profusely.

I woke up screaming.

And, of course, my nose was bleeding too.

CHAPTER NINE

MEET THE CREEPER

MARSHALL

"Wait, wait, wait," said Malcolm.

He sat down and put his head in his hands.

"This is too much," he said. "Too much for The Board."

He was right. It was too much for The Board.

He had been furiously scribbling words like UNICORN MAN, RUNNING, WAYCROSS STREET, WINDHAM WOODS, TERROR TREE, and for some reason NEED NEW PANTS.

"Because I think I peed in my pants a little," he explained.

Brigham burst out laughing.

I think he was joking.

Maybe not.

"Calm down, big guy," said Quinn as she patted her magical bag. "Crazy Board all you want. I've got purple yarn for days."

Brigham shook his head.

"I can't believe you scaled the Terror Tree."

"Like a pro," said Quinn, arms folded. "Regular Alex Honnold over here."

Brigham looked confused.

"The rock climber guy," Quinn explained. "Didn't you guys see *Free Solo*?"

"The Han Solo movie? Of course."

"No, no, that's *Solo: A Star Wars Story*."

"Yeah, there was no rock climbing in that," said Malcolm.

"Never mind," said Quinn. "So, after Forest Batman over here led me up to his sketchy hiding spot—" She looked at Brigham.

"Nice construction work, by the way."

"Thank you," nodded Brigham.

"After that, the creepy dude's cell phone rang, and it was like he was following orders."

I nodded.

"Yeah. I got the feeling he was kind of in trouble for wasting his time running after us."

"So maybe chasing us around was just his terrifying idea of fun?" said Quinn.

"Like a warm-up before the big game," said Malcolm.

"If the big game is most likely assault and battery, yes," I said.

Malcolm was pacing back and forth in front of The Crazy Board.

"So," he said, "if we can figure out where the Running Man was headed, then maybe we can figure out who else is being targeted. Then, we can catch the bad guys in the act and maybe film them and then we can—"

"Ahem."

We looked at Brigham.

"I hate to be the responsible one here, but couldn't this job be bigger than The Board?"

Malcolm stopped mid-pace.

"Nothing is bigger than The Board."

"Maybe this is," said Brigham. "This is getting dangerous. What if Running Man had caught up with them? What if . . . he had attacked."

His voice trailed off.

A chill ran down my back.

"The police," said Brigham as he turned to me. "You need to go to the police. They will help."

MARSHALL

The police did not help.

And as I stood in line in the fluorescent-lit lobby I began to understand the term "minor offense."

On the stained yellow wall next to me, there were methed-out mug shots next to words like manslaughter, kidnapping, and murder.

Somehow the words "chased by a possible Unicorn Man" seemed much less menacing once I said them out loud.

An attractive soccer mom-looking receptionist was sitting behind a pane of plexiglass scrolling through Instagram when I walked up and reported my less-than-impressive crime.

"What was that, honey?"

Behind her, a hardcore-looking cop with a 1980s action movie flat-top was leafing through a manila folder and sipping on coffee.

He glanced up at me for a moment and looked me up and down as though scanning my biometrics. Then he went back to his folder, no doubt tracking down a kidnapper or a serial killer.

This man was familiar with true crime.

Me. Not so much.

"I, um, got chased," I said. "By a man through the forest."

The soccer mom clacked a few things into her computer. She was wearing a pair of gaudy jewel-encrusted rings that must have been weighing down her fingers.

"Did he catch you?"

"No," I said. "Because I got away."

She nodded and typed and glanced back at her phone. She was playing Candy Crush now.

"But a couple weeks ago, I got punched."

I pointed to my nose helpfully.

"Punched in the face."

Again I pointed to my face, just in case she forgot where faces are on people.

"It hurt," I added.

She nodded, typed some more, glanced at her phone, and then shifted back to her computer again.

"Case number?"

Case number? Yes. Yes, I had one of those. But I didn't remember it.

I told her that.

And that pretty much took care of it.

She scribbled my name on a post-it and said an officer would call me at a later date.

We both knew that the later date would be the first of Never.

MARSHALL

"Okay, bad suggestion," said Brigham. "I just got worried."

We had reconvened in the basement that night.

I hadn't slept a wink due to visions of Unicorn Men dancing in my head.

From the looks of it, Quinn hadn't either.

She had bags under her eyes which somehow managed to make her look glamorous.

Like a model who had spent the night partying too hard.

I, on the other hand, just looked like a guy who had spent the night in a dumpster.

"It was a nice suggestion though."

Malcolm looked relieved. He was the small-town detective who feared he'd lose his jurisdiction to a big-shot federal agent. He didn't want to come off the case.

"So then," he said. "It's up to us. Completely up to us. And that means one thing . . ."

He stood up.

"Drum roll, please."

No one drum rolled, but he said it anyway.

"Stakeout time!"

MALCOLM

"Stakeout time!" I said. "Tonight!"

Brigham and Marshall leaned away from Quinn, as though they were waiting for her to explode.

She didn't.

And she didn't have to.

I had a plan.

MARSHALL

Quinn raised an eyebrow but Malcolm was ready.

"There's no car involved in this one!" he said. "Just bushes!"

"What?" said Brigham.

Quinn's eyebrow raised higher.

"We'll use the hedge bushes!"

"Are we doing his landscaping?" I said.

Malcolm shook his head and warily eyed Quinn as he pulled out a printed photo of a Google map of Coach Craig's neighborhood.

"See, we'll use these hedge bushes," he said as he pointed to an overhead shot of shrubbery. "Since cars are out of the question."

He glanced at Quinn again. She smiled and nodded regally at his subservience.

"Our next best bet is to establish our surveillance headquarters here."

He circled the shrubbery with a red pen and stuck it to The Board.

"It should provide the cover we need to keep an eye on Coach without him seeing us."

Brigham looked as though he'd been asked to scrub the urinals in C-Wing.

"We need to bring supplies," said Malcolm. "And make sure you go to the bathroom before we leave because, you know, there's no toilet and we can't come back until—"

"Wait, wait, wait."

Brigham threw a hand up.

"You want us to spend all night, squatting in the bushes, watching the neighbors like perverts?"

"Well, not like perverts. Nobody said anything about being perverts."

"Yeah, but it seems like something a pervert would do, right? Watching the neighbors from a hedge bush?"

"But we have a girl with us," said Malcolm sagely as he gestured to Quinn.

"Yeah, but girls can be perverts too," I said because messing with Malcolm is always fun.

"That's true," offered Quinn. "Many of us are very perverted."

"See!" said Malcolm with a satisfied grin. "Perverts can be anyone!"

He crossed his arms and nodded as though that settled everything.

He picked up a pair of overly large binoculars and slung a backpack over his shoulder.

"So, let's get to walking, perverts!"

"Now?" I said. "You want us to walk two miles and go sit in the bushes . . . right now?"

"Sure, why not?!" said Malcolm. "It's Saturday night. What else do we have to do?"

I looked at Quinn and Brigham.

Quinn shrugged.

I wished I had an answer for him. I was just planning on a couple of rounds of Mario Kart and Smash Bros.

Might as well not fight this one. We knew it was going to happen eventually.

We all stood up except for Quinn who propped her feet on the coffee table, put her hands behind her head, and leaned back.

"Sure, we could do all that . . ." she said. "But why walk?" She pulled out a set of keys and dangled them in front of us. "When you can drive?!"

And just like that, we had a Mystery Machine.

QUINN

I stole the Astrovan.

That's right. I, Quinn Carswell, stole the Astrovan.

It wasn't that hard really.

The plan went like this.

Step one: Walk over to the key hook.

Step two: Take the keys to the minivan.

Step three: Put the keys in the ignition.

Step four: Drive away.

Grand theft auto in four easy steps.

Do I feel bad about this?

No.

Not at all.

Not one bit.

Okay. Maybe a little.

It feels kind of like a violation of family trust.

But my sister probably won't notice anyway since she's currently dating a guy who drives a ridiculous red Camaro.

And another guy who drives a Ford Mustang.

And another guy who drives a Tesla.

The Astrovan was getting lonely.

Well, now it's not.

"Shotgun!" yelled Malcolm as he opened the big green sliding door and dove into the front seat.

Brigham wrestled him for a minute but gave up when Malcolm started squealing about "squatter's rights."

He took the middle row next to Marshall who had his hands between his knees and an eager look on his face like a puppy going for a ride. It was adorable. It's okay, you can tell him I said that.

As the only licensed driver among us, I was the Wheel Man . . . or Wheel Woman.

I cranked up the engine and put it in drive.

"Gentlemen," I said. "I would like to introduce you to our 1989 Chevy Astrovan. Better known as the Creeper."

"Awesome," said Malcolm. "It has a name."

"We call it that because it looks like the exact type of van that children and female joggers should avoid at all costs."

"So will we be giving out free candy?" said Marshall eagerly.

"No, sorry, I'm fresh out. But since it's Sloan's car you might find a rolled-up joint or two between the seat cushions."

The inside of the Creeper smells like Bonnaroo.

"This is amazing," said Malcolm as he ran his hand over the peeling upholstery. "This is our Batmobile."

Brigham grabbed the nearest Bic and flicked it on.

"And the Batmobile has multiple cigarette lighters on the floor."

We picked up donuts, the fancy kind with unidentified creams in the middle, and then we headed to Coach Craig's.

Technically, we were following Siri, but you didn't need GPS to find Coach Craig's house once you got close.

Just follow the glow.

He had multiple beer signs in his windows.

Mostly domestic light beers.

Water beer, according to Sloan.

"Is that a house or a liquor store?" said Malcolm as he shielded his eyes from the blue-neon lights.

I pulled to the curb at a wooded lot that was diagonally across the street from Craig's shaggy yard.

It gave us the perfect view of everything going on up and down Maynard Street.

Which, we soon found out, was absolutely nothing.

"What do we do now?" I said as I turned off the engine.

"We watch," said Malcolm. "And we eat donuts."

QUINN

The donuts were gone in twenty minutes.

"Okay," said Brigham as he leaned back in the middle row and patted his stomach. "What do we do *now*?"

"We watch," said Marshall. "And slip into a diabetic coma."

The scene on Maynard Street wasn't exactly action-packed.

So far the most exciting moment was when an old lady in a bathrobe opened her door and called for her cat.

Malcolm took notes.

Brigham took note of that.

"Did you just take notes on the cat lady?" he said.

"Of course I did," said Malcolm. "Nothing escapes my attention."

"*9:13 p.m.-Old lady opens door,*" said Marshall as he peeked over Malcolm's shoulder and read aloud. "*Old lady calls cat. Cat's name is Sprinkles.*"

A few seconds later, Sprinkles showed up at the doorstep.

Malcolm dutifully scribbled in his notebook.

Marshall leaned forward again.

"9:14 p.m. Old lady lets Sprinkles inside."

"Guys, I think I figured it out," said Brigham. "The old lady and Sprinkles were behind it all along."

Marshall nodded solemnly.

"I forgot to tell you. I was attacked by an old lady and her kitten."

I snorted and laughed.

"Clawed or de-clawed?"

"Claws, man. Sprinkles was all claws."

Twenty more minutes passed.

Much of that was spent with Brigham and Marshall reliving old Framptonworth campaigns and Malcolm taking notes on the very non-noteworthy events occurring within view of the Creeper.

I looked over his shoulder.

"9:36 p.m. Coach Craig's air conditioning unit turns on. Outside temperature is in the low sixties. Coach Craig hot-natured?"

Eventually, even he got bored with that and clapped his book shut.

"Okay," he said. "I think it's time . . ."

"Time for what?" said Marshall with a hint of dread in his voice.

"You know."

"Oh no," said Marshall.

"Please no," said Brigham.

I had no idea what they were talking about.

"You know you want it," he said. "It has to happen."

"We don't want it," said Marshall. "And it doesn't have to happen."

"It completely doesn't," nodded Brigham in agreement.

"Oh, yes it does," said Malcolm. "It's time to play . . . The Last Time I Peed My Pants!"

Marshall facepalmed. Brigham groaned. I nearly spit my iced coffee onto the dashboard.

"What?!" I said. "What is that?"

"Oh, it's just what it sounds like," said Marshall.

Malcolm smiled and nodded.

"Yes, it is, but it's more than that! If you agree to play The Last Time I Peed My Pants, you *have* to promise to tell everyone the last time you peed in your pants. No exceptions!"

"And . . ." I managed, "And this is a game you play often?"

"Too often," moaned Brigham.

"It's the perfect icebreaker!" said Malcolm.

"We don't need icebreaking," said Brigham. "The ice has already been broken among us long ago."

"Ahh, you can always break more ice."

"No, no," said Brigham with a hint of pleading in his voice. "It's a one-time thing, you break the ice and then it's just broken!"

Marshall was nodding alongside him frantically.

"Yeah, and some ice . . ." he said sincerely. "Some ice we don't need to break."

As for me, I was struggling to breathe as I was gripped in a fit of laughter that actually physically hurt.

"Wait, wait, wait," I said as I gasped for breath. "Wait . . ."

They turned to me and stared, bemused. Now they were laughing at my laughing.

"It's just . . ." I trailed off as I worked to get the words out. "In order to play this game often . . . wouldn't you have to pee in your pants often?!"

"Ideally, yes," said Malcolm, in all seriousness.

And I lost it.

And then it happened.

No, Malcolm didn't pee in his pants.

Coach Craig emerged.

"SHHHHHH!" spit Malcolm in a spray of donut crumbs. (He had resorted to eating the one that had rolled under the seat.)

"Dude!" said Brigham. "That was louder than anything we were doing!"

"Sorry!" hissed Malcolm. "I just got excited."

I worked hard to compose myself as we hunched low in the van and watched Craig walk out onto his front porch.

No, not walked . . . limped.

"Guys," said Malcolm. "Coach Craig is on crutches."

"And he's, um, looking directly at us," said Marshall.

"Nah," said Brigham. "Why would he look at us? We've got tinted windows."

"Maybe that's why he's looking at us," gulped Malcolm. "Tinted windows are suspicious."

"Yeah, but we're in a soccer mom van," said Brigham. "That's very unsuspicious, right?"

Then it occurred to me.

"Oh no," I said.

"Oh no, what?" said Marshall.

"What if he dated Sloan?"

"What?!" they all three blurted.

"Did he?" asked Brigham.

"I don't know! Probably! Sloan has dated everyone! I lose track!"

"He recognizes the Creeper!" said Marshall. "Let's get out of here!"

"Abort!" said Malcolm. "Abort! Abort!"

I propped the seat up and cranked the ignition.

The van let out a dry sputter and nothing more.

"Noooo."

I put my head on the steering wheel and tried again.

More sputtering.

I knew I was asking too much from the Creeper.

He only starts when the temperature is just right, the barometric pressure is low and there's no sense of real urgency amongst his passengers. Well, there was urgency, because Coach Craig was off the porch and hobbling in our direction.

Though in the darkened street and through the tinted windows, I couldn't tell if he recognized us.

"HEY!" he yelled, and we jumped in unison. "Did Amazon just drop off a van full of dorks?!"

He recognized us.

MARSHALL

Malcolm cranked the handle and slowly lowered the window.

"Heeey, Coach," said Malcolm.

"Heeeey, dorks," said Craig. "What are you doing here?"

"What happened to your leg?" asked Brigham.

"Your mom happened to my leg."

Brigham cocked his head to the side.

"My mom broke your leg?"

"Shut up," said coach.

He shifted on his crutches and grimaced.

"What are you guys doing outside my house past your bedtime? Going to a dork convention?"

Quinn laughed brightly.

"Oh, you live here?" She pulled a strand of hair behind her ear and giggled some more.

Was she flirting? It seemed like she was flirting.

"We didn't know! We were just going to . . . a party!"

I cursed under my breath.

Malcolm groaned quietly and slid low in his seat.

Everybody knew that we didn't go to parties. In order for us to go to parties we would have to get invited to parties.

"A party," said coach flatly.

Quinn nodded. She realized her mistake but there was no going back.

"Yep . . . Yep, just partying," she coughed. "With our fellow classmates. We like to party because of the great, really great, party scene here."

"On Maynard Street?" said coach. "There's a great party scene on Maynard Street?"

"Um . . . yes?" said Quinn.

"And you suckers were invited to a party? On Maynard Street? My street?"

Quinn was drowning, so I decided to dive in with her.

"Well, you know, it's not a cool party," I added. "It's like a Dungeons and Dragons party."

"For dorks," added Malcolm helpfully.

Craig let out a sharp laugh and bounced on his crutches.

"Ahh, now that's more like it! You guys wouldn't know a real party if it bit you on the butts, right?"

"No," replied Brigham. "Because parties don't do that."

Craig cackled some more. He seemed relieved that the natural order of the world was still as it should be.

"Which one of you is the Dungeon Master? Wait, wait, lemme guess, lemme guess. Buckle Shoes Boy, right?"

"We still haven't decided," said Malcolm. "Want to join?"

At this, we were expecting ridicule of enormous proportions. We didn't get it.

Coach Craig paused mid-insult windup and seemed taken aback.

"Um . . . no," he said. "No, no I have to . . ."

He leaned forward on his crunches as he stared at the pavement in front of him.

"Nah, man," he said. "Thanks for the invite, though."

We stared dumbly. And Craig's cheeks reddened when he realized he had accidentally been a nice person.

He took a tottering step backward and then swung around in the direction of his house.

"Anyway, you kids have fun at your nerd party," then he turned and ambled away. "And drive safely on your way home."

As Coach Craig clacked back up his driveway, there was about thirty solid seconds of stunned silence in the Creeper.

Then Brigham spoke. "Um. What was that??"

"Yeah, he told us to drive safely. Where was the insult in that?" said Quinn. "Was that some kind of higher form of yo momma joke we're not aware of?"

Malcolm leaned over his notebook and busily scribbled, NO INSULT—NEW YO MOMMA JOKE?

I slapped it out of his hands.

Because I knew it was no joke.

I knew exactly what had happened.

The injured knee.

The stooped shoulders.

The haunted gaze.

My turn to be Sherlock.

"Well, it's obvious, isn't it?" I said. "Coach Craig has been at-tacked by the Unicorn Man."

MARSHALL

Tonight, the dream was different.

It started with Sloan.

We're sitting on a park bench. It's twilight.

Malcolm, Brigham, and Quinn are all sitting a few yards in front of us at a banged-up wooden table playing a game of Founders.

They aren't speaking to each other. Their heads are bowed. Their hands are folded in their laps and their noses are all bleed-ing profusely.

Sloan says she wants to make out—hey, I told you it's a dream—but I'm too worried about my friends.

"Shouldn't we help them?" I ask Sloan.

Sloan starts to laugh.

"We can't help them," she says. "They have no septums."

I turn and look her full in the face and she has a horse's head.

And then I wake up.

Screaming again.

Look, I know this isn't exactly a dream journal, but this kind of thing is therapeutic for me.

My nightmares are now your nightmares.

I thank you for that.

CHAPTER TEN

SAVED BY THE SUMMIT 5000

MARSHALL

"But how can you be so sure?" said Malcolm during lunch on Wednesday.

He was taking notes and chewing on a carrot stick he had just dipped into chocolate pudding.

Gross.

I was still arguing my theory that Coach Craig was recovering from a Unicorn Man fight.

It was a theory that had been tested severely since Coach Craig had told everybody on Monday that he'd strained his knee training for a half-marathon.

"C'mon," I said. "Coach Craig's not an endurance athlete unless he's on a pub crawl! It's a cover story!"

"That could be," said Brigham. He was supposed to be tutoring Brody Engel in the chem lab but had skipped out for this very important meeting. Quinn was off getting a second round of chocolate milk. "Maybe he's afraid he'll get in trouble with the administration for fighting again."

"Yeah, he could have gotten into a fight," said Malcolm. "He always gets into fights. I heard he got into a brawl last month with some dudes at Planet Fitness over who was next in line for the elliptical machine."

"It's all on his face. Literally," I said. Trying out my best Angela Lansbury. If Malcolm could do it, so could I.

Really, I gathered by the haunted look in his eyes that he'd been through something traumatic. Just like me.

"He seemed kind of scared. Defeated, right? Coach Craig fights for fun. This wasn't fun. Unicorn Man has a professional hitman fighting style. And it's probably something Coach Craig hasn't experienced before."

Malcolm took another chomp of his chocolate carrot. Brigham made a gagging sound.

"It's a good theory," said Malcolm as he wrote, HITMAN FIGHTING STYLE-GOOD THEORY in his notebook and then slapped it shut.

"But," he said, "we need more evidence if we're going to put it on The Board."

"You need more evidence?" I said. "You've got a three-by-five glossy of Winky Jeff under the main suspects section just because he winks a lot! Since when do you need evidence?!"

"Well, to be fair, his winks are creepy," said Quinn who saddled back next to us.

"Hence the more popular name, Creepy Jeff," said Brigham.

Dang, poor Winky Jeff can't catch a break.

Quinn cocked her head to the side.

"Though, I have been thinking about something," said Quinn as she opened her carton of chocolate milk with ease. "Remember when the Running Man in the forest said he was going somewhere that looked like a pool hall?"

My mind flashed back to that night of terror, romance, and nosebleeds.

"Yeahhh," I said.

"Well," she said. "Coach Craig's house is practically bathed in neon."

Malcolm snapped his fingers and reopened his notebook.

"Ohhh," said Malcolm. "It does look like a pool hall!"

"So, Running Man was getting orders to go take care of Coach Craig that night?" said Brigham.

Quinn nodded. "But Coach Craig was able to fight him off since, you know, he's Craig the Concusser."

"Yeah, he can actually fight!" said Brigham. "No offense, buddy."

"None taken," I said. "I'm terrible at self-defense."

Really, I was just excited they were coming around to my detective work.

But Malcolm shook his head and made a *tsk-tsk* noise.

"Still," he said, "we need a bit more evidence if we're going to attach some yarn to it."

I opened my mouth to argue but then I realized exactly where he was going with this. It was his plan all along.

"Ah, all right," I said. "How do you propose we find 'more evidence'?"

I knew full well what the answer was.

Malcolm's face slid into another ear-to-ear smile.

"I'm so glad you asked," he said. "Because we're going to need more donuts."

MALCOLM

Yes, they groaned. Yes, they moaned. But they had to know.

The stakeout business isn't a one-and-done thing.

I told them that and Brigham, as usual, cracked wise.

"How much more do we need to know about the nighttime bowel movements of Sprinkles the cat?"

"We can never know too much," I said.

Once again, Quinn was the easiest to convince. She seemed to have developed a taste for grand theft auto.

"I'll get the Creeper," she said. "Who's got the donuts?"

MARSHALL

Breakfast was strange on Saturday morning.

Because it was normal.

It was the kind of breakfast you see families on television having, with placemats and silverware and big bowls of cereal.

For the Fairbanks home, the odds of my mom, me, and Tribal

Ted eating actual meals at the same place at the same time on non-holidays are quite slim. But I woke up that morning to the smell of bacon and eggs.

It had been a couple of days since our last Crazy Board meeting. There was lots of business to attend to but more mundane matters, like Mr. Bank's relentless AP Calculus, kept getting in the way.

I walked in and Mom was standing at the stove with a smile, while Tribal Ted was reading a newspaper.

A newspaper!

Something was up.

"Hey, tiger," said Ted.

He has never once called me that before.

Something was really up.

"Um, hey, Ted," I said.

I walked by Mom, and she gave me a kiss on my messed-up bedhead.

"G'morning, tiger," she said.

What's up with all the tigers?!

I was about to question it, but she handed me a plate of delicious food and I dove in. Most of my morning meals consist of cold Pop-Tarts or Chewy granola bars. I was starving.

I sat down at our much too-small kitchen table and noticed that Ted was looking at me with a strangely concerned look on his face. It was the kind of look he always got at the end of the *Fast & Furious* movies when he wasn't sure if Dom and the family were going to make it out unscathed this time. (Spoiler alert: They always did.)

"How's it going, sport?" he said.

"Um . . . good."

"Yeah?" said Ted. "You doing okay these days, kiddo?"

"Um, I was," I said. "Until you started talking like the dad from *Leave It to Beaver*."

Tribal Ted laughed and tossed the newspaper to the side.

"Yeah, you're right, I can't do this."

He leaned forward. "Here's the deal, you've been saying some extra freaky things in your sleep lately and your mom and I are kind of worried because it's some really weird stuff."

I probably turned white. Or bright red. Or a variation of both.

A sixteen-year-old male can dream about . . . a lot of things.

What was I saying? What was I doing? What did they hear?

Mom laughed.

"Nothing that bad," she said. "Just . . . weird."

She gave Ted a look and he hopped up.

"Welp, gotta head to work or something," he said as he gave my mom a much too lengthy kiss and ruffled my hair before leaving the room. "Glad I could clear things up. See you around, tiger."

Mom casually took a seat next to me and began to butter her toast.

"So," I said. "What am I saying?"

"Well, you talk about snot a lot."

Ahh.

"And Quinn."

Uh-oh.

"And unicorns? I get the sense they're not nice unicorns since you very loudly scream at them to go away."

That tracked.

"Me, personally, I've always loved unicorns," she said. "You know I collected *My Little Ponies* as a kid and Moonstone Rainbow ranked in my personal top five. She's not as cool in the reboot though, so if you get the chance, watch the originals. Nothing against the new stuff but I'm just more of a fan of the old-school ponylore from the '80s. It wasn't as hyper and self-aware and . . ." She went on like this for a while. If you wonder where I get it from, there you go.

I gave her a smirk.

"Yeah, this isn't a *My Little Pony* unicorn," I said. "I wish it was."

I had to be careful what I revealed here. For some reason, I didn't want to get into the matters of our secret society.

For starters, there just wasn't enough time. But also, I liked having it all to myself. It was like some kind of strange mystery-solving therapy. Also, there was the thought that we were beginning to meddle in things that perhaps the police should be handling. A responsible parent would probably sense this and simply call 911. Like Malcolm, I didn't want to share with the authorities. This was our case to solve.

If he could have read my mind at that moment he would have wept with pride.

So, I kind of lied. Sorry, Mom, if you're reading this.

"It's just the attack," I said. "I still dream about it every once in a while."

Mom furrowed her brow.

"That makes sense. And what's up with the snot? You seem very concerned about it."

"I do?"

"Last night you distinctly yelled, 'Give me back my snot!'"

I was mid-drink with orange juice and nearly choked.

"I did?" I said, sputtering out a laugh.

Mom laughed too.

"Ted seemed very concerned," she snickered. "He turned to me and said, 'Why is he so protective of his snot?'"

I chuckled and grabbed some napkins.

Mom leaned forward again. She was on the case.

"So . . ." she said. "Why are you so protective of it?"

"Well, you know, I lost a lot of snot in the attack. I guess Dream Me wants it back? Personally, I'm okay without it."

"And then the unicorns?"

Here, she seemed even more concerned. Was she on to us?

"Yeaaah," I said. "Yeah, I don't really know about that."

Okay I didn't *kind of* lie, I *full-blown* lied. Mom didn't believe me one bit, but she let it slide.

"And Quinn?" she said, her eyebrows raising.

I groaned and pushed my plate forward.

"Quinn is kind of self-explanatory," I said. I could feel my cheeks turning red and I hated it.

My mom knew about my infatuation with the beautiful Quinn Carswell. And she fully supported my slow-motion courtship since they had once bonded over a shared love for *Doctor Who* during a quick conversation in the carpool line.

"Any girl who knows that much about the Time Lord is good enough for my sweet Marshall," she had said.

The rest of breakfast was spent on this topic. Safer ground. She told me about how she was named shift manager, which means more money but also more work. I told her about how I was named project manager for LEGO Robotics Club in the spring, which meant, well, just more LEGO robotics.

Then, as I stacked up the plates and started to bring them to the kitchen sink, I glanced at Ted's newspaper. It was a crumbled copy of *The Tucker Times*. And with one glance, I knew it was destined for The Crazy Board.

Because on the bottom right-hand corner was a headline that nearly made me drop all the plates.

INCREASE IN VIOLENT CRIME TIED TO UNICORN GANG.

BRIGHAM

"Maaaan," I said. "I knew I shouldn't have let my subscription lapse."

I grabbed the paper from the gaming table just before Malcolm could get his hands on it.

Marshall had slapped down a copy of the latest *Tucker Times* in front of us and the headline brought the Saturday BrainForce meeting to a screeching halt.

Prior to that, we had been waiting for Marshall to arrive and were discussing whether or not we should order matching T-shirts.

Malcolm was all for it. I told him I had the feeling they might hinder our ability to work undercover.

"Yes, but color coordination is important too," he said.

"In that case, shall we get matching sweatbands?" said Quinn with a grin.

"Ohh, yeah," said Malcolm. "And maybe trucker hats?"

"Should the trucker hats say, 'Undercover Investigators at Work' then?" I said.

"No, that's ridiculous," said Malcolm. "But I like where your head's at."

And then the newspaper arrived, folded under Marshall's arm.

"Do you like apples?" he said as he hopped down the stairs.

"No," I said. "I'm slightly allergic."

"I know that," he said. Then he slapped the paper down on our gaming table. "But how do you like them apples?!"

I'm sure you guys have that article in an evidence locker somewhere, right? Next to a rubber unicorn mask and a bloody rock from the Windham Woods stone pile. But I'll still summarize it for continuity's sake.

The details were scarce. But it looks like the reporter had noticed that the series of "muggings" had occurred in a high-crime side of town known as the Burrows. No surprise there.

Growing up in Tucker, you don't go into the Burrows unless you have to.

And if you do have to go into the Burrows, chances are you're there for a casual drug purchase and/or routine assault and battery.

The surprise, of course, was that the culprits were wearing "horse-like" masks and that the victims said in each incident no money, jewelry, or valuables were taken.

One victim, who was unnamed, said a man dressed like a "trick or treater" had repeatedly punched him in the face "for sport."

"*Officer Hank Bridges speculated that the attacks were part of a violent initiation for a newly formed group called 'the Unicorn Gang,'*" stated the article.

"Wow," said Malcolm as he snatched the paper from my hands and read on.

"*The Tucker city police would like to encourage any citizens with information about these crimes to contact the department right away,*" he read.

"And that's just what I did," said Marshall.

"And they seemed kind of bored by it, right?" said Quinn.

"Yeah," said Marshall. "The Terminator cop just looked right through me and the receptionist lady never took her eyes off Candy Crush."

"Welp," said Malcolm. "Good thing The Academics are on the case then, right?"

He tacked *The Tucker Times* to The Crazy Board and spun around.

"So, two questions," he said, clapping his hands together. "Who's buying the donuts? And what's your T-shirt size?"

MARSHALL

I bought the donuts. Gas station brand. C'mon, I'm not made of donut money!

"Ugh, these are below stakeout standards," said Malcolm snootily as he opened the box.

He ate six of them.

We parked in our normal stakeout spot and hoped Coach Craig would leave us alone and let us properly stake him out.

"So, what are we hoping to see tonight?" said Quinn brightly.

She was wearing a faded yellow sweatshirt stretched over her shoulder, her hair was in a side ponytail, and it was the most beautiful thing I'd ever seen.

"Today, we are hoping to test Marshall's theory that Coach Craig was actually attacked by the Unicorn Gang," Malcom said as he pulled out a red notebook from nowhere. "We need further evidence."

"And we're testing that theory by watching Coach Craig's collection of front yard garden gnomes in the middle of the night, right?" said Brigham.

"Hey, it is an impressive collection," said Malcolm, as he eyed a seventh donut.

I snatched the box away.

"Well, while we wait . . ." said Quinn with a sly grin, "Why don't we talk a little bit about . . . Katherine Underwood?!"

We all looked at Brigham simultaneously.

It was dark but I could tell his cheeks were turning bright red.

Poor fellow.

"Um, what?" he said.

Quinn snickered.

"I've heard from Sam Hammond who talked to Lily Taylor who talked to Max Munson who talked to Katherine's best friend, Carly Trammell, that she might not say no if you asked her out sometime."

Brigham nearly choked on his off-brand donut.

"Ask her out?!" he said. "Where would I ask her out to?"

"Um, on a date," said Quinn.

"Wow," said Malcolm in awe. "A date."

"How do you do a date?" said Brigham.

"Yeah, how would that work exactly?" said Malcolm. He leaned forward and uncapped his pen.

Quinn cocked her head to the side.

"Geez, do I need to put together another Crazy Board for you guys?"

"Yes, that would help," said Malcolm.

"Guys overthink dates," she said. "It doesn't have to be all flowers and formal dinners with tablecloths. Fun is the key."

Her eyes met mine for a second. Only a second.

Um, was this directed at me? Our lone date consisted of walking through the neighborhood and running from a deranged alleged drug dealer. I suppose she was thinking of something more romantic?

Brigham stared out the window.

"Well, I like fun," he said.

"Good," said Quinn. "Your like of fun is a good sign, Padawan."

"What do you think she thinks is fun?" said Brigham.

"Well, that's what you need to find out."

"How do you find out?"

"You talk to her."

"Oh," said Brigham. "We talk sometimes."

I had to interject here.

"Um, are you still counting the time you asked her what time the pep rally was happening?"

"Yes," he said. "That always counts."

"What happened then?" said Quinn.

"Oh, it's a great story," said Malcolm. "Brigham asked Katherine what time the pep rally was happening and then . . . she told him."

We laughed.

"No, there was more!" said Brigham. "There was the joke!"

"Ah, yes don't forget the joke," I said. The Legend of the Joke has been told and retold many a time in the Ringold basement.

"She said she wasn't feeling very peppy that day, so she didn't want to go to the rally," said Brigham. "And I said I wasn't either. And then I said maybe that's why the school administrators prescribed a rally because our pep levels were at an all-time low."

"Bahaha!" laughed Quinn. "That's awful!"

"I know, right?!" said Brigham. "But she laughed! And she laughed a lot!"

"Oh man," said Quinn. "If she laughed at that, that's definitely a good sign."

This is the theory that Brigham has argued multiple times in the retelling of the Legend over the past year or so.

"Right?!" he said, finally vindicated. "But how do I ask her out?"

"I heard she likes mini golf," said Quinn.

"Oh, I like mini golf!" said Brigham.

"Well, there you go! Ask her to mini golf! And you can fall madly in love in front of the little windmill!"

Brigham didn't seem convinced, and I could tell he had more questions, but Malcolm was ready to move on.

"Glad we settled that," he said. "Now if we can stay on topic, we have a neighborhood to watch."

We sat in silence as we watched Sprinkles saunter by.

Malcolm dutifully took note of this in his book.

"So, how do I ask her?" said Brigham.

Malcolm tossed his notebook in the air.

"Geez, man. Are we going to have to start holding separate Academic meetings on relationship advice?"

"Well, yeah, that would help," said Brigham. "But for BrainForce . . . Think about it. We know nothing about the mysteries of girls—but we have a girl right here! She can tell us all the secrets."

"Oh," said Malcolm. He looked at Quinn as though she had some kind of magical power.

"I've never thought of it that way."

Quinn began to snort laugh, which had everybody else laughing.

Except me. I stopped hearing them at this point.

Because that was when I noticed him.

At first, I thought he was only a shadow.

A shady shape on the edge of the wood line in Coach Craig's backyard.

Then the shadow moved.

"Is that?" I asked. "Is that a person?"

The snort laughing stopped mid-snort.

"Where?" said Malcolm.

The minivan rocked to the side as we all shifted to the big window, peering into the darkness.

"Just next to the tool shed. I think that's a man? Or a woman? Or . . . something."

"Nah," said Malcolm. "I think that's just a shadow or it could be a—"

He stopped mid-sentence.

He dropped lower in the van.

"That's a person."

A tiny pinprick of orange light appeared in the midst of the shadow.

"There's someone else staking out our stakeout," he said.

MALCOLM

Someone else was watching Coach Craig.

Or were they watching us watching Coach Craig?

The cigarette gave them away.

A tiny dot of light slowly faded in and out.

"Well, that's also creepy AF," said Quinn.

"What do we do?" said Marshall. "Call the cops?"

"Noooo," said Brigham shaking his head. "What do we say? We're watching a guy who's watching a guy?"

"In a kind-of-stolen family minivan?" added Quinn.

"Good point," said Marshall. "Then what?"

"We need to call Coach Craig and tip him off," I said.

They protested, which is understandable. But we had his number from the AirDrop, and before they could talk some sense into me, I was calling.

The phone began to ring.

"Don't use your name!" said Brigham.

"Or your voice!" said Marshall.

"My voice?" I said. "How am I supposed to not use my—"

"Hullo?" said Coach Craig.

His voice was gruff, and it sounded as though I woke him up and it occurred to me that I had no idea what I was going to say.

"Umm—"

"Disguise your voice," whispered Quinn.

"Who is this?" mumbled Craig.

"Never ye mind who this be," I said.

Never ye mind. That's what I said. Because for some reason I was speaking in a Scottish accent.

I was going for old-school Sean Connery, but I think it came out more like a leprechaun.

"What?" he grumbled. "Is this some sort of prank call? If so, it's lame."

"Nay, tis not," I said. "Tis but a warnin'!"

Okay, now I sounded more like a pirate.

"I'm about to warn your face in a minute," said coach, more alert now. "You know I can see who's calling right?"

Good point. But my phone was registered to my stepdad anyway. Different last name.

"Ne'er mind about that," I said. "Somebody's watchin' ya, mate."

Okay, now I was shifting to Australian.

Coach Craig said nothing.

"And they're standing in tha shadows in yer own backyaaaard."

"What in the—"

Click.

I disconnected and threw the phone onto the seat next to me as though it was going to explode.

There was a beat of quiet as we all looked at each other.

"Um, good work?" said Marshall. "But why were you the pirate guy from *SpongeBob*?"

I shrugged.

"I was going more for *007*."

"Sorry, mate," said Quinn. "It didn't work."

But the warning sure worked. Because within seconds Coach Craig was out the door.

Angry.

Baseball bat in hand.

And ready to fight a unicorn.

MARSHALL

Coach Craig charged outside.

Or rather he hobble-charged, since he was still on crutches.

"How's he gonna swing a baseball bat on crutches?" said Malcolm.

"And he's more of the football type, right?" said Brigham.

This wasn't good.

Coach didn't look our way but tottered down his front porch and then headed into the side yard.

He stopped with his back to us and stared into the shadows.

"Coming back to finish the job, you one-horned freaks?!" he yelled. "Bring it on!"

There was no response from the shadow man.

Just that pinprick of orange light. And then it was gone. The cigarette was tossed to the ground.

And there he was.

My "further evidence" strode right out of the shadows, right out of my nightmares, and into Coach Craig's backyard.

He was just as I remembered him.

Silent.

Surreal.

Abnormal.

The Unicorn Man.

And he was staring straight at Coach Craig.

QUINN

It was like watching a cheesy horror movie.

The one where the slow-walking killer could easily kill much more efficiently if he'd just go about his business at a light jog.

We all knew the Unicorn Man could run.

But not today.

Today, Unicorn Man opted for the menacing slow walk.

Poor Coach Craig couldn't have run away if he tried.

He muttered something that sounded like, "whathafuzza," dropped his bat, and then frantically hobbled back toward his front door.

He was the prey.

Unicorn Man was the predator.

He was on him in seconds and went straight for the good knee.

Craig let out a wail and went down hard.

It was a strange, sad sight to see Coach Craig, bully of all bullies, brought to the ground so swiftly and efficiently.

The Unicorn Man said something low, grumbly, and chillingly casual.

"Call the cops," said Marshall. "It's about to get bad."

Brigham picked up his phone and dialed 911 and stammered something about a fight in Coach Craig's front yard.

Unicorn Man was hunched over Craig now. He punched him in the face, a quick lightning strike that resulted in an explosion of blood.

"Yikes, there goes the septum," said Marshall as he grabbed his own nose.

The Unicorn Man said something else indistinguishable, and Coach Craig shook his head and yelled something back.

The Unicorn Man must not have liked it because he kicked him in the ribs.

Once. Twice. Three times.

"It's getting bad!" said Marshall.

Then he went for the head. Craig curled into a sad, broken ball.

Coach Craig tried to cover his face, but the Unicorn Man's swift kicks landed with cruel precision. He really was a professional.

"He's gonna kill him!" yelled Brigham.

"What do we do?! What do we do?!" screamed Malcolm.

"We gotta help!" said Marshall.

"What if he's got a gun?!" said Malcolm.

"I know karate!" said Brigham. "Has anyone else been watching the Master Kensei links I've been sending to the group text?"

"No one does that!" shouted Malcolm. "When will the cops get here?"

"I just hung up!" said Brigham. "They can't teleport!"

Teleporting policemen and internet karate wouldn't save Coach Craig. But the Creeper might.

"Hold on!" I yelled.

I cranked the Astrovan and miraculously it caught on the first try.

The Creeper doesn't come with many amenities. It's got crank windows, manual locks, heck, we're lucky it has seatbelts.

But there is one modification that my sister insisted on after we pulled out of the parking lot of Gibson's Used Cars two years ago.

I put my hand in the center of the steering wheel and leaned.

AOOOOOOOOOOOGGGAAAAAAAAAAAAAAAAAAA!

An obnoxious old-timey airhorn exploded into the night.

The Unicorn Man froze over Coach Craig's crumpled body.

I leaned on it again.

AOOOOOOOOOOOOGGGGAAAAAAAAAAAAAAAAAA!

Dogs barked.

Porch lights turned on.

Shades went up.

Marshall held his ears and looked up at the ceiling as though we were being divebombed by German forces.

"What is that thing?!"

"It's a Summit 5000!"

AOOOOOOOOOOOOOGGGGAAAAAAAA!

"Loudest custom car horn on the market!"

AOOOOOOOOOOOOOGGGGAAAAAAAA!

"It also plays 'Dixie' and 'La Cucaracha'!"

AOOOOOOOOOOOOOGGGGAAAAAAAA!

"Sloan likes to use it when she's tailgating slow grandmothers!"

AOOOOOOOOOOOOOGGGGAAAAAAAA!

"Cause she drives like a complete psychopath!"

And for once, I was grateful for that.

Because the Unicorn Man was gone.

He receded into the shadows and left Coach Craig clinging to life and a stalk of tall grass in his front yard.

We left the safety of the Creeper behind and ran to help.

MALCOLM

I expected blood. But not that much blood.

We ran across the street and found Craig the Concusser unconscious and in a sad heap next to his lawn decorations. The yard gnomes were swimming in red stuff.

"Aw no," I said.

I stepped back reflexively.

"That's a lot of blood."

I'm not proud to say it, but I froze. I didn't want to touch him. Blood is not my thing.

Marshall, Quinn, and Brigham, on the other hand, leaped into action like a trained teenage medical team.

"Unicorn Man broke his nose," said Marshall. "Probably broke his ribs too."

"Make sure there are no cuts or gashes on his head," said Quinn. "That's most important."

"We need to bandage his wounds. Do you need a shirt?"

Brigham took off his stained pocket tee in a *Baywatch* rush. "This will help stop the bleeding."

How did they know how to do this stuff?

Why weren't they freaking out?

And where did Brigham get those abs??

Coach Craig's face looked like hamburger meat. He let out a moan that sounded like a wounded calf and we all jumped.

It was loud.

Too loud.

We knew Unicorn Man couldn't be far away.

Shirtless Brigham crouched down and stared into the street-light shadows like Tarzan.

"We need to get him inside," he whispered.

"Should I go back to the car?" I said.

They looked at me like I had grown my own unicorn head.

"I mean, to blow the horn in case he comes back?"

Yeah, that's what I meant.

"Forget the horn," said Quinn. "Grab a leg."

Remember what I said about trained-teenage medical professionals?

Forget that.

It took us five minutes to carry/drag Coach Craig across his front yard.

At one point his foot got hooked on a garden hose and we kind of sort of dropped him.

The unconscious Coach Craig was now semiconscious. And loud.

"CHEAPLLAMAAS! THANK YOU FOR THE LOVELEE DAYSEES!"

"Did he just call us cheap llamas?" said Brigham.

"Did he just thank us for the lovely daisies?" said Quinn.

"Whatever he said, if Unicorn Man's still around, he heard it," said Marshall.

We made it to the front porch and pulled Coach Craig through the door by his blood-stained Nikes, closed the door behind us, bolted it shut, and turned around.

And this is where things got weird.

QUINN

Did Malcolm tell you it was weird?

Yes, it was weird.

Weirder than a nightmarish nose-breaking Unicorn Man?

Yes.

Oh, yes.

Weirder than that.

Though, at first glance, the inside of Coach Craig's home was pretty unexceptional.

A couple recliners, a big leather couch, a big blue sectional, and a flat-screen TV that's nearly bigger than the wall that's supporting it. It's pretty much what you'd expect from a frat boy-man that never got into a frat.

Minus one glaring exception.

Malcolm actually screamed a little when he saw it.

The rest of us froze.

And then Brigham stated the obvious.

"You guys," he said. "Coach Craig has a Crazy Board."

BRIGHAM

Coach Craig had a Crazy Board.

And it was even crazier than ours.

Malcolm whistled through his teeth.

"Now that's a nice-looking board," he said under his breath.

"Wow," whispered Quinn. "And it's way bigger than yours."

"Hey!"

"It's okay, buddy," said Quinn. She patted him on the shoulder. "It's not all about size."

But if it had been about size, Coach Craig would have won handily. A crazy collage of papers, photos, newspaper articles, and yarn took up the entire wall of his living room and then stretched farther around the corner and into the kitchen.

Marshall wandered that way, entranced by the treasure trove of new evidence.

"Oh, and he's got the good *red* yarn," said Malcolm, flashing an accusatory glance at Quinn.

"Hey, purple is regal!" she said.

"Um, guys," said Marshall.

He had just followed a particularly long strand of yarn into the hallway. "Come here. Now."

He was white.

Staring.

Shaking.

We gathered beside him, and together we looked into the dead eyes of a rubber unicorn mask.

MARSHALL

The craziness of Coach Craig's Crazy Board could not be contained to one room.

First, I saw a picture of the Unicorn Man. It was a large photo of the AirDropped file that originally sent me into Panic Attack Town. I felt my heart speeding up as I stepped closer to it. I stared at the blurry picture and a shiver ran up my spine. Tacked to the Unicorn Man pic was a red strand of yarn. I followed as it zigged to *The Tucker Times* article we had just read, (good on Coach Craig for supporting local journalism). Then it zagged to a scrap of paper with an address on it (34 Skyline Drive). And then zigged again to something large and floppy and skin-like hanging from the board.

It was the mask.

There was no head inside that Unicorn Mask. No murderous hooligan hiding within it. But it still felt like staring into the eyes of my nightmare. All the hurt, all the cruelty, all the pain of that night came flooding back. A scream bubbled up in my throat.

Instead of screaming, I actually slapped it.

Maybe that was silly, but I was kind of proud of that slap.

Did this mean my fight-or-flight tendency was shifting toward something less resembling a scared rabbit? I hoped so.

I called for the guys, and they crowded around me in Coach Craig's neon-green St. Paulie Girl-lit kitchen.

Next to the mask were the words: UNICORN DUST PUSHERS and MISTER HAPPY'S CREW.

Malcolm looked like he was going to faint from excitement.

Brigham, who was still shirtless, uttered some creative curse words.

Quinn was all business.

"Okay," she said. "First things first. We need to get help for Coach Craig. He's lost a lot of blood and is most definitely concussed."

We nodded, though no one really took their eyes off the collection of amazingness and terror sprawled before us.

"And then second," said Quinn. "While we wait for the ambulance to show up, we all get out our cell phones and take pictures of every single inch of this board."

We nodded, pulled out our phones, and got to work.

"Crazy Board plagiarism," said Malcolm as he shook his head and snapped away.

I looked over at him.

"I mean, I'm not above it," he said. "It's an impressive display of Crazy Boarding."

Behind us, Coach Craig lay on his back and hummed a John Denver song.

MALCOLM

As we followed the thread it was clear the epicenter of the craziness was in the kitchen.

And it was there that the plot thickened. Because two words were about to up the danger factor considerably for our small team of crime fighters.

Two hastily scrawled words next to the picture of a menacing, thick-necked man with a buzz cut.

BAD COP.

His photo was circled several times.

"So, there's a bad cop now?" said Brigham.

"Apparently," said Quinn.

"But," said Brigham. "I just called the cops."

"Wait," said Marshall, snatching the photo from the wall. "That's the guy from the police station. That's the blond Terminator!"

Coach Craig let out a startled snore and we all jumped.

The red strand continued downward and toward a tattered yearbook page on the lower section of the board. It was crumpled and looked as though it had been hastily ripped out. The rows of frozen smiling faces on the page seemed somehow menacing under the green glow of beer-hall neon.

"That's not Carter High," said Marshall. "I don't recognize any of those people."

Quinn leaned in.

"Look at the template. There's a shamrock next to the page number. Which team is the Shamrocks again?"

I actually knew that.

"That's Druid Hills High."

They all looked at me.

"Remember when we played them at homecoming and the pep squad hung that banner in the gym that said, 'Druid Hills is a Sham (rock)'? It never quite made sense to me."

"Oh yeah," said Brigham. "That's because it doesn't."

"Look," said Marshall. "Coach Craig circled a name."

Indeed, he did. In fine red pen, he had circled the name Caroline Mae Henderson. She had dark hair and darker circles under her eyes. She was the only kid on the page not smiling and she looked somehow older than her classmates. It was as though she was weighed down. If they were looking to the future with hope, she only saw dread . . . despair. And maybe she was right.

Next to her name was a single scrawled word.

Taken.

A chill went up my spine.

"Taken?" said Quinn.

Marshall swallowed hard.

"They're . . . taking people now?"

"Or worse," said Brigham. "Look . . ."

His hand was shaking slightly as he pointed to the far side of the board and to another clipping from *The Times*.

This one wasn't a story though. It was a death notice.

Quinn groaned.

"Oh no."

A few lines summed up the life of the sad-looking teen on the torn-out yearbook page.

"Died at the age of nineteen," said Brigham. "Drug overdose."

We stared at each other in silence.

"A drug overdose," said Marshall.

We were all thinking the same thing.

"Or was it . . . more than that?" I said.

The red yarn ended there.

In the next room, Coach Craig's snoring had subsided.

The tinny hum of the neon lights was the only sound. Then another light began to flash. Brighter. Blue and red. And from outside.

And then it all kind of happened at the same time.

The knock on the door.

The glance outside.

The photo of the face on the board.

That same face, staring stone-jawed and cop-like through the window of the door.

"Oh no," I stepped back from the blinds. "Bad Cop is here."

Behind us, Coach Craig softly warbled a soothing tune.

"Country hoooome. Takemeroaaaads."

CHAPTER ELEVEN

BAD COP

BRIGHAM

Bad Cop was standing at the door.

And, man, he looked like a bad cop.

Straight out of Bad Cop casting.

Thick neck.

Thicker biceps.

Severe 1980s-era *Terminator* buzz cut.

Cold hard suspicious eyes.

Chewing gum quickly.

Patting his holstered gun slowly.

He knocked on the door with a *ratatatat* and we all jumped.

"That's the guy!" said Marshall while peering through the blinds. "He might recognize me. He stared right at me at the police station."

"So, what do we do now?" said Quinn. "If he sees all this stuff and he truly is a Bad Cop then . . ."

"Bad things will happen," said Malcolm.

"So, he won't see it," I said.

Believe it or not, I knew what to do.

Because believe it or not, I've been in similar situations.

Domestic disputes and all.

Mom and dad fought a lot.

A lot.

And it was loud.

Though it was thoroughly traumatizing, thankfully it never came to blows, but the cops showed up a lot. Nobody wanted to see Dad or Mom hauled off to jail, so when that happened, we went into family crisis mode.

Our most popular bit was a routine we called the Cop Out.

So, I guess all of my broken home training had come to this.

"You guys stay low," I said as I opened the kitchen window, flashing back to home life on Dowdy Court. "I'm going to sneak out the back and talk to him out front. I'll make him think I'm just a concerned bystander."

"A bystander in the middle of the night?" said Marshall.

"It'll work," I said. "It has before."

"Wait!" said Quinn.

But it was too late. No turning back. I was already out the window and into the dark backyard.

QUINN

"Wait!" I said.

But it was too late.

He was already out the window and in the backyard.

"Um," said Malcolm. "Doesn't he need a shirt?"

BRIGHAM

I needed a shirt.

I really, really needed a shirt.

They could have warned me, right?

By the time I realized I was half-naked it was too late.

Bad Cop was peering into the darkened windows of Coach Craig's front porch when I looped around the yard and approached him from the street.

"Hey!" I shouted from the streetlights.

Bad Cop swiveled and for a moment I thought he was going to pull out a baton, chase me down, and beat me with it.

He pulled out a flashlight instead, jumped the porch railing, and was on me in two seconds.

His gun was holstered but I instinctively put my hands up.

I felt really shirtless at that moment.

"Stay where you are, sir," he said.

His voice was higher and twangier than I expected, but no less menacing.

"Um, don't shoot," I said with a chuckle.

He didn't chuckle back.

Bad Cop said nothing and kept the blinding flashlight beam in my eyes.

Time to do some lying.

"Um, I was just passing by, and I think I saw a fight between two guys out here," I said. "I'm not sure because it was dark. At first, I thought it was just two dudes wrestling. But then it kind of looked like one of them was getting mugged so I called the cops — I mean, the police department."

"Where's your shirt?"

"Where's what?"

"Your shirt. You going for a swim?"

"Oh, well, that's a good question . . . um."

Bad Cop's flashlight beam was peering into my soul.

"I was on a run."

"A run?"

"Yes, sir. A three-mile run. I'm on the Carter High cross-country team and this is part of my usual route."

I'm not. But I was banking on the hope that Bad Cop wouldn't check the CHS XC roster as part of his investigation.

Being shirtless was not ideal, yes. But it wasn't completely bad.

One of the rules of the Cop Out is that an unexpected detail can help distract the cop from the obvious lie you're telling while you tell it.

For example, one night during one of our better performances, my brother Bryan rode around the corner of our house on a unicycle. I followed him, yelling that he had stolen my unicycle.

Actually, my mom had been yelling at my dad because he filled up the DVR. But the unicycle thing was just strange enough to be believable.

In theory, the same principle would work against Bad Cop.

Except this time, I wasn't Brigham: Unicycle Theft Victim. I was Brigham: Shirtless Nighttime Jogger.

Bad Cop didn't say anything but swiveled his flashlight beam out of my eyes and to the ground. That had to be a good sign.

The darkness was all blurry spots.

"So, do you often run without a shirt on?" he said.

"Yessir," I said. "Almost all the time."

Bad Cop stared and chewed his gum.

"Sensitive nipples," I explained.

More staring. More chewing.

"My coach said it's best for nipple sensitivity. To wear no shirt. He also suggested Band-Aids. But . . . ouch, amirite?"

Bad Cop apparently didn't think I was right.

I felt like he was using some kind of Jedi mind trick to keep me talking.

It was working.

"Nipple sensitivity . . ." I said, "has been one of the biggest challenges of my cross-country season so far. Also, side cramps. Sometimes bananas are good for that because they say the potassium provides enough fuel for the muscles to process."

More staring.

"I have a teammate who uses raw honey."

"For his nipples?"

I barked out a high-pitched laughing sound that I've never made in my life.

"No, no. For cramps, sir! He eats raw honey before every race so he doesn't get cramps! I tried it once and it didn't work, and I puked in the woods at mile two."

Was I really talking about cramps and nipples?

In my hyper-aware state, I honestly didn't know what I was going to say next. It was like my mouth kept moving and I was just along for the ride. Was this the best performance of my life-time? The worst? Was I having a stroke?

"What's your name, Speedo?" said Bad Cop.

"Brigham Weaver, sir."

Bad Cop flipped out a small notebook and wrote this down.

"Where do you live?"

"Tayfan Drive," I said.

Bad Cop stopped mid-scribble and swiveled his flashlight back into my eyes where it peered directly through my brain.

"Say again."

I gulped, immediately realizing my mistake.

"Tayfan Drive, sir."

"Tayfan Drive is more than six miles from here," said Bad Cop. "I thought you said you were running three?"

I was lying to an officer! I was lying to an officer, and I was caught! I was lying to an officer, and I was caught and I was going to jail!

He knew it. I knew it. Obstruction of an officer is a real thing.

He was going to arrest me.

I was going to lose all future scholarships.

Worse, I was going to prison with no shirt.

"Oh, yeah, sorry," I said. "I run a double route on the week-ends."

Bad Cop closed his notebook.

"So, let me get this straight. You're on a six-mile run at eleven thirty p.m. You're shirtless because of your sensitive nipples. And you saw 'two dudes' wrestling in the front yard over here, but they ran away."

"Um," I said. "Yes."

Bad Cop knew something was amiss. And he was going in for the kill. And then the radio blared to life.

"All units we have a 10-17 at the Bank of Tucker parking lot. We need all responding officers in the area."

He sighed and radioed back.

"This is Unit 103, headin' that way," he said while staring directly at me.

He reached into his back pocket and handed me a card that had the contact info for Tucker Police Department.

"If you see something else," he said. "Let me know."

There seemed to be genuine concern in his voice that took me off guard.

Maybe this Bad Cop wasn't so bad after all.

He hopped into his patrol car, slammed the door, and then leaned out the window.

"And make sure you tell Marshall I said hey."

His eyes lit up in red then blue then red then blue.

"What?"

His lips peeled back into something resembling a smile.

But it was more like having a hyena grin at you.

"Make sure he stays safe and keeps his nose covered."

He gunned the engine.

"And good luck with your nipples."

Then he turned on his siren. And he was gone.

MARSHALL

"Okay new plan," said Malcolm as he peered through the window and watched the police cruiser pull away.

"We take Coach Craig to urgent care and drop him off at the waiting room. Somebody will take care of him. Then we get to my basement and hide and eat fudge brownies and—"

"How about another plan," said a raggedy voice from the couch.

We turned around to see Coach Craig sitting upright and half-dead.

"Get out," he said.

We looked at The Board, and then back at him.

He clutched his obviously wounded head and leaned forward.

"Get out now. And forget what you saw here."

He knew we knew. And we knew he knew.

"Coach, you might have a concussion," said Quinn, soothingly. "We need to make sure that you didn't fracture anything or—"

"GET! OUT!"

We got out. We got out of there fast.

We ran across the street, grabbed a shirtless, stammering Brigham in the front yard, and dove into the Creeper.

Quinn cranked it. The engine actually started. And we raced to safety.

Or, well, since it was the Creeper it was more like we race-walked to safety, but still.

MARSHALL

Quinn hit a speed bump at forty-five miles per hour and the box of donuts scattered across the floorboards.

Brigham didn't notice.

He had his head in his hands.

He still needed a shirt.

"Dude," said Malcolm. "Take my hoodie. Please."

He was experiencing obvious ab-envy. I was right there with him.

He unzipped his red sweater and tossed it to Brigham, who was noticeably shaking.

"I hate to ask," I said as I patted him on the back. "But how'd it go?"

"Well, not good at first," he said.

He drew in a ragged breath.

"And then really not good after that."

"Uh oh," said Quinn. She peered through the rearview mirror into the backseat. "Why really not good?"

"Well . . ." Brigham's voice shook and he drew in another deep breath. "I talked about my nipples a lot."

I stopped patting him on the back.

"Your nipples?"

"Yeah," his voice went up an octave. "Yep, yeah, there was more talk about my nipples than I expected. And also kind of a sidebar on potassium and how to avoid side cramps?"

"Well, that's weird," I said. "But not necessarily bad."

"And maybe even helpful and informative?" said Malcolm.

"No, no," said Brigham. "The bad part was at the end. After my lesson on muscle fuel and nipple friction . . ."

The Creeper stopped at a red light next to the old Matthew's Cafeteria.

"What happened at the end, Brigham?" said Quinn.

"He said hey . . ."

He trailed off and looked at me. He was shaking even more now. "He said hey . . . to you. Hey specifically to you."

I didn't quite catch his drift.

"How could he say hey to me," I said. "I wasn't even out there and—oh."

"Yeah," said Brigham. "He knows you."

I kind of felt like I jumped into a pool of icy cold water.

You know when it's so cold and you can't catch your breath? It was like that.

"He knows me?"

"Yes."

"How?"

"I don't know."

"Well, he probably knows you from the police station, right?" said Malcolm. "Maybe he overheard your report and started looking at your case file and—"

"Yeah," interrupted Brigham. "But I never mentioned Marshall. I just talked about nipples and potassium but somehow, he knew."

"How does he know?" I said.

"I don't know."

"That's not good."

Brigham nodded.

"Really not good."

It was hot outside, but inside the Creeper, I was freezing.

"He's Bad Cop," I said. "And he knows my name."

MARSHALL

That night, I didn't go home. Following Malcolm's recommendation, we dove into the quiet darkness of the Ringold family basement as though it was a warm blanket.

There were no fudge brownies, but we made Bagel Bites.

We turned away from The Crazy Board and turned on *The Fellowship of the Ring*.

All the while, I felt myself sympathizing with poor Frodo more than ever. Outmanned. Outgunned. Shellshocked and unprepared for the awful challenges ahead of him.

Poor hobbit Elijah Wood was lamenting about how he wished he didn't have to deal with all this crap. Gandalf, of course, knew just what to say.

"So do all who live to see such times. But that is not for them to decide. All we have to decide is what to do with the time that is given to us."

Was Gandalf talking to me? To us?

I'm pretty sure we all thought so.

After the movie was over, we sat there in silence. Malcolm had passed out on a couch. Quinn had missed curfew by a mile and needed to return the Creeper. We were tracking her phone to make sure she made it okay.

"All right," I said with a sigh of relief. "She's back in her driveway now."

"Good," said Brigham.

For the first time in hours, my body actually untensed. I could feel my eyelids getting heavy and I leaned into the old orange sofa.

Brigham was sitting upright in the beat-up brown La-Z-Boy, as though keeping watch.

I was just about to doze off when he spoke.

"If it makes you feel better," he said, "he knows my name now too."

That did make me feel a little bit better.

Misery loves company, yes. But so does mind-numbing terror.

CHAPTER TWELVE

A NEW NIGHTMARE

MALCOLM

Okay, this is the part of the investigation we will call the Disappearance.

Mysterious sounding right?

We walked into Coach Craig's study hall on Monday and he wasn't there. But we kind of expected that.

Instead, Coach Sydney Conner was sitting in his usual rolling chair. Coach Conner is in many ways the female version of Coach Craig.

Just substitute football for cheerleading.

Like coach, she ruled Carter High as a student. And so, she decided not to leave. Now she's a regular roaming substitute and assistant cheerleading coach who is also a minor celebrity on TikTok.

Her thing is dancing in front of a classroom with students following along in the background.

Some might say her moves are a bit suggestive for a public-school classroom.

Of course, I follow her account but, um, that's purely for academic purposes.

On day one, she made us all do the Dougie.

Simple enough.

On day two, it was the Cha-Cha Slide.

Still, pretty easy but hard to do in the middle of a crowded classroom.

On day three, it was a classic: the Electric Slide. She was not happy with our lackluster performance and analyzed the footage on the smart board.

"You have to *feeeel* the rhythm," she said while pacing back and forth in front of a half-asleep study hall.

"Man," said Quinn. "I never thought I'd say it, but I miss Coach Craig."

"Yeah, how many sick days do you think he'll use for his unicorn beating?" asked Marshall. "I only used three."

"Seems like that should be the industry standard for unicorn beatings," said Quinn.

Marshall snickered.

"Want to know something weird?" said Brigham. "I don't think he's called in sick."

"How do you know that?" I asked.

"This morning, I was doing TA work in the office, helping Mrs. Alford make copies, and I saw the big white board where they list the teacher's schedules. There was a big question mark next to his name. Like the administration doesn't even know where he is."

"So he never called in?" said Marshall, hiding behind his book bag so Coach Conner wouldn't call on him to participate in something called "the Kangsta Wok."

"I don't think so," said Brigham.

"And when did you plan to tell us this information?" I said.

"I was going to save it for the next BrainForce meeting," confessed Brigham. "I've got calculus, you know."

Quinn shook her head in exaggerated seriousness.

"Calculus does not exist on The Crazy Board," she said. She was mocking me I think. But I agreed wholeheartedly.

"Okay, so how do we find out where he is?" said Marshall. "Oh no, does this mean another stakeout?"

Of course it meant another stakeout—and I was about to inform him of that when Quinn interrupted.

"I have a better plan," she said. "It's pretty complicated though. See if you can follow along here . . ."

We leaned forward for what I was sure was going to be another Crazy Board-worthy caper.

"We ask," she said and then leaned back.

"And then what?" I said.

"That's it," said Quinn. "That's the whole plan."

"Brillant," said Marshall, putting his hand up for a high five.

"Thank you," said Quinn, returning that high five.

"We are good students. People trust us. So, we just ask."

"Well . . . that's kind of disappointing," I said.

"Yes, but we save money on donuts," said Marshall.

MARSHALL

It was our most simple of plans.

And yet it backfired immediately.

BRIGHAM

"Why do you want to know?" said Mrs. Ricardo.

QUINN

"It's not my business to discuss personnel matters with students," said Mr. Bellinger.

MALCOLM

"You need to be focusing more on your side-to-side transitions in the Electric Slide," said Coach Conner.

I kind of took offense to that.

MARSHALL

"Go sit down and stop bothering Coach Jensen," said Coach Jensen.

He talks in the third person a lot.

So it turns out, we asked one too many questions.

And that led us to uncharted territory: A trip to the principal's office.

"Quinn Carswell, Marshall Fairbanks, Malcolm Ringold, and Brigham Weaver. Please come to the front office," said Mrs. Alford through the school-wide intercom.

Ooooooh, said the entire lunch room in unison. Even the lunch ladies joined in I think.

The shame was great.

"We're good students," said Malcolm in a high-pitched mocking voice as we traveled down the hall. "Why don't we just ask?"

"Okay, sorry," said Quinn. "It was a lazy plan. I just figured we could do something, anything, that didn't require a meeting and twelve steps worth of planning on The Crazy Board. And my voice doesn't really sound like that."

"Everything requires twelve steps of planning on The Crazy Board," said Malcolm. "Otherwise, it's not worth doing."

"Okay, but we need a plan now right?" I said.

"Too late for that," said Malcolm. "I have no access to a Crazy Board."

"But what do we say? Are we gonna tell them about the unicorn?"

"No," said Brigham. "That means police. And police means Bad Cop."

"Yeah, but what's Bad Cop going to do to a bunch of teenagers?" said Quinn.

"Um, he's a cop," said Brigham. "What can't he do?"

I now realized that multiple cops—um, police officers—are reading this. So, sorry for this part.

On the walk to the principal's office, we determined that we would hold strong and deflect. We were only interested in Coach Craig's whereabouts because we're good students who care about the well-being of Carter High staff and faculty.

Mr. Chang would believe us. He had to believe us.

We sat two rows deep in his office.

Brigham and Quinn took the front row. Marshall and I took the back.

"Good afternoon, students," said Mr. Chang.

He was busily typing on his desktop and had yet to completely turn in our direction.

"Good afternoon, Mr. Chang," we said in unison.

He smirked.

"I hear you've been asking a lot of questions today," he said. "Is that right?"

We nodded.

"It's not school policy to discuss personnel matters with students," said Mr. Chang. "But why do you ask?"

"Well, we were just wondering," said Malcolm. "He's our favorite teacher."

Mr. Chang raised an eyebrow.

"Why are you lying?"

He was still typing. He wasn't looking at us. And it was unnerving.

I felt my ears warm. This is not a situation I've ever been in, in the hot seat at the principal's office. But I've seen it happen while TA-ing alongside Brigham and Mrs. Alford, and I've seen that the stone-wall method is the best way to go.

Say less.

Always say less.

I did that.

We all did.

We said nothing and Mr. Chang typed on.

"Some students consider Coach Craig their favorite *teacher*." He threw air quotes around the word teacher. "These are students who skip class. They wear letters on their jackets. They drive cars that are too loud. They get into fights in the hallway for recreational purposes. And they're often in my office, sitting right where you are."

He finally stopped typing and looked our way. When he did, it was as though he could see straight through us.

"You have the highest test scores in the school. You're straight-A students. You wouldn't know anything below a 4.0 GPA if it bit you on your rear ends."

He looked at me.

"Marshall Fairbanks, you're a junior star student, for crying out loud. Coach Craig is not your favorite teacher. You could teach Coach Craig a thing or two about teaching."

He lowered his voice.

"There's a reason the door is closed right now," he said. "I'm telling you this in confidence. And I know I can, because I trust you four more than I trust some of my own employees. Or at least my janitorial staff."

We all knew who he was talking about. Poor Winky Jeff can't catch a break.

"The truth is no one knows where Coach Craig is right now. That's why you've been summoned here. An email went out this morning asking all staff members to let me know if they have any information on his whereabouts. The fact that you all asked different teachers at nearly the same time leads me to believe something is up."

He leaned back in his chair and crossed his arms.

"So," he said. "What's up?"

We may be reasonable teenagers. But we're still teenagers. And that means when an adult asks us "what's up," our first response is usually to say two words and two words only.

"Nothing much," said Malcolm.

Principal Chang leaned forward. He smelled blood in the water. He shifted his gaze.

"Malcolm Ringold," he said. "I've worked in the teaching profession for twenty-three years. And if there's one thing I've learned, it's that it's never 'nothing much.'"

He looked at each of us individually. Which one of us would crack first?

"It is always something."

Brigham cleared his throat.

"Okay," he said. "It is something."

Mr. Chang smiled and nodded.

"We miss Coach Craig because we can't take any more of Ms. Conner's TikTok choreography. I need to study for calculus, but I'm more worried about not embarrassing myself doing the Swag Bounce."

A brilliant move by Brigham. And it was actually true.

Mr. Chang shook his head and his shoulders dropped.

"I have no idea what that is," he said. "But this is not the first TikTok-related complaint I've received regarding your substitute. I will talk to Ms. Conner about eliminating social media dance parties from her curriculum . . ." He sighed. "Again."

I began to realize we might pull this off.

"Anything else to add?" He looked at us. And through us. He knew. And we knew. And he knew we knew. But we weren't going to let him know we knew he knew, you know?

"Okay," said Mr. Chang. "You're dismissed."

We sprung from our seats and headed for the door.

"But, guys . . ." he said.

We turned. He dropped the principal demeanor and for a moment just seemed to be talking to us like a regular person.

"If you know something, you need to say something, okay? His mother is very worried. And I'm a little worried too."

We nodded and said that we would.

But would we?

We weren't so sure.

MARSHALL

That night, I had a completely different nightmare.

This one was more subtle but still equally nightmarish.

I was in Principal Chang's office. By myself this time. And he was typing.

I was in my back-row seat, waiting for him to talk when I realized his mouth was hanging open.

There were flies buzzing around his screen.

"Mr. Chang?" I said.

He didn't respond.

I stood up, walked behind his desk, and looked over his shoulder.

I leaned in and saw that his fingers were decomposing. Flesh exposed. Bone showing. He was still clacking away on the computer.

He was typing one single phrase over and over.

Ding Dong the Coach is Dead.

Ding Dong the Coach is Dead.

Ding Dong the Coach is Dead.

"What does this mean?" I said.

"It means you killed me," said Mr. Chang slowly and calmly.

I took a step back.

Mr. Chang rose from his weathered desk chair.

He stood for a moment with his back to me. Then he turned. And I realized he wasn't Mr. Chang at all. I was staring at a dead, decaying zombie Coach Craig.

"IT MEANS YOU KILLED ME!" he screamed.

And I woke up.

Screaming.

Okay, that last part wasn't so subtle.

MARSHALL

"I have a problem," I said.

Brigham nodded.

"You have multiple problems."

It was midnight and we were playing old-school *Mario Kart* on Malcolm's Nintendo 64. He was upstairs somewhere.

"Unicorn stalkers . . . crazy drug dealers . . . corrupt cops . . . also you're about to get hit by a red shell."

He hit my Yoshi with a heat-seeking shell and I cursed.

"Yes," I said. "All that is bad. But this is worse."

"Worse than unicorn stalkers?"

"Yes," I said. "Yes much worse."

I tried to toss a banana peel his way, but wound up only slipping on it myself.

"I will never be able to kiss a female."

Brigham snickered.

"You and me both, buddy." He smacked me with a green shell. "But that's not breaking news."

"No, no," I said. "I'm not *physically* able. Every time I get close to almost kissing Quinn, my nose starts bleeding. We were this close to actually making out in the forest last week, but the bleeding began and . . . that was it."

"Ahhh," said Brigham.

He was currently in first and unfairly firing off a series of mushroom boosters.

"First off, congrats on *almost* being able to kiss a girl," he said. "Most of us would just like to be in that arena."

I nodded.

"Yes, I'm happy to be here."

I ran off the edge of Rainbow Road and switched to smart steer.

"But eventually we'll all be here," I said. "Even Malcolm. Meanwhile, I'll still be sad and alone having to bring along a jumbo-size Kleenex box on all my dates. If I ever go on dates."

"That is a problem," said Brigham.

"Like I said."

"I'm very experienced in this topic. It's wise that you came to me."

"Ha."

"Okay, here's the thing," he said. "Quinn likes you."

I nodded.

"That's a very, very big thing."

I skidded through an oil slick.

"If Katherine Underwood actually wanted me to kiss her, I would literally be doing backflips off this nasty sofa right now."

"Yeah," I said. "But what if she wanted you to kiss her and you literally couldn't do it?"

He fired off another green shell and pondered this.

"That's a whole different problem. But it's a problem I wish I had."

He paused the game and turned to me.

"What I'm saying is, Quinn will understand. You're dealing with some stuff, man. Some really, really sucky stuff. She realizes that and she'll wait until you get it all figured out. She likes you that much."

He was right. Things were better now, and I felt less alone. But I still felt . . . haunted. Literally haunted by the Unicorn Man. Normal dating right now was like trying to go on a picnic at the Overlook Hotel from *The Shining*.

"I'm telling you, she'll wait for you to figure it out."

"Yeah," I said, feeling a little better. "I guess that's half the battle."

"Nah, man, that's the whole *entire* battle," he said. "You are a lucky man."

Then he unpaused the game.

"Except for now."

"Why?"

"Because, turtle shell."

He smacked me with another red shell and cruised across the finish line.

"Thanks, buddy," I said.

BRIGHAM

"Speaking of Katherine Underwood," said Marshall.

It was about one a.m., and we were following up a full *Mario Kart* grand prix with a heated round of *Smash Bros.* in Malcolm's basement. He must have fallen asleep upstairs.

"We weren't speaking of her," I said.

"Well, still," said Marshall. "I think we should."

He was Donkey Kong, I was Samus. He hit me over the head with a barrel.

"What's to talk about?" I said.

"How about the fact that we have solid inside intel that your dream girl would not completely shoot you down if you asked her on a romantic mini-golf date?!"

Donkey Kong nearly knocked me off the ledge. I tried to counter with a pulse blast, but he blocked it handily.

"I know we've been busy with detective work and there's a lot going on. But still, this is headline news! Katherine Underwood likes you!"

I shook my head.

"How do we even know that info is reliable? It's like fifth-hand intel."

"Well, there's only one way to find out."

"How?"

I knew the answer.

"Ask her."

Donkey Kong smashed another barrel on my head.

"Dude," I said. "I don't think I'm the dating type. That takes a car and nice clothes and—"

"And what?"

"Money," I said. "It's well known I don't have any."

"Eh, who does these days?" said Marshall. "With the global economy and all."

"Katherine Underwood does," I said. "Her parents own a hardware store."

Donkey Kong tossed me into the air and kick-flipped me off the ledge.

"I'm currently wearing hand-me-downs from the Obama administration."

"And you wear them well," said Marshall.

"I don't have a car."

"We have the Creeper. Quinn can give you a ride."

"I have no money."

"We'll take up a collection."

"I don't want to be a charity case."

"Dude."

Marshall paused the game mid-body-blow and looked at me.

"You're not a charity case. You're my best friend. And if Katherine Underwood isn't interested in you because you're not the heir to a hardware store fortune, then she doesn't deserve you."

I couldn't help but grin.

"Ah, shucks."

"For real," he said as he unpaused. "Nobody cares that you're not rich. Nobody that counts, anyway. These are crazy times right now. We're all confronting our fears. We're all living for the yearbook . . ."

"Did you just quote Malcolm?"

"Yes, please don't tell him."

I managed to land an uppercut.

"But, in this case, he's right," said Marshall. "At least you're not in danger of any make-out nosebleeds. You just have to make up your mind to do it and then throw yourself out there, man."

He blocked my leg sweep and tossed me off the screen.

"Just like I'm going to throw this barrel directly at your face."

And that's exactly what he did.

"Thanks, buddy," I said.

QUINN

"Should we get out?" said Marshall as we pulled in front of Coach Craig's house on Thursday night.

It was dark, quiet and apparently abandoned.

Without the ever-present neon-glow of light beer signs, the house felt . . . dead.

The black windows peered back at us as we stared from the safety of the Creeper. It was a chilly night, so we had the heater on. It made the whole car smell like gasoline, but it was worth it.

"Um, maybe we should just call this a drive-by stakeout?" said Brigham.

We all looked at Malcolm.

Surprisingly, he was okay with that.

"Yeah, either he's hiding from the Unicorn Gang and doesn't want to be found or . . ." His voice trailed off as he made more notes in his book.

"Or he's already been found," said Marshall.

"Right," I said. "So, whose job is it to find him?"

As I pulled away from the haunted home of Coach Craig, I think we all knew the answer.

And no one wanted to say it.

Of course, Malcolm said it anyway.

"Us . . . That's who."

MARSHALL

The Unicorn Man took the night off for this nightmare.

Instead, Caroline made a guest appearance.

Yes, Caroline Mae Henderson was standing in the exact spot on C-Wing where I normally find my nightly visitor. She had the same sad forlorn look from the yearbook. Shoulders hunched. Eyes downcast. She stood alone in the hallway. A stark silhouette beneath the greenish flickering fluorescents.

Then I blinked, and she was in front of me.

Inches from me.

And then, slowly, she began to smile.

"What will they say?" she said.

Her smile grew.

"What will they write?"

I shook my head and tried to reply but no words came out.

"I know," she said.

Strands of long dark hair fell in her face.

"Taken," she said in a whisper.

Her smile spread further, unnaturally so, as though some unseen hands were pulling at her cheeks.

Then, a crackling school intercom came to life overhead with a jolt.

"Taken," she whispered again.

A staticky female voice came over the speaker and began to repeat the same words over and over:

Marshall Fairbanks, sixteen. Died of a drug overdose.

Marshall Fairbanks, sixteen. Died of a drug overdose.

Marshall Fairbanks, sixteen. Died of a drug overdose . . .

She cocked her head to the side.

"So sad."

Her smile grew impossibly wider as I realized with fresh horror that she had a unicorn horn sprouting from her forehead. She lowered her shoulders and, knowing what was about to come next, I finally screamed.

And I woke up in a tangle of *Star Wars* bed sheets.

I was sweating.

I was shaking.

And, well . . . I was kind of missing the Unicorn Man.

Chapter Thirteen

Doing Parties

Brigham

Okay, I had made up my mind.

I was going to do it.

I was going to throw myself out there. I was going to "live for the yearbook."

If Marshall could confront his unicorn nightmares, and if Malcolm could become an amateur sleuth, I could do this.

I could ask a girl out to mini-golf.

The approach would be the trickiest part.

She was on the other side of B-Wing, surrounded by beautiful friends who were all talking animatedly.

I opened my locker, stared at the back of it, and then peeked around the side of the door.

I was trying my best not to put out a stalker vibe.

Eventually, only Lily Taylor remained. But then, magically, she left. And Katherine was alone.

And then, even more magically, she dropped her books.

This was my chance! I could sweep over there, pick up her books and propose a date!

I still wasn't sure what to say but I was surprised to find that my feet were moving in that direction.

How would I go about this? I had no idea. I just hoped that

when I opened my mouth, actual words would come out. Bonus points if they were intelligible words.

She dropped down to gather her books, saw me coming, and actually smiled.

At me!

This was happening!

And then, there was Malcolm's face.

Malcolm's big, smiling face.

"We got a clue!" he said.

"What?" I said. I tried to sidestep him but Quinn was there too.

"A clue!" she said. "We think we might know where to find Coach Craig!"

"Oh, really?" I said, craning my neck to see past them. The coast was still clear. I still had a chance.

Malcolm moved back in front of me.

"Quinn was looking at her phone when a calendar update popped up."

Quinn shoved an iPhone in my face.

"Only it wasn't my calendar! During Operation AirDrop, some of Coach Craig's contacts and notifications crossed over to mine. And this was the reminder!"

She tapped the screen and held it up for me to see.

Hell Party Part II. Skyline Drive. Oct. 31.

"Hell Party II!" said Malcolm. "Doesn't that sound terrifyingly awesome?"

It did. And I was now sufficiently distracted.

"And it's on Halloween, so we can disguise ourselves!" said Quinn.

The bell rang.

She was gone.

And I was late for class.

Okay, maybe next time.

Though, to be honest, I think Hell Party II sounds less scary.

MARSHALL

Four words.

Malcolm wrote four words on the top right corner of The Crazy Board.

HOW TO DO PARTIES.

Yes, how to do parties.

How to do, indeed.

Judge us if you must. But this was crucial.

Because, as a team, we had no idea at all how to do parties.

For that, one would need to, well, be invited to a party.

"Should we watch a movie about parties?" said Brigham. "Like *Animal House* or *Weekend at Bernie's*?"

"I don't know," I said. "Is *Weekend at Bernie's* really a party movie?"

"Yeah," said Brigham. "I think there are parties in it."

Malcolm leaned over the sofa.

"But it's mostly a dead guy at the parties, right?"

He had wandered away from the board.

"That's the irony I think," said Brigham. "A dead guy is the life of the party."

"Ahhh . . . haha! That's clever!"

Malcolm chuckled and wrote DEAD=LIFE OF THE PARTY on The Board.

"That's good stuff," he muttered.

Quinn shook her head.

"That is not good stuff," she said. "That is not good stuff at all."

QUINN

Marshall put his hands on his head and leaned back in his favorite plastic chair.

We were entering the second hour of our "How to Do Parties" seminar and somehow we were back on Bernie.

"So," he said. "Bernie just wears sunglasses and bright clothes. He doesn't talk but he looks cool. So maybe that's the secret. Maybe we just need to look cool and say as little as possible."

"I think he also dances," said Brigham. He was halfheartedly working on calculus homework.

Malcolm turned.

"Are you kidding me? If he's dead, how does he dance?"

"There's something with a voodoo curse that makes him dance every time he hears music I think," explained Brigham.

"So we have to dance at this party?" said Marshall.

"Couldn't hurt," said Malcolm.

He headed over to the board and added a subset to the main topic.

HOW TO BE GOOD AT DANCING. Then he opened up his laptop.

"What are you typing?" I said.

"I'm doing a Google image search for Bernie," said Malcolm. "For The Board."

"No," I said.

"No?" said Malcolm.

"Just . . . no."

"Why no?" said Marshall. He had a cute, concerned look on his face that almost made me lose my train of thought. Almost.

"First off, he only dances in *Weekend at Bernie's II*. It's not nearly as good as the first. Second off, you can't learn 'how to do parties' from Google. And if you're using the phrase, 'do parties,' you don't know how to do parties."

"Okay," said Marshall. He looked relieved. "So, no dancing then."

I shook my head.

This was bad.

Very bad.

And it was bad because I knew exactly what I had to do.

And I knew exactly where to go for help.

I couldn't believe I was saying it while I said it.

Six words.

Words that stopped my fellow Shadow Guilders dead in their tracks.

Bernie-pun intended.

"We need to talk to Sloan."

Malcolm

Sloan Carswell.

Sloan Carswell was coming back.

Sloan Carswell was coming back to my basement.

Not as an intruder, but as a guest.

As a guest of *honor*.

The promise of an unholy alliance of Quinn and Sloan Carswell was almost too much to bear. I just hoped she knew about the Hell Party.

But then, this was Sloan Carswell. Of course she would.

Quinn

"Yeah, I know about the Hell Party," said Sloan.

Of course she did.

I was standing in her room while she was sprawled on her bed and staring at her cell phone.

It was awkward. I hadn't been in her room in more than a year and I wasn't sure whether to sit or stand.

"That's not really a starter party," she said. "Why does the Scooby gang want to go there?"

"Coach Craig is missing," I said.

"And?"

"We think we can find some clues as to where he is," I said with a shrug.

"And?"

"And what?"

I found myself stifling the usual urge to strangle her. Don't be alarmed. That's normal.

"*And* why are you asking me for help?" she said. "You almost jumped me in the basement the other day."

She tossed her phone to the side and looked at me for the first time.

"You were ferocious. I thought you were going to throw me through a wall down there to keep me away from your precious boyfriends. Or at least try to. Why are you inviting me back as a guest of honor?"

Well, that was a valid question. And I'd been asking myself that as well. Really, I'm not sure. I just knew we were probably headed into some dangerous waters. My sister, for all her faults, knows danger. And I felt as though we'd be safer with her there. Of course, I wasn't going to tell her all that. But I was about to do something that went against all my sibling instincts. I was going to apologize.

I took a deep breath and did what needed to be done. It was for the Shadow Guild. *They better name it that.*

"Look," I said, I sat down on the corner of her bed, on the same flowery bedspread we used to make blanket forts out of when we were both home from school on sick days. "I'm sorry about that. I overreacted a little."

"A little?"

"A lot," I said. "I just was being—"

"Crazily territorial?" said Sloan with an obnoxious grin.

"Um, I was going to say *an alpha female* but yes, that too."

Sloan picked up her phone and started texting again.

"So, we were trying to figure out who attacked Marshall. But there's more to it than that. There's weird gang members and drug dealers involved. One of them chased us through the woods. I think we may really be onto something here. And I don't think we can call the cops."

"I can relate to that," said Sloan.

"Um, yeah . . . well, it's getting shady. And we need your help. Because you're the shadiest person we know."

Sloan let out a snort laugh identical to my own. It runs in the family.

"It's a good thing you came to me," she said. "But there is one problem."

"What's that?"

Sloan broke into a wicked Sloan-smile.

"How's Malcolm's basement gonna hold *two* alpha females?"

MALCOLM

Sloan Carswell.

Sloan Carswell was back.

Sloan Carswell was back in my basement.

Not as an intruder but as a guest.

As a guest of *honor*.

I think I've already covered that but I'm just very excited.

I tried to keep my voice from shaking as I stood in front of The Board that night.

"Ladies and gentlemen, we have a guest speaker tonight," I said.

Sloan was draped over the orange sofa as though she was taking a break from a Vogue photo shoot. I locked the basement door as soon as she entered to keep Martin out. He had long since lost interest in our "dork conventions" but I had the feeling he would crash directly through the ceiling if he knew the legendary Sloan Carswell was mere feet below him in the basement. Instead, he was upstairs playing *Super Smash Bros.* online.

Ha! Loser! (Nothing against *Smash Bros.* though, it's awesome.)

"Let's give a warm Academic welcome to . . . Sloan Carswell!"

We all applauded except for Quinn who rolled her eyes.

"Thank you everyone and welcome to my TED Talk on how to do parties," she said as she walked to the front of the room. "First off . . . If you call it 'do parties,' you are doing it wrong."

"See, that's what I said!" said Quinn.

"Yes, and you were right for once." Sloan paused for laughter. We were too frightened to laugh.

"Second off, when you *do parties*, you need to blend in. Especially for the kind of detective work you're planning. The key to blending in at a party is to not make it obvious you are trying to blend in. Grab a drink, but don't drink it. You're lightweights, I'm sure. Lean against the wall. But not like you're a cool kid in *High School Musical*. More like you're buzzed and trying to make the room stop spinning. Then you will look like 99 percent of the people at this party."

I raised my hand.

"Yes," said Sloan. "You, sir?"

"Yeah, so, for costumes we were thinking we'd all be Stormtroopers and we were wondering if you wanted to get in on that?"

"What?"

"It's the store-bought kind not the full armor so it's not that expensive."

"Right," said Quinn. "And also it's a nod to when Luke and Han snuck into the Death Star disguised as Stormtroopers. Get it? The Hell Party is our Death Star!"

"No," said Sloan.

"No, you don't get it?" said Quinn.

"No, I get it. Just no to . . . all that."

She reached into her bag and pulled out a four-pack of tacky, glittery Mardi Gras masks. "You shall go as this."

"What is this?" said Brigham. "It's just boring masks."

"Right. You shall go as four people wearing boring masks."

"Um, well, no offense," I said. "But that's lame."

"Exactly," said Sloan. "And lame is good because it shows minimal effort. People at these parties don't go there for festive costumes and *Star Wars* cosplay. They go there to do . . . other things. Anything that shows effort will only attract attention you don't want."

Quinn let out a *grrr*. She looked miffed but probably because she knew her big sis was right.

"Look," said Sloan. "At these parties, girls wear as little as possible and a mask. And guys wear whatever they found in the hamper that day . . . and a mask."

"But . . . in Coach Craig's party video, we saw a guy dressed like a chicken and it wasn't even Halloween!" I said.

"And there was also a bear," added Brigham.

"And did you notice them?" said Sloan.

"Of course," I said.

"I rest my case," she said. "You guys need to be wallpaper. Not Stormtroopers."

"Dang," said Marshall. "She's got a point."

"Of course I do," said Sloan. "That's why you brought me in as your wise party sensei. Any more questions?"

I raised my hand again.

"Yes," said Sloan. "You again, sir?"

"What if a lady asks us to dance at this party?"

"A lady?"

"Yes."

"Asks you to dance?"

"Yes, do I take her by the hand and lead her to the dance floor?"

"Yes, do exactly that . . ." She took a few long-legged steps forward and smacked me on the head. "If you're wearing a powdered wig and a lace collar!"

She touched my head! I couldn't believe she touched my head.

"This isn't a cotillion! People don't *ask* at these kinds of parties. They just do."

Marshall frowned.

"Seems kind of caveman-like."

Sloan smiled.

"Exactly."

Mental note. Sloan likes cavemen.

I raised my hand again.

"How will we know how to do that?"

Sloan grinned, walked slowly across the room, and turned off the lights.

"We practice."

A small blacklight flickered to life and a Bluetooth speaker began to play.

Sloan Carswell brought props!

The song: "Bump n' Grind."

The artist: R. Kelly.

The mood: awkward.

But Sloan didn't seem to notice that. Or maybe she did and thought it was hilarious.

Sloan paired us up.

Marshall and Quinn.

Naturally.

Sloan and me.

Miraculously.

And Brigham and . . . nobody.

"What about me?" said Brigham. "Should I dance with a mop or something?"

"No, no," said Sloan over the thudding '90s R&B. "You're the standing-in-the-corner guy."

"I can do that," he said, looking relieved.

"We'll need you to be on the lookout for Coach Craig in case he shows up. You're our eyes and ears," she nodded. "As long as the girls leave you alone."

"Why would the girls not leave me alone?" said Brigham dumbly.

"Because you're hot, dummy."

Brigham looked like he'd been shot with a stun gun.

He took his place in the corner.

Stupid, hot Brigham.

I'm not sure what happened from that point.

It was a blur.

There was slow grinding.

There was fast grinding.

There was in-between grinding.

I think I became a man that day.

MARSHALL

In our section of the basement, there was no bumping and grinding.

Just awkward shuffling back and forth.

"How do you dance to this?" I asked.

"Um, like they did in the '90s?" said Quinn.

"Great. What was that like?"

"You bump and grind maybe?"

Was this an invitation? I took a step closer and then a step back and then put my hands up.

"I've gotta be honest. I have no idea how to bump and/or grind."

Quinn let out a loud laugh.

"When in doubt, I always start a lawnmower." She mimed a classic lawnmower-starting dad-dance move.

I laughed and shook my head.

"Not my style. I prefer to shop for groceries."

I pulled out an imaginary shopping cart and perused the invisible aisles.

"Well, after mowing I always like to water the lawn," said Quinn.

She busted out an impressive sprinkler. I topped that with a rodeo lasso. She dusted her shoulders off. I fired back with the robot. There was some popping, then some locking, then a really bad moonwalk on both sides. This was turning into a true nerd dance-off.

She was laughing. I was laughing. At one point she flipped her hair back and smiled directly at me and I almost had to hold onto a wall so I wouldn't pass out.

Then the music slowed and it was TLC, "Red Light Special."

I know this because Sloan stood on a chair and announced it.

"Slow dance time!" she yelled.

She gathered both Malcolm and Brigham together and took turns dipping and spinning them.

We looked at each other and shrugged.

"Now we do the sixth-grade dance, right?" I said.

We put our arms out straight and awkwardly held each other at arms-length.

Her hands were on my shoulders.

Mine were just barely on her waist.

Then she took a full step closer to me. And there was no distance between us.

She put her arms around my neck.

I put my arms around her waist.

It felt warm. It felt right.

We swayed back and forth slowly.

"Well, this is easier," she said.

"Yeah," I said. "This feels . . . perfect."

Did I just say that?

My heart was beating out of my chest.

Could she feel it?

Was this the time to kiss her?

Right here? In front of everyone?

I silently prayed that my septum would keep it together.

Then she laid her head on my chest and my mind shut down all at once.

No thinking.

No worries.

Just bliss.

Just the moment.

It's a five-minute long song but it might as well have been five seconds. Or five decades.

The music came to an end, and we kept swaying in our corner of the basement.

Then Sloan flipped the lights on, and we realized everybody was watching.

Sloan slow-clapped.

"Now *that's* how you do a party."

MALCOLM

Once the lights came back on, I looked at Sloan.

"Does this mean we're dating now?"

She slapped me on the shoulder.

But she also laughed.

And she also didn't say no.

She pivoted and turned to The Crazy Board.

"Anyway," she said. "People don't really dance to '90s R&B at these parties."

"What? What was all that then?" said Brigham.

"I just thought it'd be fun."

She winked at Marshall and Quinn. They were sitting suspiciously close on the orange couch. Both turned bright red.

"The Hell Party, however, is not fun."

"But it's a party, right?" I said. "Isn't it supposed to be kind of fun?"

"Only if your idea of fun is something illegal. People at these parties are there to hook up and get high. Most likely at the same time."

I raised my hand.

"How do you know this, ma'am?"

"Well, because I've done both."

We let that sink in for a moment.

"One last question," said Brigham. "Since we're not Stormtroopers, what do we wear with our masks?"

"Yeah, are there some guidelines or dress code we should follow," I said.

"Of course there is," said Sloan. "Write this down."

I grabbed my notebook and pen.

"Khaki slacks, white polo shirt, blazer, an ascot, a pocket square, and you're an idiot."

I stopped writing mid-polo shirt.

"No, there's no dress code!" she said. "There are no rules. Just blend. But blend without looking like you're trying to blend."

"I will try my best," I said.

Sloan slapped me on the back of my head, and I took it as a sign of affection.

"I mean, I will not try at all."

I gave a thumbs-up to the group.

"Blend," I said. "Just blend."

I quietly erased "khaki slacks" from my notebook.

We probably should have realized right then, we were in trouble.

Marshall

There was more dreaming that night.

But this was an actual dream.

There was Quinn, '90s R&B, and a world without the Unicorn Man.

I'll keep this one to myself.

HELL NIGHT

CHAPTER FOURTEEN

ATTACK OF
THE PARTY ZOMBIES

MARSHALL

Tucker is mostly a safe town. Mostly. Unless you're on the south side.

If anything bad happens—assault, battery, thievery, murder, potential coach-nappings—it happens there. And the sketchiness reaches full sketch in a series of neighborhoods on the south side known as the Burrow.

Well, we were in the very heart of the Burrow Saturday night.

And the Creeper looked right at home.

We parked beneath a flickering streetlight a few weedy blocks away from the party spot. It was a one-story cinderblock house that seemed to be physically vibrating with the *thump-thump-thump* of electro-bass.

Inside the van, the smell of body spray was overwhelming.

"Dude," said Brigham as he held his nose and looked at Malcolm. "Did you use a whole can?"

"Don't be silly!" said Malcolm. "Just a light spritzing!"

He adjusted his ridiculously glittery purple mask. I did the same.

"A little light spritzing goes a long way," I said between gasps.

"A little bit of that goes nowhere," gagged Brigham.

"I think it smells like a real man in here," said Sloan.

Malcolm looked like he'd just won the lottery.

"Yes, it does," said Quinn. "It smells like a dozen real men in here."

She was wearing a yellow mask, yellow sundress, and purple Converse All-Stars. I don't think I've ever seen her in a dress before. She frowned, pulled it down over her knees, and smoothed it.

"Was a sundress a good choice?" she said. "The sun isn't even out."

I nodded and tried to think of the right words to convey how amazing she looked without accidentally saying that I wanted her to wear that exact same dress to our wedding one day.

"Oh, shush," said Sloan. "You know you look like Dorky Boy's dream girl right now. Own it."

Quinn stuck her tongue out at her big sister. But I noticed she didn't deny it.

Sloan was uncharacteristically complimentary right now.

Brigham was the hot boy.

Quinn was the dream girl.

Malcolm smelled like a sexy man even though he really smelled like a drug store fragrance aisle.

She was trying to build us up before whatever was about to happen . . . happened.

Also, weirdest of all, she seemed a little nervous.

Maybe I should have taken that as a sign that things were about to go horribly awry.

QUINN

Sloan pulled me aside as we got out of the van.

"Hey, sis," she said.

There was a tone of sincerity in her voice that I hadn't heard since pre-middle school days.

"Be careful in there."

"Okay," I said. "I'll just blend, right?"

"It will be harder for you," she said. "Since you're, you know, adorable."

I was shocked by the unexpected niceness. Not fair, really.

"Oh, stop," I managed.

"I mean it," she said with a frown. "This is a party with people who are . . . not good people. These boys that you hang out with? They're good guys. They think you're a literal goddess. They would never hurt you or take advantage of you."

There was a bit of resigned envy in her voice that made me sad. She's never had that kind of friendship and protection. She deserves it though.

"The guys in there," she motioned to the darkened house that was pulsing with the same ominous bass beat over and over. "They're the opposite of that. Get it?"

I said I did.

But maybe I didn't.

Sloan could tell.

"Just stick close to me," she said. "You're too good for those people in there. I want to keep it that way."

I nodded and pulled a strand of fuzz off of her scandalous crop top. She was wearing fuzzy ears and that was the extent of her costume. She was supposed to be "a mouse." Really she just looked like an off-duty runway model with fuzzy ears.

"And hey," she said. "Save some of the dudes for me."

She slugged my arm and sauntered over to the guys.

Just like that, Party Sloan was back.

I rolled my eyes at the ridiculously abrupt transition.

But as we walked to the front lot, around a gaunt passed-out shirtless guy and a scattering of crushed beer cans littering the yard, I stuck close.

MALCOLM

"Cell phones," rumbled the man standing at the door.

He was as big as the actual door we were trying to walk through and was wearing sunglasses at night. I recognized him from the Coach Craig video.

"We left them in the car, Carl," said Sloan coolly. "We know the drill by now, sweetie."

The big man brightened up.

"Sloooan," he growled. He gave her a side hug. "I didn't recognize you there."

She turned to us, and his expression hardened.

"I trust you. I don't trust these guys."

"I can vouch for them," she said. "They're not as attractive as you but they're legit."

He actually grinned.

"I still need to pat you down. Mister Happy's rules."

Apparently, there had been a crackdown since the Coach Craig incident. Sloan had warned us that this was a possibility. So, yes, pretty much everybody left their phones in the Creeper. Pretty much everybody—except for me.

"Full disclosure, sir," I said raising my hands. "I do have a phone."

He held out a large cardboard box.

"In the box," he growled.

Gladly.

Sloan gave me a look. But she didn't know my secret plan. In a last-minute *Murder, She Wrote* moment of inspiration, I got the idea to leave the recorder on and toss it in with the other smartphones.

A real live wiretap! Without the wires!

Angela would be so proud.

BRIGHAM

We opened the door and walked smack into a wall of mumble rap, darkness, and sin.

This was no party. This was a sensory deprivation chamber.

It was loud and dark, with the only light coming from a few scattered blacklights and some pulsating purple strobe lights.

It was also packed.

As my eyes adjusted to the light I saw things.

Things I'd never seen.

There was a girl with no shirt.

There was a guy with no pants. (Thankfully, boxer briefs

though.) There were drugs. Obvious drugs. Mostly smoking drugs but I saw a guy in the corner snorting something off a busted-up coffee table. Cocaine? Real life cocaine?!

The blacklight cast a biohazard sheen on everyone as their eyes and teeth glowed brightly.

Halloween masks were few and far between. Some were wearing them. Most people looked like they had no idea what day it was.

I pushed mine farther onto my face.

There wasn't much dancing. Just a lot of writhing. Did I mention there was a girl with no shirt??

And I realized Sloan was right. This was not a party where people went to socialize and swap stories about their Framptonworth battle-gear inventory. This was a party for people who were here to have their needs met. And those needs were whatever they were addicted to at the moment.

For a minute, I wondered if I'd bump into my dad here.

MALCOLM

This was no party. This was a zombie mosh pit.

There was no punch bowl or Twister game or *Weekend at Bernie's* dance-off.

Immediately, I was in the crowd and I was by myself. We were supposed to fan out a bit, but I fanned too far.

I'm not sure how it happened, really. Okay, I was distracted by the shirtless girl.

Quinn, Brigham, Marshall, and beautiful Sloan disappeared into the mob.

I traveled in the current of people through a pulsating dance floor where people didn't dance as much as sway to the point where they looked like they were going to fall flat on the ground. In fact, one guy wearing a pajama onesie fell directly onto a coffee table. No one seemed to notice. I stayed in the current and was spit out at a kitchen next to a keg. A stoned-looking dude handed me a sloshy cup of something. I stared at it. He looked at me without really seeing me.

I flashed-back to Sloan's party training:

"Remember, if someone offers you something, just take it and go," she said. *"This isn't the type of party where people use discretion. It's not an after-school special."*

I took the cup and kept moving, keeping in mind the second half of Sloan's sage advice:

"Just don't eat, drink, or smoke anything. Everything is spiked with something or laced with something."

I had no plans to eat, drink, or smoke anything in this cup. Even though it kind of just smelled like light beer.

I continued to travel through the river of people to the back of the house. Along the way, I got wedged between a man and a woman making out. I'm not sure what happened, but things were grabbed.

I leaned against a wall and tried to recover.

As I did, the Chicken Man sauntered by and waved a wing at me. A coven of rail-thin vampires glided by. An obviously blitzed man in a bright glowing sombrero took a much-too-long swig on a bottle of tequila.

Then, suddenly, there was an elf girl.

She was breathless and smiling. I looked behind me because surely she was smiling at someone else, right? Her ears were pointed. Her eyes were wide. And her pupils were abnormally huge. She was beautiful but in an unhealthy way. Kind of like a drugged-out elvish space alien. She didn't need to be here. She needed sleep and soup and a sandwich and a warm blanket. The beautiful alien girl slung her arms around my shoulders and stared into my face with her giant eyes.

"You've got it, don't you?!" she said.

"What?" I said.

She poked my chest playfully.

All I saw was her face.

It was a pretty face.

"I can telllll," she said sing-song-ish. "I can always tell. You've got it, right?"

Her giant eyes looked hopefully into my regular-sized eyes.

No girl has ever looked at me like that.

So I nodded. Yes. Yes, I did have it.

I wasn't sure what I had or what I was nodding about. But it's better to have it than not have it, right? Whatever it was.

She grabbed my hand and led me away.

I went with her willingly.

I shouldn't have.

BRIGHAM

Sloan led us through the front room of what would probably be considered a living room in a non-dope house.

Then she motioned for me to take my place against the wall.

I did as instructed. And, somehow, I forgot how to stand discreetly. Hands in pockets? Arms crossed? Hands-on hips? Did it look like I was posing for a sassy senior portrait?

I remembered the words of Sloan, our Party Jedi Master.

"When in doubt, look at the ceiling and smile."

I tried it out. It felt weird.

Really, it didn't matter what I was doing. No one at this party was noticing anything. I could have ripped a giant fart and set off a smoke bomb and no one would have blinked an eye.

There was a feeling of frantic desperation among the crowd.

Everyone looked kind of . . . hungered.

Except, that is, for one guy.

He was in the back corner. Looking well-fed and sitting on a velvet purple couch smoking something like a cigar and holding a kind of goblet. From the looks of it, Sloan was headed his way.

He was putting off legitimate Jabba the Hutt vibes. I was half expecting him to motion for his guards to seize us and have us thrown into the rancor pit. Instead, his face split into a wide grin and he nodded at Sloan as she walked by. This had to be Mister Happy, right?

I sunk back in the crowd as she sauntered over, slung an arm around his broad shoulders, and whispered in his ear.

Who was this woman?

A secret spy?

A double agent for the foot clan?

Black Widow herself?

He laughed and his whole body moved up and down. A bright gold crucifix toppled out from his shiny purple shirt and dangled on a gold chain.

He placed a meaty hand on her thigh.

She didn't flinch, but I did.

And that's when I saw him.

Through the black light and the fog and the flashing strobe lights, he emerged.

The Unicorn Man had entered the party.

MALCOLM

I followed her to a room with several mattresses on the floor. There were people-shaped shadows doing . . . all kinds of things.

"Want to share?" she said.

"Share what?" I said.

Her wide eyes expanded to an impossible size.

"You said you had some. If you can share . . . I can share too."

And then we toppled to the ground and landed in a tangle on the one of the mattresses.

She leaned over to kiss me and it tasted like fruity beer, ashtray, and sadness.

Did I mention this was my first kiss? Did I mention this was the moment I'd been dreaming of since I first saw Padmé sporting a strategically ripped jumpsuit in *Attack of the Clones* on DVD?

Did I mention she was beautiful? Maybe not Padmé beautiful, but still beautiful?

And what did I do?

I tucked and rolled. Yes, I put my hands over my face and rolled to the side. She toppled off of me and, in an instant, her pretty face transformed into a vampire-like sneer.

I let out a startled scream.

She tried to scratch me and then she screamed too. It was a horrible deep scream from the gut.

"Give it to me!" she said. I NEED IT!"

We were on the floor, her face inches from mine. Did she have fangs?!

"I NEED IT! I CAN'T GO WITHOUT IT!"

I somehow managed to slide away, stumbled to my feet, said something like, "sorry, ma'am."

Then I ran for the door and closed it behind me.

Despite the constant bass, I could still hear her screaming on the other side.

This kind of thing never happened to Angela Lansbury.

QUINN

There was no mistaking it.

Unicorn Man had entered the building.

The party seemed to ebb and flow around him. He didn't interact with others. And people instinctively made space as he passed, as though he was the biggest shark circling the aquarium.

Brigham was leaning against the wall and from the looks of it we saw him at the same time. We locked eyes through the haze and knew, we needed to get to Marshall before it was too late.

I looked to my side and saw him, eyes wide, sides heaving, struggling to breathe, as he was swallowed by the crowd . . .

Too late.

MARSHALL

I know we've been over this before.

It's a panic attack. It isn't real. It feels like you can't breathe, but you can. But at that moment, I'm telling you, I could not breathe.

I stumbled a bit and a pair of arms reached out from the crowd and grabbed me.

I fell backward and wound up in the arms of a woman.

It wasn't Quinn.

She was probably just a bit older than me but she looked as though she had lived twenty years more.

She sat me down in a damp yellow chair and let out a raspy laugh.

"Ooooh, you're riding it aren't you?"

I was shocked into forgetting about the Unicorn Man for a moment, though I could still sense his presence in the room somewhere.

"Riding what?"

"Shut up," she grinned, and I could see she was missing a tooth. "The best part's when you can't breathe. Ride it as close to death as you can. But don't go too far."

I looked into her glazed eyes and saw the person she might have been if . . . whatever happened to her hadn't happened.

She slid a hand up my knee.

"Want to share?" she said.

I stammered something that sounded like, "umwhatno," and another hand suddenly clapped down on her shoulder.

"Pardon me," Quinn said.

She looked taller, stronger, and more powerful than ever.

"This gentleman's taken."

The girl stooped and let out another raspy laugh that sounded like a chainsaw.

"Lucky girl," she said, giving me a hopeless grin before shuffling away into the crowd.

And somehow, someway, for that split second, I didn't care one bit that I was in the exact same room as the Unicorn Man.

QUINN

This was not a party.

This was a hellscape.

Imagine those Dante's *Inferno* paintings with writhing bodies and weeping and gnashing of teeth.

It was that. Except with Drake songs and strobe lights.

We'd lost Malcolm immediately.

Marshall nearly disappeared into the arms of a zombie-vampire woman.

Unicorn Man was slowly pacing the room.

And Sloan was getting cozy with Kingpin from *Spider-Man*.

I pulled Marshall up from the chair and we clung together for a moment.

"You're my hero," he said.

I laughed and slugged him on the arm. We held hands as we moved to the kitchen, where there was a little breathing room.

We found a small cove next to the pantry where we could finally hear each other over the thudding bass.

"Seriously!" I shouted. "What is happening right now?!"

"I don't know!" shouted Marshall.

A stoned-looking kid came out of nowhere and handed me a red solo cup of something. I took it without making eye contact.

"Drink wench!" he blurted before stumbling away.

I contemplated dumping it on his head.

Marshall stiffened as though he was about to spring into some of Brigham's internet karate moves. I put a hand on his chest. He relaxed.

He looked at me and shook his head.

"I don't think I like parties!" he shouted.

I snorted.

"I don't either! When does the '90s dance-off start?"

"Ahh, shoot these people aren't ready for your lawnmower!"

We laughed and I almost took a drink of the mystery liquid before stopping myself.

The crowd parted and Sloan appeared out of nowhere.

"Sup, losers," she said.

"What is going on?!" I shouted. "Who was that big dude you were talking to?!"

She put a finger to her lips and shook her head.

"Don't talk about that big dude," she said. "You never saw that big dude."

MARSHALL

I saw that big dude. And I had many questions about that big dude. But now was not the time. More importantly, I had another question.

"What happened to Malcolm?" I yelled. "We lost him!"

"Yeah this place is too crowded!" shouted Quinn. "We gotta get out of here!"

Sloan rolled her eyes.

"This place is not too crowded. It's the perfect level of crowded, because you losers don't have to worry about blending in. It's so crowded nobody can tell you obviously don't belong."

She had a point.

I suppose it would have been much harder to intermingle if the only people who showed up were us five and the Kingpin making awkward conversation about felonies and jail time and twenty-sided die over dinner.

"Follow me," she said.

She turned and casually walked away, leading us down a hallway that was significantly less crowded than the rest of the house. I got the strange feeling that the drugged-out partygoers were instinctively giving this place a wide berth. We had crossed an invisible line.

Then I saw the door.

The floating purple door from Coach Craig's video.

I took a step back.

"We're not going to talk to Crazy Eyes, are we?"

"You have to be more specific," said Sloan. "Everybody at this party has crazy eyes."

She turned to the right and stopped at a silver metallic door that looked completely out of place for a ranch house.

She looked to the left and the right and then opened it. There was only darkness inside.

"Where are you going?" yelled Quinn.

"Where are *we* going," said Sloan.

She turned and motioned for us to follow her into the inky blackness.

We went inside.

I don't know why.

But we went inside.

MALCOLM

Technically, the last party I was invited to was Noah Grizzle's eight-year-old birthday blowout.

The theme was: *Pokémon! Catch 'Em All!*

It was awesome.

The theme of this current party was: *Drugs! Let's Do Some!*

It was not awesome.

I sat in a weirdly damp chair in a semi-daze, and watched the hordes of party zombies trudge by. I needed a moment. I was still recovering from my make-out session with the space alien elf girl. We were technically dating now, right?

I felt like I should know her name.

MARSHALL

"Wait, why?" I whispered to the back of Sloan's head as we journeyed downward. "Why??"

It was much quieter and the shift in sound was jarring. The basement door wasn't the kind you'd find in most normal, everyday ranch homes. It was heavy and metal and mostly soundproof.

Something made to keep people out.

Or something made to keep people in.

"Um, yeah, big sis," said Quinn. "Why are we voluntarily going into the deep, dark drug house basement?"

Sloan put a finger to her lips and led us downward.

"No time for a Nerd Force meeting," she said. "We have to move fast."

It was extremely dark and I almost fell once. And then again. The pitch blackness actually made me miss the seizure-inducing strobe lights up above. We turned a corner and that's when I was hit by the Smell. It needs to be capitalized. It was that bad. I instantly gagged.

It smelled like, well, how can I describe it? Like poop. Mixed with vomit. Mixed with something else foul and cursed.

It smelled . . . wrong. As though we were entering some ancient, haunted catacomb hospital wing hidden beneath the vinyl flooring upstairs.

Quinn and I stopped on the same step.

"I'm telling you," said Quinn with a gag. "Parties suck."

"Breathe through your mouth," whispered Sloan. "Keep it together guys. This is what we came here for."

The stairwell turned back to the right and opened up into a large room lit only by a small, cracked floor lamp in the corner.

It was stark and dingy and gray and littered with trash.

It was the evil Upside Down version of Malcolm's comfy basement.

The room was empty except for several large, haphazard piles of rags and clothes, which lined the cinderblock walls.

Sloan put a hand out to stop us. She made a snake-like motion with her other hand to indicate we were to weave around the piles.

"Stay quiet," she whispered. "Whatever you do."

As we crept through the foul-smelling darkness, I nearly stepped on a pile of broken glass that used to be a liquor bottle at the exact same time a ferret-sized rat shot out of nowhere and ran over my foot. Any other time, any other day, I would have screamed bloody murder and jumped up on a table. Instead, I muffled that scream and kept moving. As I looked back at the rat, I wondered for a moment if it was actually some kind of raccoon. Or a mutant possum? Or El Chupacabra? And those horrifying thoughts distracted me just long enough so that I didn't see the discarded beer can directly in front of me. Not until I kicked it straight across the room, crashing and clattering along the concrete floor.

Sloan and Quinn froze.

And then one of the piles sat up.

Straight and rigid.

And then another.

And then the piles began to scream.

And the lights went out.

BRIGHAM

I watched Marshall, Sloan, and Quinn duck into the dark doorway and disappear. Where were they going? And how was I supposed to find Coach Craig in this DayGlo madness? How could I find anyone? Scanning the crowd was like staring at a constantly moving neon *Where's Waldo?* book, if Waldo ever got lost at a drug shack.

Though I was able to pick out some patterns in the madness.

There were the junkies who were high on something, the other junkies who were desperately looking to get high on something, and the predators in the mix working hard to take advantage of that. They were the shady-looking fellows handing out neon purple baggies in exchange for cash.

From the looks of it, the demand overran the supply. Or maybe that was the design of it.

In the center of it all was Jabba the Hutt.

A.k.a. Mister Happy.

It had to be him.

He even kind of looked like Jabba, with a wide satisfied grin that never left his face.

I overheard the name of the drug. Unicorn Dust. And I realized Coach Craig was onto something.

And then I realized something else. While I was keeping watch, I was being watched.

MARSHALL

There was horrible screaming and groaning in the darkness. I screamed too. The smashed light in the corner flickered on for a terrifying second, and there was a face.

Inches from my own.

It was haggard and bug-eyed and full of terror. It moved even closer and screamed again. A blood-curdling horrifying shriek that filled my eardrums until I thought they would burst.

The other piles of clothes stumbled to their feet and began to wail.

A hand grabbed me from behind. Another slithered into my hair and held on, yanking me backward.

I felt a pair of arms slide around my waist. And though I screamed too, any sound I made was drowned out by the horrible yells coming from the suffocating piles of basement zombies pulling me to the ground.

Remember when I said monsters were real? I didn't mean that metaphorically. They were right here, in this Hell House basement. And they were climbing on top of me, clutching and moaning, as I fell to the floor.

QUINN

The lights went out. Horror erupted. And I just started kicking. Kicking and punching and clawing and fighting.

I hit a lot of things. I heard a lot of screams of pain and sorrow and terror all around me. I wanted to join in their terrible wailing but was afraid if I did, I wouldn't stop. I wouldn't stop screaming. Ever. I'd just sink into this pit of despair in this basement hell.

The busted lamp in the corner of the room flickered off and on and I saw Sloan, ponytail swinging back and forth, as she worked her way through the wailing crowd.

"IT'S OKAY!" she yelled at the zombies. "WE'RE HERE TO HELP!"

It was not okay. I did not know what was happening. But this was not okay.

I looked down and saw Marshall on the ground beneath a tangle of legs and limbs and hair and dirty blankets.

I windmilled my way through the zombies, grabbed ahold of him, and pulled.

MARSHALL

I was in hell.

A literal hell of screaming and flailing and grabbing and poop smells.

And at that point, an angel by the name of Quinn Carswell appeared above me in the flickering light. She reached out, grabbed my hand, and pulled me to safety.

Well, actually, she pulled my ear first, then my elbow, then my hand as she yanked me out from under the horrible pile of screaming bodies.

It was about that time that I realized the zombies weren't actually attacking me. They were just kind of flailing. They were panicked and in pain.

"What's wrong with them?!" I yelled.

"Everything!" said Quinn.

"Follow me!" yelled Sloan.

She led us down another black hallway and then pushed us into a tiny room. She pulled the door shut with a slam and for a moment there was only darkness. Then a fluorescent light buzzed on in a tiny bathroom that would have made the film set for *Saw* look like a four-star hotel.

"What?!" hissed Quinn. "What is happening?!"

If you can scream and whisper at the same time that's what she did. "Who are those people?! Why are we down here?! What is going on?"

All valid questions. I was just trying to breathe again so I sat on the dirty toilet and let Quinn do all the whisper-screaming on our behalf. Sloan stared wide-eyed into a cracked mirror and pressed her palms into her forehead.

She turned to us and I could see her arms quaking.

"That . . . that didn't go as planned."

"Who are they?" whispered Quinn. "What are they?! Are they zombies?"

Sloan put a shaky arm on her sister's shoulder.

"They're junkies," she said. "They won't hurt us. We just need to be quiet and they'll settle down out there."

As she said this, the screaming began to fade into moans and groans on the other side of the door.

"Those people upstairs . . ." Sloan motioned to the ceiling and the dull thump of bass. "They're all here for one thing. A drug called Unicorn Dust. It's something new. Something you can only get from Mister Happy."

"And Mister Happy is . . ."

"The dude we don't speak of."

"What, is he Voldemort?" hissed Quinn.

"Pretty much. Except he has worse manners. And he's killed a lot more people. And, well, he's real."

I shuddered on the rusty toilet seat and nearly slid to the floor as it completely detached from the toilet.

I preferred my villains to be fully fictional, not a few feet above us in a hellish ranch house.

"The dust is supposed to push a person as close to death as possible without being dead. The people down here, the people outside of that door, are all having bad trips. They don't know where they are or what's happening. They probably don't even know their own names. They might never remember. That's why they call this the Hell Party. The junkies who start to have a bad trip are always dragged down here by Mister Happy's thugs where they can flip out for a while and eventually snap out of it and sleep it off or . . ."

"Or what?" said Quinn.

"Or they don't . . ."

"How do you know all this, sis?"

"Does that matter right now?"

"It matters."

Quinn stared at Sloan.

Sloan stared at Quinn.

There was something going on here. Something I didn't quite understand.

But my airway had opened up again and I finally was able to speak. I cleared my throat.

"But why?" I said. "Why are we down here?"

Sloan looked at me, crossed her arms, and leaned against the dirty sink. A semblance of her normal coolness returned.

"Because," she said, "we know one of the zombies."

CHAPTER FIFTEEN

THE PRISONER

MALCOLM

Meanwhile, I was still sitting in the stanky yellow chair, watching the ghouls and ghosts pass me by and wondering what that smell was.

Wet dog?

Curry powder?

Dumpster?

I knew I should probably get moving but my mom always said if you get lost, stay put. So, I was staying put. I figured I'd eventually see a friendly masked face, right?

But no. There was only a steady wall of stoned and wasted party people trudging by. I could tell they were getting more and more stoned and wasted as the night progressed.

I also knew that I had to get ahold of myself. Here I was, in the middle of a full-blown undercover Academic investigation . . . and I was hiding on the sidelines?!

It was time to man-up. Or rather, it was time to Angela Lansbury-up.

So, I stood and plunged back into the party. And then I walked directly into the path of the Unicorn Man. He glided up through the crowd, out of nowhere, and seemed to hover above me. He was tall and thin and horrifying. I stared into his dead horsey eyes and then I stepped backward and sat down again.

The Unicorn Man floated onward, and I sank farther into the stanky chair.

Urine. That was the smell. Definitely urine.

QUINN

Quiet finally returned to the Chamber of Horrors beneath the ranch house.

Hopefully that meant we were safe enough to leave the tiny, dirty, awful bathroom that probably gave us all hepatitis B.

Sloan cracked the door, peeked out, and made a motion for us to follow.

"I've fallen for that before," I whispered.

"Shhh," said Marshall. "Please don't wake the zombies."

Those zombies were now silently trudging around as the cracked lamp flickered in the corner. I counted five in total. Some were mumbling. Most had returned to their spots amongst the filth on the floor.

We tiptoed our way across the room and to another long hallway.

It would have been pitch-black if it wasn't for one source of light coming from underneath a doorway.

Sloan opened the door and walked in.

Marshall and I paused at the threshold.

"What's next?" said Marshall. "Werewolves?"

No, but it wasn't much better.

MARSHALL

There was another cracked lamp in the corner of the small room.

No lampshade. They weren't much for home décor at the Hell House.

In the opposite corner was another heap of rags. But, of course, it wasn't. I was wise to that by now.

I took a step back. I really, really didn't want it to suddenly transform into another undead pile and scream in my face. Sloan had no such fears.

She strode forward, kneeled down, and whispered something I

couldn't quite make out. She placed her hand on the shoulder of the sleeping junkie with the patience and concern of a long-suffering nurse. And it made me realize these people in the basement weren't monsters. They weren't the bad guys.

The real monsters were the ones upstairs. They were the ones profiting off this death and addiction and madness.

Then the basement zombie rolled over and let out a wet, retching cough.

But this was no zombie.

This was Coach Craig the Concusser.

BRIGHAM

So, yeah, someone was watching me as I was watching everybody.

A warlock in a black hoodie. And he was doing exactly what I was doing, but from the opposite wall of the room.

He was leaning and scanning and trying to act like he wasn't.

I'm not sure what tipped him off. Did I look too alert? Too observant? Was I not staring at the ceiling enough?

I tried to blend in further by striking up a conversation with a spaced-out girl next to me wearing cat ears.

"You come here often?"

She smiled at me and spoke in a sped-up language that I first thought was Spanish and then realized was complete gibberish.

She was as high as a kite. A satellite actually.

I glanced back over and the warlock was nowhere to be found. And then he was right behind me.

A long bony hand clamped down on my shoulder.

I turned and looked into the somehow familiar face of a man with bulging eyes.

"Sup, bro," he said.

It was Crazy Eyes, from Coach Craig's spy video.

I nodded and tried to look disoriented. It was easy because I was.

"You need to come with me," he said. His grip tightened on my shoulder and his eyes bulged further.

I know I've mentioned my karate training right? Master Kensei? YouTube?

Well, I've never actually used it in the real world.

But I figured this was it.

No time like the present.

I pushed Crazy Eyes directly in the chest. He fell into a guy in a gorilla suit. Then I stepped back and assumed the imperial tiger stance.

Knees bent. Hands forward. Crouched low.

Crazy Eyes grinned a crazy grin.

It was about to get really crazy.

MARSHALL

The mighty Coach Craig was on the floor, balled up in the fetal position.

"NerdPants?" he said weakly. "Is that really you?"

"Yes, Coach," I said. "It's me . . . NerdPants."

He tried to sit up and coughed violently.

He looked at Sloan and then Quinn. His eyes focused in and out like old-fashioned video camera lenses. He was definitely on something.

"If you guys are real, you need to get out of here," he said. "It's not safe."

"Relax," said Sloan. "They're with me."

"Doesn't matter." His voice cracked. "Doesn't matter if they're here with the Navy Seals. They'll kill you as soon as they'll look at you. And not in a nice way."

A chill ran up my back.

"What do you mean?"

"People that come down here, they don't make it out. They usually don't use guns and knives. They're too smart for it. They use the drug."

I realized with a sickening jolt that those piles of clothes-people out there could be us if we got caught. My first instinct was to run. Run and never look back. I swallowed down that fear.

"Well, we're your rescue team," I said, realizing how ridiculous that sounded. "We're getting you out of here."

He rolled over and started to cry.

"How's that for a vote of confidence?" said Sloan.

I tried not to take it personally.

Craig sniffled and stared at the ceiling.

"But do I even deserve to get out of here?"

Sloan, Quinn, and I exchanged looks.

"Um, yes," said Quinn. "Nobody deserves to die in this nasty ranch house basement."

He shifted on his dirty mattress and looked up at me.

"Remember that time I called you a loser, NerdPants?"

"Um, you'll have to be more specific," I said.

If I had a dime for every time Coach Craig called me a loser I'd have . . . at least a crisp two-dollar bill. That doesn't sound like much but he mixes in other non-loser-based insults to keep it interesting.

He looked at me with bloodshot eyes.

"I'm sorry," he said. "I truly am sorry. You're not a loser. I'm the loser, NerdPants. You guys got your whole lives ahead of you and you're doing it right. If I ever make it out of here, someday I'll be asking you guys for a job. And I'll be lucky if you let me clean the toilets."

"I would let you clean the toilets," I said stupidly.

Quinn elbowed me in the ribs.

"Listen," said Sloan as she scanned the room. "This is a really nice chat and all. But we'll have much more time to talk about career plans and feelings when we get out of here, all right?"

Coach Craig didn't seem to hear her.

"My whole life I did what other people wanted me to do. That's all I did. My dad didn't really like me, but he sure liked football. So, I played football and, hey guess what, it made him like me. For a while. And other people liked me too. They cheered for me. They chanted my name. It made me feel better than everyone else, so I acted that way. I acted like I was better than everybody else. When really I'm just worse than everybody else. "

He shook his head.

"They lifted me up, and you know what I did? I pulled them down."

I couldn't disagree with that assessment. But now was not the time to pile on.

"Speaking of lifting up . . ." said Sloan as she motioned for us to take position around his mattress. I groaned. Man, were we really going to have to drag around 250-plus pounds of Coach Craig again?! My obliques were still strained from the last time.

Coach ignored us completely and kept talking to the ceiling.

"After graduation, I figured I'd play college, you know? But I didn't have the grades to get in and I didn't have the scholarship. So I decided to do something important. Something that helped people . . ."

"Teaching?" said Quinn as she crouched alongside me and Sloan. I was trying to figure out if I needed to grab him by the armpits or his shirt collar.

Coach Craig let out a choked cough that might have actually been a laugh.

"No, no, no way. I'm no good at that. And I'm just doing the same thing I did in high school. Pulling down the people that are better than me."

He coughed violently and continued.

"I wanted to be a cop. A good cop. A cop that makes a difference. Saves people. A cop that saves lives. So, I applied to the Tucker Police Department. I passed the physical easily. Couldn't ever pass the written exam. Too much to memorize. They told me to apply again in a year. Some kind of waiting period. I didn't want to wait. So, I figured if I cracked a case for them they'd have to hire me . . ."

"Wait," said Quinn. "What do you mean?"

He grinned for the first time, and I could see he was missing a tooth.

"While I was there, I swiped a file from the desk of some detective. It was a case about a drug called Unicorn Dust."

Quinn looked at me. We both looked at Sloan.

"It's what they're all hooked on up there. And down here. And now I am too. I went undercover, filmed it all on my phone. But then I broke my phone and . . ."

"And then you gave the phone to me."

"I'm sorry, Marshall," he said. It may have been the first time he had ever used my actual name. "I didn't realize these guys were so dangerous. I thought they were just small-time dealers like Creepy Jeff."

Creepy Jeff is a dealer? Geez, c'mon Creepy Jeff.

"I got away with it but it wasn't until I went back to the police with the evidence that those unicorn freaks started showing up at my house. Bad Cop must have tipped them off. He's on the take. It's an inside job. That's why I yelled at you guys to get out of my house. You're safer not knowing this stuff. I wish I could go back to not knowing. There's no way you can get me out of here. I'm stuck. And even if you do, they'll come for me."

His voice cracked. And he began to weep. Coach Craig the Concusser wept like a frightened child.

Quinn crouched down and put a hand on his shoulder.

"Listen, that's really sad and all," she said. "But I need you to do something for me Coach Craig . . ."

"What's that?" he said with a sniffle.

"Suck it up, NerdPants!"

Craig jumped, jolted out of his weepy stupor.

"Remember when you were playing that big game and nobody thought you could win?!"

Coach Craig nodded.

"Homecoming? Against Dawson County?"

"Um, yes, sure," said Quinn. It was obvious she had never attended a high school football game in her life.

"You could have quit, right?! But when things got tough . . . what did you do instead?!"

"I did not quit?"

"That's right! You did not quit! And you did not quit because you're no quitter! And you're definitely not going to quit now! When the deck is stacked against you, and the chips are down, you're going to fight! Because you are Coach Craig the Concusser!"

"Yeah, but . . ."

"NO BUTS!" shouted Quinn startling me and Sloan.

Quinn took his hand.

"It's time," she said.

Coach Craig the Concusser let out a grunt of determination.

Sloan and I both took a shoulder, and we bolstered him to his feet.

"C'mon, Coach, fight!" she said. "We're getting you out of here!"

Then we all took a step forward and Coach Craig fell straight backward, as though yanked from behind.

"Yeah, but . . ." he said meekly as he looked up at us from his dirty mattress. "There's this."

He held up his leg and showed us a dull iron clasp clamped around his ankle.

Coach Craig was in chains.

"Ahhh," said Sloan. "Now I see the problem."

MALCOLM

Meanwhile, there's me in that chair.

Yep, I'm still in that chair.

But all that was about to change.

I don't know what started the fight, but it happened right in front of me.

A dude wearing a sombrero bumped into a dude wearing a banana suit.

Words were exchanged and there was some pushing and some shoving. At first, I thought it was kind of funny since the Banana Man was, you know, dressed like a banana. But then he pulled out a gun. And it was less funny.

BRIGHAM

As I prepared to strike, Crazy Eyes looked me up and down and smiled.

"You train under Master Kensei?"

He stepped back and matched my stance with an iron claw stance of his own.

"Nice to meet a fellow subscriber!"

He knew the ways of the imperial tiger too!

I regulated my breathing. I crouched even lower. And I waited for him to strike.

And then the shooting started.

MARSHALL

"What is this, Dracula's castle?" said Quinn as she tugged at the heavy metal chain.

It was attached to the cinderblock wall and it wasn't budging.

Then—*KA-BAM!*—there was a deafening crack of thunder from above.

We all hit the floor.

Then another.

KA-BAM!

"What was that?!" I yelled.

"That my friends, is gunfire," said Sloan. "This might be a good time to leave the party."

BRIGHAM

Good news: Crazy Eyes forgot about me completely.

Bad news: There was a gunfight taking place a few feet away in the living room.

I abandoned my post and headed down into the basement.

MARSHALL

Sloan grabbed the chain alongside Quinn and pulled. Craig and I joined in. There was plenty of grunting and groaning, but nothing moving.

"Just go," moaned Coach Craig as he slumped down on his mattress. "You gotta get out of here. You guys gotta go before they realize you're here."

"Don't be so selfless," grunted Sloan as she kept tugging.

It was no use though. Craig wasn't going anywhere. She pulled us aside.

"He's right though. We have to get out of here, now. If the party empties out it'll just be us and Mister Happy and his goons. And that could get . . . awkward."

Just then, Brigham showed up over our shoulders and I screamed.

He screamed in reply. Sloan and Quinn shushed us.

"There's shooting upstairs!" he yelled. "I almost got into a karate fight! Malcolm disappeared! Is that Coach Craig?!"

Coach Craig waved weakly.

"Is he chained to the wall?"

"Yes," said Sloan as she pulled on the rusty chain. "We heard the gunshots, a karate fight sounds awesome, hopefully Malcolm will turn up, and, yep that's Coach Craig."

She yanked on the chain again.

"Now that you're caught up, got any ideas?"

KA-BAM! The roof of the basement shook and it sounded as though a buffalo herd was stampeding above our heads.

"Wait!" said Quinn. "I actually do!"

She dropped to the ground and started untying her shoes.

"Oh, this is gonna be good," she said with a grin.

She pulled out a small metal contraption from her sock and began unfolding it until it was a much larger metal contraption. It was long and pointy and dangerous looking.

"Perhaps this could be of assistance," she said proudly.

We stared at her blankly.

"Collapsible knitting needle! Top of the line! I figured we'd need it if we got into a knife fight or a knitting party along the way."

Sloan looked supremely impressed.

Quinn shrugged.

"It actually belongs to Sam Hammond's mom," she said.

"Okay, great," said Sloan. "Does anybody know how to pick a lock?"

I looked at Quinn, Quinn looked at me.

"No idea," she said.

"Um, yes we do," said Brigham. "AP physics. Mr. Rembrandt's class? Remember the lesson on leverage when he had us lift that big linebacker dude, Grayson Sanders, with the platform and the metal pole?"

"Ahh, yeah," I said. "But this seems much different."

"Nah, same mechanics," he pointed to the steel knitting needle. "That's our metal pole. We just need a big enough surface for all of us to stand on for leverage."

We glanced around the dingy room and there was nothing but trash, Craig's mattress, and soiled clothing.

"Hold on," I said. I bolted out the door and into the nasty Saw bathroom. There, I found the broken toilet seat I had nearly fallen off of. I grabbed it and sprinted back, making sure to weave around the now-slumbering zombies along the way.

Another series of gunshots rocked the house but somehow the junkies seemed completely unperturbed by WWIII up above.

"Perfect. Also nasty," said Brigham when I presented him with the filthy toilet seat. "Jab the point of the needle into the space next to the shackle."

"What's the shackle?!" said Sloan. "I'm not a locksmith."

"The curvy *u*-part," said Brigham.

"Ahh, why didn't you say that, hot-stuff?" She jammed the needle into the lock and stepped back. Brigham placed the dirty seat down carefully on the end of the needle and balanced on it.

"Okay," he threw his arms out. "Everybody, crowd around me."

"What should I do?" slurred Craig. "I can bench 250!"

"Yeah, that's not gonna help right now," said Brigham. "Just stay real still."

We all stepped onto the toilet seat and squeezed together as close as possible. I took Quinn into my arms instinctively. Sloan did the same thing with Brigham.

"Okay, on three we all jump. One, two, JUMP!"

Another gunshot shook the house at the exact moment we came down in unison. The lock let out a satisfying *pop* and the iron clasp fell off of Coach Craig's ankle with a clatter.

"That worked?" blurted Craig. "How did that work?!"

"That's science," said Brigham with a nod.

"And Knitter's Pride brand needles," said Quinn. "The best money can buy."

"Wow," said Craig in awe as he rubbed his ankle. "Saved by Nerd Powers."

MALCOLM

Okay, I was no longer in the chair.

I was now behind the chair.

Chunks of the wall were exploding around me.

A glass bottle hit me on the head.

A girl in a cheetah body suit scrambled completely over my shoulders and kicked me in the jaw.

I stayed put. Partially because I didn't want to get shot or stampeded, but also because I was frozen in complete terror.

Hell Party was in full swing. And it was living up to its name.

MARSHALL

Coach Craig stumbled to his feet and then hit the ground again.

We helped him up and he steadied himself.

"Maybe I'm not dead yet," he croaked.

"Maybe," said Sloan grimly. She glanced up at the ceiling.

The bass was still thumping but it sounded like the world was ending above our heads.

"Are there any doors or windows down here?" said Quinn.

Coach Craig nodded and almost keeled backward again.

"There's a little window at ground level," he said. "I saw them push a dresser thing in front of it one of the times they thought I was dead."

We shuffled around the corner and, sure enough, there was a big, battered china cabinet against the wall in the next room. I glanced back and the zombies weren't even stirring. They seemed oblivious to us and the ruckus above.

"I kick one beer can across the floor and it's an all-out riot. Meanwhile, it's *John Wick III* upstairs and they all take a nice nap."

"It's the dust," grunted Craig. "Just doesn't make sense."

I threw a shoulder into the cabinet, and it only moved a few inches.

"C'mon," said Craig. "Use all ninety pounds of those muscles."

I shot him a look.

"Sorry. Force of habit."

"I think you're going to fully recover since your a-hole levels have stabilized."

He let out a chokey laugh and slapped me on the back.

"Good one, Marsh!"

I countered with a playful slug to the arm.

Were Coach Craig and I becoming . . . friends?

Meanwhile, Quinn and Sloan handily worked together to move the cabinet to the side, revealing a small window of tinted yellow glass.

Sloan pushed it open.

"This way to freedom," she said.

I stopped.

"But what about Malcolm?"

Sloan dragged an old chair over to the window so we could reach it. It would be a tight fit, especially for Coach Craig, but we could make it.

"We just have to hope he's smart enough to know when to leave the party."

MALCOLM

No way I was leaving the party.

Not without my friends.

Meanwhile, the stream of panicked partiers continued to stampede by. But since most of them were high, they were doing nothing more than making laps around the living room. Some of the more lucid ones, like me, had found hiding places behind furniture. Others had actually found their way to the door. And the unlucky ones were on the ground. Bleeding.

This was an actual shoot-out. But not an organized one like in the Westerns. People were yelling, screaming. Seeing someone shot in real life is not like seeing them shot on TV. It's confusing. It's less clear-cut. They don't grab their chest and groan and tumble over. They just . . . stop moving. At one point, I saw a man's arm explode. At another point, I saw a man lying in a pool of his own blood, he stood up like it was only a scratch and then got shot again.

Then Jabba entered. And the room froze. The shooting stopped as he strode directly into the line of fire.

"Who's responsible for this?" he said while staring at a bleeding man on the floor.

Banana Man stood up from behind a couch.

Sombrero Guy did too, though he was now missing his sombrero.

They both moved to the center of the room like two disobedient children who knew they were about to be grounded.

Turns out, it was much worse than that.

Jabba pulled out a handgun. It was small and compact. Banana Man quivered. Sombrero Guy pleaded. Jabba mocked him and smiled and then fired a bullet directly into his kneecap.

BAM.

He did the same to a screeching Banana Man.

BAM.

They both fell to the ground.

Screaming. Writhing in pain. Blood poured out of their legs.

Pandemonium erupted again and another wave of partygoers stampeded for the exit.

"PARTY'S OVER!" thundered Jabba with a grin.

I jumped in with the crowd and booked it for the door.

It was time to leave the party . . . while my kneecaps were still intact.

Chapter Sixteen

The Call of Fergie

Marshall

We parked the Creeper three blocks away.

At the time, it seemed like a good idea.

Now that we were lugging a half-drugged Coach Craig down the street and scrambling for our lives, not so much.

"Okay, so now can you tell me where he came from?" huffed Brigham as he propped up the sagging Coach Craig. "Why was he in the basement? And is he high?"

"Good to see you too, Brigham," said Craig.

Brigham nearly tripped.

"And did he just use my actual name??"

"Yes, he did," I said through puffing and panting. "He's nice now, and very sensitive, we'll explain later. Hey, Malcolm!"

Malcolm appeared out of nowhere and he had me in an awkward bear hug from the side.

"You all right? You're not hurt are you?"

"No, no. I'm fine," he said. "It's just. I've seen things."

More on that later.

The Creeper was in sight.

Then there was a shout from down the street and I turned to see my nightmare directly behind us.

Silhouetted below the streetlight.

There were three of them.

Three men running our way.

All with unicorn heads.

"Um, we need to go, now," said Sloan.

We went. As fast as we could, we went. But with a deadweight Coach Craig clinging to our shoulders, it was like running a three-legged race with a drunken hobo.

"C'mon!" grunted Brigham." We can make it!"

It was clear we weren't going to make it. I glanced over my shoulder and the Unicorn Men were moving fast.

Panic, like I've never felt, gripped my body as I realized what was going to happen. They were going to catch us. They were going to take us back, kicking and screaming. I envisioned each one of my friends in piles of dirty blankets underneath the Hell House as they injected us with that unicorn poison. We would fight it at first but, eventually, we would smile, and we would accept it. And we would become the zombies in the basement.

There was that old familiar feeling of my throat closing up. That old familiar feeling of oxygen not making it to my lungs. I started to choke and wheeze and spit as we staggered along.

And that's exactly when Coach Craig stopped and planted his feet onto the ground.

Both Brigham and I stumbled forward. Coach stood on his own. He looked at me, then at Brigham and he grinned.

"I've got this, Nerd Squad," he slurred. "Duty calls."

He saluted us. And then he turned and ran straight toward the danger.

Well . . . he ran straight into a trash can. But then he straightened out and began to run toward the danger.

"Coach!" I yelled.

He ignored me. He was limping but moving faster now.

And then he sang. It was an indistinguishable warble at first but then I realized what it was.

We all did.

"GOOO THE COUGARS OF CARTEEEER! GET UP AND WIN THAT GAAAAAAME!"

It was the Carter High School fight song. Or at least a very butchered version of it.

"WIN OR LOSE, WE'RE WITH YOU AND WE'LL CHEER YOU JUST THE SAAAAAAME!"

It had the same effect as the Creeper's foghorn.

Dogs howled.

Crickets stopped chirping.

Lights turned on behind barred windows.

And it was just crazy and distracting enough that the Unicorn Men stopped in their tracks.

Coach Craig sped up still.

Years of conditioning and practicing and father-pleasing football training powered him forward, onward, upward, and through his pain.

Except, this time, he wasn't running for his dad. He was running for himself.

And us.

Just before he reached our evil pursuers, he lowered his shoulder and delivered the kind of blow that only Coach Craig the Concusser could.

Unicorn Man number one folded like a tackling dummy.

His rubber mask went flying to reveal an evil-looking man with a sharp pointy goatee who kind of looked like the devil.

At the same time, Craig threw an arm out and clotheslined a second Unicorn Man who went down hard into a trash can with a clatter.

The third Unicorn Man stumbled on the curb and Craig grabbed his leg and yanked him backward. His horned head scraped against the asphalt.

We should have been running. But at that point, we could only stand and watch in awe.

"Wow," said a stunned Malcolm. "Now I know why they call him the Concusser."

"C'mon, losers!" yelled Sloan. "This is our chance!"

We sprinted the final few yards to the Creeper, Quinn threw open the sliding door and we dove in.

Sloan jumped into the driver's seat.

"C'mon, Creeper!" she shouted as she put the key in the ignition.

Of course, we were asking too much of the Creeper's poor lawnmower engine. It only made a whiny shudder.

Sloan tried again.

"C'mon, Creeper!"

She turned the key, and it made a semi-choking sound.

The devil man was back on his feet and sprinting toward us, leaving his mask behind.

He was yards away. Then feet away.

"C'MON, CREEPER!" we yelled in unison.

Then he was right there. Right at the window. He didn't look angered or alarmed. There was a chilling mechanical deadness in his eyes as he reared back and punched directly through Sloan's window.

Glass popped and sprayed everywhere.

I screamed.

The Devil Man grunted and reached for the steering wheel.

And as if offended by this treatment, the Creeper finally roared to life.

Sloan floored it and caught the Devil Man's shoulder with the side-view mirror. He went spinning as the mirror clattered to the ground and the Creeper sped into the night.

All the while, we could still hear the triumphant, strangled sounds of Carter High School's beloved fight song.

QUINN

Sloan ran a red light. Then another one. No one seemed to notice.

Marshall and I were holding hands. Normally this would have been the equivalent of second base for us, but now it was just a necessity.

Brigham pressed his face up against the window and Malcolm shook violently and stared into nothingness.

Once we were a few more red lights away from Hell, Sloan swung the Creeper into an empty side street and slammed on the brakes.

She clutched the steering wheel and breathed heavily. She said nothing. And for a second I thought she was going to hyperventilate. I reached forward and put a hand on her shaking shoulder.

"Nice driving, Wheel Man," I said. "Just keep breathing."

Sloan nodded.

It felt strange to be the calm, cool sibling for once.

Brigham put his head in his hands.

"I never thought I'd say it," he said. ". . . But Coach Craig is my hero."

MARSHALL

We didn't know where to go. What to do. Who to call.

Sloan was still performing some kind of breathing exercise. Quinn was holding my hand and it was amazing. Brigham was shaking his head and muttered something about Master Kensei's training "failing him."

And Malcolm was staring into the void. Silent. Emotionless.

In a night of disturbing things, this had to be the most disturbing of all.

Malcolm was actually quiet.

I patted him on the back, and he jumped, then looked at me as though he'd just realized I was there.

"Hey, buddy," I said. "You want to talk about it?"

"No," said Malcolm. "I don't want to talk about it."

He rocked back and forth slowly. Then he reached for this backpack.

"I want to Crazy Board about it."

Sloan shook her head.

"Sorry, kiddo. We don't carry Crazy Boards in the Creeper."

Malcolm gave her that same blank look.

"That's why I always carry my own."

He pulled a yellow legal pad out of his backpack.

"Travel size."

He then brought out a variety pack of Sharpies.

The tension in the Creeper eased a bit. Yes, we had just visited the seventh layer of Hell. Yes, there was still a good chance we'd be murdered tonight. But the sky was still blue, the world was still round, and Malcolm still wanted to Crazy Board.

He flipped open the pad and began to scribble.

"Okay, first," he said. "There was this girl . . ."

He wrote THIS GIRL in Sharpie and flipped the page.

"She was an elf. She was tall and terrifying and on a lot of drugs."

He wrote that and flipped again.

"And I think she may be my girlfriend now? Or at least my lover?"

He wrote GIRLFRIEND? LOVER? and flipped onward.

Sloan opened her mouth and then closed it. Quinn cut her off with a quick shake of the head and pat on the shoulder.

She knew what we all knew. Once the Crazy Boarding begins, it's just best to let it run its crazy course.

And, in this case, it was truly crazy.

BRIGHAM

Malcolm slowly picked up speed and his tone brightened as he walked us through the horrible events he had just witnessed.

"So, in conclusion," he said, "this is bad. People may be dead. Coach Craig is in big trouble. The Unicorn Gang is most likely looking for us. But we still have advantages. Because we're smarter, we're not on drugs and they don't know where we are right now."

He then flipped the legal pad under his arm.

"Questions?" he said, as though he had just finished his own TED Talk.

In that TED Talk he also laid out the supposed hierarchy of the Unicorn Gang operation.

Mister Happy was on top. The Unicorns were his goons. The other creepy dudes were his pushers. The partiers were there because they were hooked on the Unicorn Dust. The poor zombies in the basement were having bad trips or had overdosed. Or, in the case of Coach Craig, they were enemies of Mister Happy. And he was intentionally drugging them in hopes of an eventual overdose.

Sloan raised a hand.

"Yes, I have a question," she said quietly.

"Yes, Sloan," he said.

This might have seemed ridiculous, but I appreciated the comfortable nerdy formality of Malcolm's presentations.

"Your cell phone," she said. "Where is it right now?"

Quinn gasped.

Marshall cursed.

Malcolm dropped his travel-sized Crazy Board to the ground.

He looked like a deer in semi-truck headlights.

"Riiight," she said. "In Carl's cardboard box. I thought so."

He stammered something that sounded like *nonononono*.

I let out a groan and slid out of my seat and onto the dirty floor.

And then, right on cue, Marshall's phone began to ring.

With a shaking hand, he held up the glowing screen.

The call was coming from Malcolm's cell phone, of course.

MARSHALL

My ringtone is "My Humps" by the Black Eyed Peas.

It's supposed to be funny since, you know, it's one of the most obnoxious songs of all time. Also because of Michael Scott.

Now, it was one of the most terrifying songs all of time, and Fergie was the harbinger of doom.

"Don't answer it!" yelled Brigham.

"You've got to answer it!" yelled Malcolm.

"Throw it out the window!" yelled Quinn.

"Shut it off!" said Brigham.

Sloan said nothing.

She extended a hand my way.

"Give it to me."

I gave it to her.

She pressed the button and switched to speakerphone.

"Hello," she said coldly.

At first there was nothing.

Silence.

Then breathing.

"Say it," said a gruff voice.

There was some muffled moaning.

"SAY IT!"

There was more silence followed by a familiar voice in torment.

"They're coming for you guys," said Coach Craig. "Sorry, guys. I tried, but they're coming for you."

And then there was a gunshot. And more screaming. Primal this time. Like nothing I'd ever heard. Sloan dropped the phone on the floorboard.

Quinn clasped her hands to her mouth.

I snatched the phone from the floor, tapped on the screen and felt the panicked urged to throw it out the window. Then there was another voice.

Deep. Menacing. Unexpectedly calm. "Hey, kiddies. Hope you had fun at my party . . ."

It was Mister Happy.

And he wasn't happy.

BRIGHAM

We said nothing, but Mister Happy knew we were there. And he laughed.

"Don't worry," he said. "You don't have to talk. Just listen."

There was another moment of silence, then he spoke again.

"I want to tell you why they call me Mister Happy. It's actually a good story . . ."

I had a feeling it wasn't.

Another pause. We could hear the screams, but they were muffled now as though Mister Happy had apparently moved to a quieter spot in his dungeon.

"You see . . . I have a lot of enemies. And there are a lot of people that want what I have. So, sometimes, they try and take it. I can't let that happen. But more than that, I have to make an example of those who try and take what I have. You see?"

I nodded even though he couldn't see me.

"Good," he said. "So, when I catch these people, I make sure things happen to them. Things that hurt. And things that they will not ever, ever recover from. Physically, maybe. Mentally? No."

Another muffled scream.

"But, of course, I don't do those things personally. The gentlemen you've seen, they like to call themselves the Unicorn Gang, which I think is a bit dramatic . . . they do those things. And here's the crazy part, the people they do these awful things to, technically they're my enemies . . . but in the end, after the Unicorns are done with them, they become my friends."

I looked out the window and into the black night. I just wanted him to stop talking. He didn't.

"Because by the time I arrive, they are always begging for it to end. And when they see me, they finally know—it's over. Sometimes they actually smile, if they still have teeth. And they're happy. Legitimately happy! That's why they call me Mister Happy. Because I am the one who ends the pain and suffering. For that last moment, their last moment here on this earth, Mister Happy is their very best friend."

There was more muffled screaming in the background but Mister Happy ignored it.

"I want you to know something . . ." His voice dropped to a little more than a whisper. "I think I've made five new friends tonight."

Ice water shot through my veins, and I felt as though I was floating somewhere above my head.

"Marshall. Brigham. Malcolm. Sloan. Quinn . . . We're going to be *best* friends. I'll be seeing you soon. And when you do . . . you'll be very happy to see me."

And then *click.*

The line went to silence.

QUINN

So, there was a good five-to-ten-minute freak-out after that.

I'll spare you the details, but Marshall had his usual panic attack. Brigham chattered a lot about how he couldn't die because he needed to know how Marvel's Phase V ended. Sloan and I took turns saying our favorite curse words a lot. And Malcolm took copious notes along the way.

"But why?" said Brigham. "Why would he give us a warning that he's going to kill us? Shouldn't he just, you know, kill us?"

I saw Marshall visibly shudder at the same time I did.

Sloan had her head in her hands.

"He doesn't know where we are," she said. "So he threatened us because he wants us to call the police."

Malcolm nodded.

"And he wants us to call the police, because if we do, Bad Cop will know where we are."

"And then Bad Cop tips off the Unicorn Gang," said Brigham.

"And then the Unicorn Gang drags us back to Hell Town," said Marshall.

Sloan and I took turns saying curse words again.

"So, we can't go to the police," I said. "We can't go home or we'll lead them straight to our families. Where can we go?"

Marshall cleared his throat.

"I think I know."

He pulled a large bronze key out of his pocket.

"Back to where it all started," he said. "It's time for this junior star student to earn a little extra credit."

QUINN

"What?" said Sloan.

"Extra credit," said Marshall. "It's time to do some."

Sloan stared at him.

"You want to do schoolwork now?"

"No, it's the key to the school, get it?" said Marshall. "It's . . . I'm a junior star student. So we can get in."

"Yeah, but why do we need to do extra credit while we're there?" said Malcolm. "I have a 4.0 across the board."

"No, no, no," said Marshall. "I was just . . . I'm just being cool. You know, it's like my catch phrase."

"Ahhhh," I said. "It's a catchphrase. I get it kind of."

Brigham cocked his head to the side.

"So, 'Let's earn some extra credit' is your catchphrase?"

"What, it's not good?"

Sloan snorted and started up the Creeper.

"It's just the dorkiest catchphrase of all catchphrases."

"What, you have something better?"

"Um, yeah," said Malcolm. "How about . . . 'School's back in session, evil-doers!'"

Sloan nodded.

"Or how about, 'It's time to get saved by the bell, suckers!'"

"Oh, I got it," I said. And I did. "How about, 'I'm about to get straight A's . . . in Butt Kicking 101!'"

I've edited that for profanity just in case my mom is reading this. But mine's still the best.

MARSHALL

Okay, Quinn's was better.

Sloan's was better too.

Everyone's was better, all right?

"Time to earn some extra credit" is not the catchiest of catch phases. But it's less flash and more substance. A thinking man's catchphrase if you will.

As we rolled through the darkened streets of greater Tucker, we discussed just that. It was a lively conversation that almost kept our minds off the fact that we were being hunted by a homicidal drug dealer.

Almost.

The drive from Moreland Avenue to Carter High School usually takes about twenty minutes, but that night it took over an hour.

Sloan was discreetly sticking to the side streets and away from any of the main thoroughfares.

"The Creeper is about as recognizable as the Batmobile to those sickos now," she said. "We have to stick to the shadows."

Malcolm nodded.

"Just like Batman."

"Yep, and that makes you Robin," said Sloan.

"Ahh," he groaned. "Robin's kind of lame."

"How about Batgirl?" said Quinn.

Malcolm considered this.

"Yes, much better."

It made no sense, but the mood had lightened considerably since Mister Happy's terrifying death threat. We were in an awful mess. But we were in this awful mess together. It was true foxhole camaraderie. And in a weird way, I felt as though our many nights spent mounting RPG campaigns against the elder witches and farm wizards in Framptonworth had prepared us for this real-life monster. Our training was kicking in.

When we arrived at the school, the parking lot was empty, as expected.

But it was even emptier than usual.

Normally, you'll see Ms. Moreland's busted Kia in the front lot, or Winky Jeff's El Camino. And there's usually a bit of noise coming from the hallways as the floor-waxer hums across the shiny linoleum.

Tonight, there was nothing.

No cars.

No humming.

Just an ominous stillness in the air that kind of made me want to run inside and hide in my locker.

But then, I suppose, the emptier the better.

Sloan parked the Creeper at the loading dock behind the lunchroom. It's dark, out of the way, and not visible from the streets. Though I didn't have to tell her that.

"This is where my old boyfriend Scottie Stanford and I used to park during junior year," she said. "He was a senior in college. We used to sneak onto the roof and smoke stuff."

Quinn gave her big sis a disapproving look.

"What?" said Sloan. "It's not like we were doing Unicorn Dust."

"No, I'm talking about Scottie Stanford," she said. "Have some standards."

Sloan shrugged.

"You've got a point there."

The key didn't work on the back door, so we had to sneak around to the front.

Once we were in, the lock clicked with an echo that bounced along the empty hallways.

"Feels like we're sealing our own tomb," said Brigham.

"Shush," said Quinn.

We moved quietly through the darkened hall and took a right at Ms. Clark's home ec class.

"You know," whispered Malcolm. "This is terrifying. But I'd still rather be here for this than one of Mrs. Ricardo's quizzes."

He was steadily regaining that old Malcolm spirit.

"Ugh, yeah I remember those," said Sloan. "Does she still call them quizzicles?"

"Yep," said Malcolm. "Makes you wonder what she calls 'tests,' right?"

Sloan's sharp laugh echoed off the walls.

"Ha! I can't believe I never thought of that!"

I shushed them viciously.

They might have felt as though we were merely visiting our alma mater. Me? I was traveling back in time. Back to the very night this all started. To the night of snot and savage beatings and one-horned man monsters.

It all looked exactly the same. That moment was frozen in amber. And, for some reason, I kept going back to it, in my nightmares and now in real life. I couldn't escape.

I led them to the darkened science lab and Malcolm flicked on the light.

Brigham flicked it off.

"Are you crazy?" he hissed. "They'll know we're in here!"

"Well, we can't sit in the dark, can we?" said Malcolm. "We've got a lot of survival planning to do."

"I got this," I said. I went to the supply cabinet, pulled out the Bunsen burners, placed them strategically around the room, and lit them up.

"Niiice," said Quinn. "Torch lighting. Good for the ambiance."

Sloan leaned against the wall as Quinn, Brigham, and I took our seats around one of the high-top tables.

Malcolm headed straight for the dry-erase board. He picked up a marker, looked me straight in the eyes, and had the audacity to say it.

"Okay, kids. Time for some extra credit."

MALCOLM

"Hey!" blurted Marshall. "That's my catchphrase!"

"True," I said. "But my delivery was better."

He made inappropriate gestures in my direction.

"Marshall Fairbanks, see me after school!"

More gestures. I was losing control of the classroom already.

"Okay, here's the plan I came up with a few weeks ago for this particular scenario," I said as I uncorked the marker and began to draw a crude map of the school.

"Whoa, whoa, whoa, wait, wait, wait," said Brigham.

I waited.

"You're telling me that you have a specific plan for this specific scenario?"

I nodded while drawing the entry foyer next to the custodian's closet.

"You mean, you had a plan in case we went to a gangster drug party, found Coach Craig in the basement, got caught in a shootout, and had to hide in the school?"

"Well, yeah, but I kind of figured we'd be hiding out in the computer lab because there's no windows there."

I looked at Marshall.

"Science lab is good too though."

Sloan hopped onto a stool and crossed her long perfect legs.

"Umm, maybe next time you should plan a scenario where you don't leave your cell phone with a crime boss?"

Ouch.

"Too soon," I said.

And that's when a new scenario began to occur. This one I never planned for.

I'd like to think Mrs. Lansbury would have seen this coming.

And she might have.

But then again, Mrs. Lansbury never hung out with Sloan.

CHAPTER SEVENTEEN

CARRIE'S REVENGE

BRIGHAM

Sloan wears short shorts.

That's not a pervy statement. It's just a fact. And I have no problem with that.

But I do have a problem with what I saw when she crossed her legs and sat on the stool beside me.

I wasn't exactly looking. But I was kind of looking.

Sloan has a collection of stylish tattoos. They are all awesome and tastefully placed. An Aztec firebird on her forearm. A lightning bolt on her ankle. A quirky gnome riding a bike on her right calf. And then a new one I had never noticed before, one I probably wasn't supposed to see because it was high on her upper thigh.

It was the tattoo that changed everything.

It was a tattoo of a severed unicorn head.

A zombie unicorn, obviously.

QUINN

Brigham let out a garbled yell and pointed at Sloan as though she was the Ghost of Christmas past.

"YOU!" he said. "You're one of them, aren't you?! You're in the Unicorn Gang!"

Sloan barely reacted. She did her bored-looking smirky-smirk that makes it look as though you, not her, are the one who's to blame. I know that look well. It meant she was the one to blame.

"What are you talking about?" said Marshall.

"Um, yeah," Malcolm said. "It's Sloan, she's on our side!"

Brigham shook his head back and forth, his eyes large.

"That's not what her upper thigh says!"

Sloan actually snickered. I knew that snicker too.

"Didn't like what you saw there, handsome?"

Brigham turned bright red.

"Stop trying to embarrass me. Left leg. It's there. A dead unicorn tattoo!"

Malcolm dropped his dry-erase marker.

Marshall froze.

Me? I felt as though I was plummeting down the first hill of a roller coaster.

Because how could I not see it? How could I have been so stupid?

Of course Sloan had a unicorn tattoo. And of course Sloan was in the Unicorn Gang.

MALCOLM

A lot of things happened all at once at this moment.

I dropped my marker.

Marshall let out a startled scream as though he had seen a unicorn ghost.

Brigham lost his balance on the stool and fell backward.

And Quinn? Well, Quinn leaped over a table and was on Sloan in mere seconds. It was as though she teleported.

Teleportation powered by pure rage.

She grabbed her sister by the shoulders. But Sloan didn't resist.

Then Quinn stopped, her shoulders drooped, and she began to shake.

And I realized, she wasn't crying. She was laughing.

It wasn't a good laugh.

Quinn

It wasn't funny. But it was. Just funny in a sad, disastrous, heartbreaking kind of way, you know?

My laughter turned to one single loud crazy sob and then back to laughter again.

"Of course you're in the gang," I said.

I could have slapped her. I could have strangled her. And she wouldn't have stopped me. Ironically, that's exactly what wound up stopping me. I love my sister, after all.

Really, I think I was most mad at myself for not noticing.

Sloan is not what you'd call a modest woman. In fact, you could call her the exact opposite of modest. But I realized that, over the past summer, I had not seen her in a full bikini at all. Whenever we'd go to the beach or the pool, she'd put on a bikini top but board shorts over her swimsuit bottom.

I was just glad she wasn't trying to show me up with her annoyingly Instagram-ready bikini body. I should have assumed something was amiss right there. I should have known she was trying to hide something. But how was I supposed to know that thing was a drug gang-affiliated dead unicorn tattoo?

My bad.

Sloan

I could tell their little nerd minds were motoring along.

"That's how you got us into the party, isn't it?" said Marshall.

"And that's how you were able to talk to Mister Happy, right?" said Malcolm.

I gave them a nod, stood up, and peeled back my jean shorts.

"Might as well get a good look."

"Are you serious?" said Quinn.

"It's a tattoo, not a sticker," I said. "Of course I'm serious."

"WHY SLOAN?!" yelled Quinn. This is usually the point in our arguments where she jumps me. Or I jump her. But this was no normal argument.

"Why Sloan?" she said softer now.

She didn't move.

Instead, she just looked at me.

And, well, she looked ashamed.

I'd rather she'd have jumped me.

QUINN

I'll be honest. I was going to lay the smackdown on my sister. WWE-style.

But then she flinched.

And she looked like Sloan again.

Pre-*The Sloan Show* Sloan.

And it made me miss her.

"You know . . . we had to leave Chicago because of you," I said.

She re-crossed her legs.

"Yeah, and it was a great move. Less traffic. No snow shoveling. More access to Chick-fil-A."

Aaaand *The Sloan Show* was back. I ignored her.

"I had friends there, you know? Not great friends, but still some friends. I was involved in things. We had a home. Dad had a good job. It was all I knew. Then you get caught with a little weed and some guy. And then another guy. And then another guy. And then more weed. And then Mom and Dad made us move one thousand miles away so you can have more 'space to grow.'"

Sloan looked bored. And while it should have infuriated me, it only made me sadder.

"I had to leave everybody. It was the end of middle school and my friends went to high school and instantly forgot about me. It was like I was erased. They moved on. They didn't care. You didn't care either."

My hands started to shake. Instead of hiding them like I usually do I let her see.

"I worried about you so much. The drugs. The boys. The nights when you would stumble in and tell me things that I was much too young to hear."

Sloan blinked. I balled my shaking hands into fists. Then I took a deep breath.

"But good came from it. So much good. I met these guys. I met Marshall. I met Brigham. I met Malcolm. They accepted me for who I am. Back in Chicago, I didn't have friends like that. I guess I was considered cool but only because I was trying so hard. Too hard. Being cool is not worth it when it all depends on the fickle viewpoints of mixed-up peers. If you let cool define you, then *they* define you."

Sloan shrugged.

"If it makes you feel better, I never thought you were cool."

I shook my head, not taking the bait this time.

"And now what are you doing? Running with an illegal drug gang? Where are Mom and Dad gonna move us to next? How much space will you need for this one?"

"Alaska maybe?"

"You joke," I said. "You joke but I think you're ashamed. I think you're scared. And I think deep down inside, you have to put on this tough-girl front so people don't see the real you."

"What's the real me then?"

She asked me like she really wanted to know.

At this point, Marshall, Brigham, and Malcolm were pretty much frozen in place as they watched our ridiculous family drama unfold.

"The real you is . . . not this. The real you is weird."

She let out a sharp laugh.

"But in a good way. Odd. But in a way everybody is, and most people are afraid to show. The real you once filmed a shot-for-shot remake of *The Lion King* with our dog, Chewie. The real you cried when her hamster died even though you were fourteen years old. Shoot, the real you kept hamsters as pets even though you were fourteen. The real you used to hug our parents. And me. The real you is dorky and sometimes scared and not perfect. Nowhere near perfect. But at least you're real. Not hood-life Barbie."

"Hey, at least Barbie has an awesome car. I drive a minivan."

"Great. Another quip."

I looked at the ground. Then I looked her in the eyes.

"Tell me . . . are you hooked on this stuff? Are you hooked on this Unicorn Dust?"

Sloan didn't answer.

She just stood up, walked over to the door, and clicked the lock.

Then she looked back at me, looked at all of us. Her sly smile was gone. It was replaced by something different.

Something hard. Something dangerous. I've seen a lot of looks from my sister, but never that one. And it frightened me.

"You guys aren't leaving," she said. "Not like this."

BRIGHAM

I was not going to fight Sloan.

But I was going to have to fight Sloan.

I mean, I wouldn't do it.

But I would have to.

And I realized that there are no Master Kensei videos dealing with how to fight a girl who's kind of a friend but also evil . . . in a chemistry lab.

Which I wasn't going to do anyway.

But I knew I had to.

These were the thoughts going through my head as I edged toward the door and prepared to take Sloan by surprise from behind.

Really, I was just hoping Quinn could overpower her sister and save the day so I didn't have to.

Turns out, it didn't happen that way.

SLOAN

Yeah, I locked the door.

Yeah, I know it scared them.

And, yeah, I liked it.

C'mon, it was funny.

Don't get me wrong. It's not like I wasn't touched by my sister's heartfelt speech. Though it was also one big guilt trip. She failed to mention that Dad got a better job in Tucker. We now live in a much nicer house, and he works better hours.

These kids are so dramatic.

They act like everybody's a hero or a villain in their dorky board game.

It's a little more complicated in real life.

Some of us are both heroes and villains.

"It's about time you little nerds figured it out," I said as I turned around to face them.

Brigham looked as though he was mentally wrestling with how to fight me and still remain a perfect gentleman.

"Stand down, soldier," I said. "You think I'm a double agent?"

"Are you?" said Malcolm.

"How do you think I walked into that party? How do you think I knew the bouncer? How do you think I got within five feet of Mister Happy without finding a bullet in my brain? Why do you think he told me where to find Coach Craig?"

I stared at them all. One by one.

I looked at Quinn who was still looking at me like a disappointed parent.

"You're right. This isn't me. But I'm also not . . . good. And I like it. I'm not good on purpose. I get bored being good. I wish I wasn't like that but—okay, I'm lying. I'm glad I'm like that."

Quinn shook her head disapprovingly. So sanctimonious.

I moved to the head of the classroom.

"After we moved here, Mom and Dad asked me to stop causing trouble. So, I naturally headed for the first bad boy I could find. And that's where I finally found the kind of trouble I didn't want."

"Scottie Stanford?" said Quinn.

"No, not that loser. He couldn't buy over-the-counter Allegra if he wanted to. His name is Connor Limehouse."

"What a name," said Brigham.

"He just introduced himself back at the party by punching directly through our driver-side window."

"The Devil Face man?!" said Brigham. "C'mon, you need a guy with better taste in facial hair."

Malcolm agreed. "He does kind of look like he's in a '90s boy band . . ." He had pulled out a piece of scrap paper and looked like he was taking notes on this conversation. "But a murderous one."

I didn't disagree.

"Yeah, I didn't realize what I was getting into with him," I said. "I met him at an actual fun party. The kegger that they throw every Spring Break Eve, when Mark Robinson's parents leave town. You know the one."

They looked at me blankly and it was obvious they didn't.

"Anyways we started talking and he seemed intriguing. Didn't say much, but also looked like he had something else going on. Something interesting. I wanted to know what that something was. Turns out, it wasn't good. He took me to a Hell Party. You know why it's called that now."

I shook my head as unwanted visions of that sick night flooded my head.

"I realized these weren't like the parties I was going to in Chicago. They weren't fun. There were no festivities and merriment. Just sadness and addiction and death."

Quinn had her head in her hands. It made me mad.

"Quinn, look at me," I said.

She looked up and her eyes were red-rimmed. Angry and sad at the same time.

"Remember when Mom and Dad made me go to that drug counselor back when they found my stash?"

"Yeah," she said. "You hid it in my Polly Pocket Playhouse."

"Oh, yeah," I laughed. "Well, it's pretty obvious it didn't work. No amount of counseling did. Because I never wanted to change. But five minutes in that trap house, just five minutes in that Hell Party, scared me so much. It scared me straighter than months and months of talking to that babbling shrink ever could have."

Quinn nodded and looked somewhat relieved.

"So, no. I am not on the Unicorn Dust. Never."

"So, why the tattoo?" said Brigham.

"Just listen, handsome," I said.

He turned bright red again. I enjoy doing that. It's like a super-power.

"First off, I just kind of like it. I like zombies. I like unicorns. I was looking for something upper thigh-ish. It was the perfect fit. But secondly, and most importantly, it's my ticket in. Nobody there doubts my loyalty to the Unicorn Gang. But they should."

I looked at Malcolm.

"I don't have a Crazy Board," I said. "But I'm on this case too."

MARSHALL

Secret Agent Sloan. It had a nice ring to it. Miraculously, Malcolm stepped aside and gave her command of The Board.

"As you know, Mister Happy is the leader," said Sloan. "And he's a bad man. But he has mini-bosses."

"Like Bowser and Bowser Jr.," said Malcolm.

My fellow dorks and I nodded along.

"Sure, whatever, like Bowser."

"And Bowser Jr.," added Malcolm.

"Yeah, whatever," she said. "Anyway, the mini-bosses are the guys with unicorn masks. They usually have something to prove. And they usually prove it through violence."

"I can vouch for that," I said as I pointed to my nose.

"It could have been worse," said Sloan.

Man, no respect for the septum. I must have made a face.

"I mean it," she said. "I've seen it."

Sloan sat down on a stool and took a deep breath.

"It happened to a girl named Carrie. At the Hell Party. I remember her first name. I never knew her last until . . . until it was too late. We started talking on the back porch. She said she wanted to be a veterinarian. She loved all dogs. She said that whenever she saw a dog in the park near her house, she made sure she found out its name. We laughed about it because she said she always remembered the dogs' names but never the owners'."

Sloan stopped for a moment and stared at the floor. Somewhere in the distance, a siren wailed.

"I was taking a shot of Fireball in the kitchen when she passed out. Turns out she had just taken a hit of the Unicorn Dust. She banged her head on the counter and fell to the ground all limp. Like a rag doll. I reached for my cell to call 911 but Conner grabbed my arm and wouldn't let go."

"Oh snap," said Malcolm.

Sloan nodded.

"Right? Normally if a dude grabs me like that, they're not getting all their appendages back in one piece. But the look in that psycho's eyes made me realize he wasn't anything like the juvenile delinquents I'd been messing around with. He squeezed my wrist so hard I could literally feel my bones bending. I looked into his eyes . . . and he looked right past me. Right through me. There was nothing there. It was like he could do anything to anyone, and he wouldn't blink."

"Michael Myers," I whispered.

"Michael Myers," said Sloan. "Chances are he's the guy who broke your nose. Mister Happy sends him out to create violence and spread fear. He knows Conner will show no remorse. No guilt. No mercy. No . . . humanity."

We all looked at each other in the flickering light of the burners. Where was this Michael Myers now? The siren had moved on and the silence in the school returned. Though the building was mostly empty, we spoke in hushed tones, as though he was standing over our shoulders.

"Anyway, he told me that calling the cops to a Hell Party is not allowed. I said 'Well, it is now.' And he drew back to punch me. Closed fist and all. Then Mister Happy appeared from nowhere. He caught his hand and snapped it behind his back."

We all simultaneously gasped.

"He pulled back on his arm until Conner actually screamed," said Sloan. "He deserved it, of course, but the look from Mister Happy still haunts me. He looked . . . overjoyed. If Conner feels nothing, Mister Happy feels all of it. And he loves it. He loves to hurt. He loves to cause pain. He's in the right business for it."

Sloan's eyes glazed over.

"Then he patted my . . . well . . . he patted me. And he said not to worry about it, he would 'take care of me.' I didn't want to know what that meant.

"All the while, Carrie lay there, bleeding. Mister Happy looked down at her and actually laughed. He told me not to worry about it because she was just another 'nameless party-girl.' The party went on around her. Around her blood. People didn't care. Sickos. They told me she would be fine, but she was dragged into the basement. Mister Happy waved at her and told her to 'have a nice trip.' That was the last I saw of her. I had the feeling I would soon be joining her down there but there was a brawl in the kitchen and I slipped out. A few days later, I saw her name in the death notices in the paper. It had to be her. Caroline Mae Henderson. Died at the age of nineteen. Drug overdose."

"Oh," whispered Brigham. "The girl on Coach Craig's Crazy Board."

Sloan didn't seem to hear him.

"I knew that something needed to be done. I knew this had to be stopped. And so, yeah, I've stuck around. And, yeah, I keep going back to the Hell Parties. Because I'm looking for a way to get even. I want to end Mister Happy. And I want Conner to feel the pain that Carrie did. That unicorn tattoo is my ticket in, but it's also in memory of Carrie."

She slid from the stool and to her feet.

"So, no, I'm not on the Unicorn Dust. And I'm not an addict. I'm stone-cold sober. Vengeance is my drug now."

She looked at us all, one by one. Defying us to argue. Defying us to tell her she was wrong.

The old clock above Mrs. Ricardo's desk ticked and ticked.

Finally, Malcolm spoke.

"See," he said. "I told you she was Batman."

QUINN

Sloan walked over to me, looked me in the eyes, and hugged me.

I wasn't expecting it.

"I'm sorry," she whispered. "Thanks for worrying about me, sis."

It was the kind of embrace we haven't had since we were kids.

I felt myself tearing up. I felt my sister returning. For the first time in a long time, she was back.

And that's when Fergie began to sing again.

MARSHALL

Yep, it was "My Humps" again.

Yep, Fergie was the harbinger of darkness once more.

"Uh oh," I said. "It's my mom."

This was strange. It was the middle of the night on a Saturday and my mom was checking up on me. I know that wouldn't be considered strange at all for most people. Most moms check up on their sons in the middle of the night on a Saturday, but not my mom. Since she works strange shifts, Fairbanks hours are different. Sometimes, I find her eating breakfast at three p.m. Other times, she's doing power yoga in the living room at three a.m. We once had Thanksgiving dinner at five thirty in the morning.

It's just our way of life.

Plus, she trusts me.

Since I spend the night at Malcolm's a lot, I usually just send her a text with a heart emoji. She responds with a winky face and a thumbs up.

But when she calls, that's different. When she calls, something has happened. And in this case, something had definitely happened.

I picked up the phone and braced myself.

"Marshall," said Mom, her voice flat and tense. "Ted has been stabbed."

I nearly dropped my iPhone into the lab sink.

"What?!"

"A man came to our door looking for you and he was . . . well, we thought he was some kind of confused trick-or-treater, but he was looking for you and—wait, hold on—"

There was muffled shuffling as it sounded as though the phone had changed hands despite my mom's protests.

"'Sup, bro," said Tribal Ted.

Ted!

I'd never been so glad to be *'sup-bro*ed by my mom's boyfriend. Tribal Ted wasn't bleeding out on the carpet! Yes!

He also sounded much too cheerful for a stabbing victim.

"You okay?!" I managed.

Ted actually laughed.

"Ahhh, bleeding a lot . . . but you know how it goes."

I didn't.

"What happened?!"

"Well, since you asked, this freak in a horse's mask came to the door asking for you and he didn't ask nicely and tried to barge his way right through me so I told him to go to hell and that's when he got the jump on me and tried to break my nose so I blocked his right but then he countered with a . . ."

I switched to speakerphone so everyone in the room could share in the Tribal Ted Experience.

"Then he pulled out a knife. Big, serrated, *Crocodile Dundee*-looking thing. Same thing happened to me in Tampa, when I used to work for FedEx, but the other way around since I was the guy knocking on the door and the guy who lived there pulled the knife because he said he didn't want to pay for his packages. Which is freaking stupid because he didn't have to pay for them since it was a FedEx delivery! That guy had more of a switchblade though, which is cooler I think. Anyway, that's how I got the scar on my right arm, you know?"

I knew that scar. It was angry and impressive and just a few inches down from his tribal tattoo.

"This guy is awesome," mouthed Sloan.

Malcolm nodded sincerely.

Ted was just getting started.

"I wasn't ready for all that in Tampa, but this time I was,

because I grabbed that big stone frog ashtray by the door. You know that big stone frog ashtray?"

I did. It's large and ugly and shaped like a frog and we keep it on the front porch. I always feel sorry for it, because the frog's mouth is constantly full of ash and Ted's plastic cigarillo butts.

"I keep that there for a reason. Not just because it looks awesome, even though it does look awesome."

He paused for the first time, either to breathe or waiting for me to agree that the frog was indeed awesome.

I did, just to be nice, and also because he had just taken a knife for me.

"Once he pulled the knife out, I pushed him backward and he slashed at my arm, like this—"

Remember, we were on the phone. I still nodded as though Tribal Ted could see me.

"So, I grabbed the ashtray and chunked it at him right in his big fat horse head!"

He let out a delighted "*ha-ha-ha*" and Malcolm put both his hands to his mouth like a shocked grandmother.

"Then he punched me! And I punched him! And I punched him again and kneed him right in the balls! And your mom came out and was screaming and there was blood everywhere that I didn't realize was mine and the neighbors called the cops and the horseman ran away like some scared little chicken! Or should I say horse!"

Tribal Ted let out a long loud laugh as though this was the most enjoyable Saturday night he'd had in years.

"Long story short, I'll now have a scar on my left arm. Hey, maybe it'll match!"

I felt dizzy.

In a night of unlikely heroes, this was the unlikeliest.

Tribal Ted.

Fatherly protector.

Before I could say thank you, my mom was back on the line. Her voice was shaky, and she said the paramedics were there and about to stitch up Ted. I told her to stay inside and stay safe and lied about where I was again. She was alarmed and had more questions, of course, but I cut her off and put the phone on silent. I hated to do it. But there was no time to waste.

Hiding was no longer an option.

The Unicorn Gang was out there.

And we needed to bring the herd to us.

CHAPTER EIGHTEEN

THE UNDERGROUND

MARSHALL

For once, I was the guy commanding The Crazy Board.

And it drove Malcolm crazy.

"Do you want me to at least draw a diagram?" he said while reaching for my dry-erase marker.

I slapped his hand away.

"Mr. Ringold, take your seat!"

He grumbled and slid behind a desk.

"Geez, I thought Mrs. Ricardo was strict," he said.

"Okay," I said as I uncapped the dry-erase marker and turned to the board. It occurred to me I had no idea how to do this.

"Okay," I said as I turned back to them and recapped the marker. "We have to call the cops."

"But . . ." said Brigham, raising his hand. "Bad Cop."

"Right," I said. "That's why I said 'cops,' plural. One cop is bad. Multiple cops are good. They can't all be crooked, right?"

"This is true," said Quinn. "There was only one Bad Cop on Coach Craig's Crazy Board."

"Right, good point," said Malcolm. "Can I just write that on the board real quickly?"

"No."

"But how can we be sure that more than one cop will show up?" said Sloan.

"Ahh," I said. "That's the question isn't it?"

"Yes," said Sloan. "That's why I asked."

I'm not good at this.

I plowed on.

"We invite everyone," I said. "All emergency services. Come one, come all."

I laid it all out for them. Timing was crucial. We call the cops. If Bad Cop tips off the Unicorn Gang, the Unicorn Gang shows up first. But soon, the other law-abiding emergency officials show up too . . .

"Hopefully just in time to catch the Unicorn Gang in the act."

"But what is *the act*?" said Brigham. "I'd rather not be a part of that act."

"That's understandable," I said. "I know it sounds crazy, but we open all the doors, find a good place to hide, and then wait for the calvary."

"Yes," said Brigham. "That does sound crazy."

"Very crazy," said Quinn. "But it does make sense. That way they come into the school and when the good police get here, they can arrest them for criminal trespass."

"Exactly," I said. "And hopefully that will lead to more arrests and raids at the Hell House and internal investigations and, well . . . justice."

I turned and wrote JUSTICE on the board.

Then I folded my arms and set the dry-erase marker on the table in front of me. Good plan, eh? Low risk. High reward.

"Okay," said Malcolm. "So the plan is to host a Bad Guy/Good Guy mixer and hide while they do all the mixing?"

"Well, yes."

When he put it that way, it didn't sound so grand.

"Good deal," he said. "But first . . ."

He leaned forward and snatched the dry-erase marker. "Plan B."

BRIGHAM

Plan B was . . . more complicated. It involved headlamps, boiler rooms, mountain bikes, and pitfalls. That's right. I said pitfalls.

We figured it wouldn't come to that. But, you know, of course it did.

MALCOLM

After a solid thirty-five minutes of Plan B planning, we all composed different texts for our families. Like soldiers at war writing letters to their loved ones. All differently worded but with the same theme. Since I didn't have a phone, Marshall texted my parents for me.

Stay indoors. Don't answer the door for anyone. If you call the cops watch out for the one who looks like a blond *Terminator*. We're fine. If you see someone with a terrifying unicorn head, don't engage. And don't worry about us. See you in the morning!

Of course, we were immediately met with alarmed replies. But we all switched to silence. And we had long since shut off location services.

We knew what needed to be done.

We needed to summon the Unicorns.

I punched the three numbers on my phone.

Took a deep breath. Looked at my friends. And hit send.

"911, what's your emergency," said a nasally voice.

I'd never called 911 and realized I wasn't really sure how to do it.

"Um, yes, ma'am," I said. "I am Malcolm Ringold and I'd like to report a kidnapping . . . and an attempted murder . . . and some shootings . . . a lot of them . . . and a bad, um, really bad drug dealer guy named Mister Happy . . . you get the drift, right?"

I looked at Brigham. He shrugged and gave a thumbs-up.

We really should have Crazy Boarded this part.

The nasally voice said nothing but I could hear clicking and clacking on the other side of the line.

"What is your location?"

Here we go. That was the question, wasn't it?

"We are at Carter High School," I said. "We're hiding from the bad guys here in the science lab. Please send help."

And then I hung up.

We all stood up in unison and headed for the door. No way we were staying in the science lab, of course, we couldn't make it that easy.

We hustled to the doorway, waited a few breathless minutes, and then Sloan reached for the fire alarm.

"Dibs," she said. "I've always wanted to do this."

BRIGHAM

Really, I'm surprised Sloan hadn't done that before. Pulling the fire alarm when there wasn't a fire seemed right up her alley.

She yanked on the red handle and the once-quiet hallways erupted into flashing lights and an ear-bleeding alarm.

"That was just as satisfying as I imagined!" she yelled as we ran to the front doors.

The plan was to hide in the janitor's closet, but not until the Unicorns were approaching. We all agreed that it seemed even more terrifying to cower in the dark with no idea whether our enemies were actually in the building. We wanted to see them coming.

We slammed the big green doors behind us, muffling the sound, and walked out to the flagpole. Inside, it was all shrieking, flashing chaos, but outside it was actually a quiet night in Tucker. There was the steady drone of traffic. A few dogs barking in the distance. A couple of jetliners gliding across the lightening sky. But no sirens in the distance just yet.

A few minutes passed.

A few more.

And still no sirens.

Quinn figured it out first.

The awful truth.

"You guys," she said. "It's 911."

We looked at her.

Quinn looked at Sloan.

"There's someone on the Unicorn's side working in dispatch," she said. "Think about it. They knew you were trying to call 911 from the Hell Party but Mister Happy didn't seem that worried.

He knew no one was coming because he has someone on the inside working for him . . ."

"Nooo," said Marshall.

He sank to the ground.

"So, if they get a Mister Happy-related call for help . . . someone at 911 makes sure no one knows about it?"

"That's messed up," said Malcolm.

"But there's still the fire department, right?" said Marshall. "We pulled the alarm so at least they'll show up, right?"

"Riiight," said Quinn, though she didn't seem convinced.

We waited for a few more minutes.

Still no sirens.

"Unless . . ." said Sloan.

"Unless what?" said Malcolm.

"Unless the alarm is routed to dispatch. In that case, they'd just ignore it. Or worse . . . shut it off."

And that's exactly what happened.

As if on cue, the alarms went silent. And deathly quiet returned to the hallways of Carter High School.

All we had done was ring the dinner bell for a bunch of ravenous Unicorn predators.

"We need to get to the closet," whispered Sloan.

We ran inside and headed for our safe room. We weren't even close when a door slammed somewhere on the other side of the building.

The Unicorn Gang was here.

And help wasn't on the way.

MARSHALL

I sensed them before I saw them.

They didn't make much noise.

No solid echoing footsteps headed our way like in an old-school monster movie. That would have actually been helpful.

These monsters were quiet. Stealthy. I heard a soft squeak of shoe soles against the floor, then the rustle of cloth that made me think of shedded snakeskin. We were moving past the lunchroom when I held a hand up for everyone to stop. Surprisingly, they did. Then I peeked around the corner and saw them.

Five of them.

All together.

All silhouetted against the Fall Fling Harvest Dance bulletin board.

All wearing unicorn masks.

Their horsey heads bobbed with each step like a nightmarish herd.

Psychos.

Luckily, we were standing right next to our safe haven. Winky Jeff's storage area.

We opened the door and dashed in.

Quinn was careful to shut us in as silently as possible as she eased the doorknob closed and twisted the inside lock with a faint click.

It was bigger than most closets and legend had it that Winky Jeff actually lived here occasionally. Hence the backward locks.

We stood silently in the inky black darkness. Malcolm was panting softly, and I wanted to shush him, but I didn't dare.

We thought the herd would pass us by, but then there was a *click-click* of the door handle.

Click-click.

I held my breath.

Click-click.

Malcolm stopped panting.

"Split up," said a gruff voice from the other side of the door. He sounded close enough that he could have been in the same room. "If you see one, they'll run. Make it so they can't."

Then another voice. This one even lower and rumbling.

"Remember, Happy wants us to bring them back to the Dungeon. So don't kill . . ." Then a pause and a chuckle. "But that doesn't mean you can't hurt."

There was relaxed laughter from the herd. What was sheer terror for us was a fun outing for them. Just another Saturday night of violence and aggravated assault. There was one more *click-click* of the doorknob and then there was nothing. No sound at all.

We sat in silence for a solid minute. No one moving. No one whispering.

Malcolm was the first to speak.

"Well," he said. "I guess it's Plan B."

MALCOLM

Carter High School was named for America's best ex-president, and Georgia's only homegrown commander in chief, Jimmy Earl Carter. But prior to 1970-something, it was known simply as Public School 145.

P.S. 145 was built in 1926. And it feels like it.

It's all brick and mortar and bomb shelter-ish.

In fact, there is an actual bomb shelter. It's in the off-limits section of the school called the Underground.

That's the cool-kid way of saying the basement.

There's lots of pipes, storage rooms, a Freddy Krueger-like boiler room, and even an abandoned indoor pool.

It's where the cool kids go to skip school and make out and, well, do other cool kid things of which I have no idea about. The best part is, it locks from the outside and we had the key. If we could lure them in, we could trap them.

Step one of Plan B.

"So, we need to get to the Underground," I said.

Sloan turned on her cell phone flashlight.

"It's a good plan," she said. "If you don't get lost. That place is a labyrinth. I spent half my senior year down there."

See? Cool kids.

"But . . ." she said. "I'm not going with you."

"What?" said Quinn. "But you're our magical unicorn spy." I sensed some sibling sarcasm even in the midst of our terror.

"Exactly," said Sloan. "And my cover is blown. They know who I am. They know the Creeper. And if I can get to the Creeper I can draw them away."

"To where?" I said.

"Where else? We stick with the plan."

She patted me on the head as though I was her faithful golden retriever. I'm completely okay with that.

"Plan B was more exciting anyway."

She looked at Marshall.

"No offense."

"None taken," said Marshall. "That's what I liked about it."

Sloan put her hands on Quinn's shoulders and looked her in the eyes.

"You can do this. You're the smartest person I know. And maybe I should be the type of big sister who shelters and protects you and sits around at home and braids your hair. But that's . . . so boring. And I don't think you want that either. I think you want adventure."

She looked at us.

"I think you all do. Well, you got it. So, man up, nerds."

She looked at Quinn.

"And woman up, nerd."

She winked.

"See you in the forest."

With that, the amazing, beautiful, dangerous Sloan left the closet behind. And then, when she hit the lunchroom, she started singing.

"GOOO THE COUGARS OF CARTEEEER! GET UP AND WIN THAT GAAAAAAME!"

MARSHALL

Quinn grinned and wiped a tear from her eye with a shaky hand.

"Well, that was dramatic," she said.

"Dramatically awesome," said a lovestruck Malcolm.

It was. But also, effective. I'm not much for school spirit, mostly since the entire school seems to enjoy pointing and laughing at my failures and shortcomings on a regular basis. But there's still something about that song. Something about the way it's sung by nerds and non-nerds alike, joined together for just a moment in harmony. And the words of that cherished anthem echoed loudly and obnoxiously off the hallways of Carter High School.

"WIIIIIN OR LOSE WE'RE WITH YOOOOU AND WE'LL CHEER YOU JUST THE SAAAAAAME!"

"Man," said Brigham. "She really can't sing."

"No, not at all," said Quinn.

We turned and grabbed headlamps from the stash of supplies in the janitor's closet. Turns out Winky Jeff's storage room offered more than just shelter. It also housed the gear from Coach Jensen's camping class, which was basically an excuse for the baseball team to hang out in the woods for course credit.

"Get an extra one," said Malcolm. "I've got an idea."

A few tense minutes followed and then we heard the signal from the Creeper.

AHHHHOOOOOGGGGAAAAAAAA.

"That's it," said Malcolm. "Let's go!"

No more sneaking. No more tiptoeing. We actually wanted them to follow us as we scrambled toward the Underground entrance.

It's a small half-door located at the end of C-Wing, of course.

"C-Wing," I muttered. "Why does it always have to be C-Wing?"

And though we were trying to attract them, I still wasn't exactly ready to see them.

Especially not back in C-Wing. Not back where it all began that quiet, awful night.

But I turned the corner and there they were.

The Unicorn herd.

BRIGHAM

There were three of them.

They were at the far end of the hallway.

And they seemed surprised to see us.

Gleefully surprised.

One was tall and spindly like a nightmare scarecrow. One was short and stocky. The other crouched with stooped shoulders and a feral stance.

"Heeey, kiddies," he said. "Time to plaaay."

"Nope," said Quinn.

We scrambled around the corner and down a little-used utility hallway. At the end of the passage was the small Underground door. Malcolm unlocked it, yanked it open and we ducked in. Then as if sucked closed by some unseen malevolent force, it slammed behind us.

And we were plunged into the darkness.

MARSHALL

My first instinct?

Panic.

Sheer, complete, arm-flailing panic.

We couldn't see. We were being pursued by a gang of horror movie extras. And we just entered Freddy Krueger's rec-room.

If ever there was a time for some arm-flailing, this was it.

But then . . . we had a Malcolm.

"Grab the pipe on the right," he said. "And run."

We did as he said. Running in complete darkness was both a strange and terrifying experience. I braced myself as I expected to sprint septum-first into a wall at any second.

"We're about to turn to the right," said Malcolm, his voice coming from the void, calm and clear. "Keep your right hand on the wall, feel the corner and keep moving."

We did that too.

We were moving fast, and I couldn't see a thing. No one could. But somehow, someway, Malcolm was channeling his inner Daredevil and guiding us forward.

"Are you using echolocation?" whispered Brigham.

Malcolm actually laughed. Was he having fun?

"I studied the schematics, bro! Don't you guys read The Crazy Board? Okay, now take a hard left. Then stop."

We took a hard left.

We stopped.

We stood in silence. I brushed up against someone and somehow instinctively knew it was Quinn. Our hands found each other, and she laced her fingers through mine. My heart, which was already beating dangerously fast, sped up even more. Was this cardiac arrest?

We huddled on the ground waiting for Malcolm to give the next command.

I've never experienced that kind of darkness.

I closed my eyes and opened them, and it made no difference.

Then *KA-KLAM*. There was the slamming of the metal door.

The Unicorn Men were in the Underground.

There was another clang followed by a clatter and muttered cursing. I smiled in the dark.

"Maybe one of them broke a nose."

We were back in Hell. But this time the underworld was working for us.

"Lamps on," said Malcolm.

Again, we did as he said. And I might have preferred the darkness.

Twisted metal monsters loomed over us as we crouched in the main boiler room. It was a valley of pipes and valves and coils. Steam leaked out of somewhere and floated across the cone of light shining from my head and into the misty murkiness.

Malcolm moved swiftly to a dangling light bulb in the center of the room as though he always knew it would be there. Which he probably did.

"Toss me the extra headlamp," he said.

I dug it out of my pocket and threw it his way. He caught it and looped it over the bulb so that it was hanging in the middle of the room.

The echoing footsteps were growing closer, and my panic levels were reaching new heights.

"Should we turn off our headlamps?" I said. "Our lights are going to attract them."

Malcolm looked in my direction and blinded me with his lamp. "Well, that's what I'm counting on."

He then heaved the lightbulb so that it swung in a wide oval, the hooked-on headlamp casting crazy spinning shadows around the metal structures that stretched to the ceiling.

"Okay," he said. "Shut 'em off now."

The shadows from the swirling headlamp spun around us as Malcolm led us though a doorway and into a narrow hallway. As we marched on through the darkness I glanced over my shoulder and realized what he'd done. The looping lamp gave the distinct impression that someone was moving and stumbling and fumbling through the room behind us. To the Unicorn Gang, it would appear we were just a panicky pack of teens with a flashlight and no clue. The perfect target.

And I began to wonder for a moment if Malcolm was a true crime-fighting genius.

That moment wouldn't last.

BRIGHAM

Malcolm's masterclass in boiler-room warfare and schematic memorization continued into another long hallway.

"We're now in an offshoot of the boiler room," he said calmly. "It's an antechamber that loops back around to the entrance. You can turn on your lamps now."

I flipped the switch and ducked a pipe that would have probably knocked me out cold a millisecond earlier.

"While the Unicorn thugs follow our light show back there, we'll head to the entrance and lock them in," he said. "Easy-peasy."

"Um, I nominate Malcolm as president of Shadow Guild," whispered Quinn as we headed down the dark passageway.

"I concur," I said. "But of BrainForce."

Malcolm led us into a larger hallway.

"I accept that nomination," he said. "But for The Academics."

We turned left and there it was, the tiny door where we started.

It was our escape from the Underground. And it was hope that we might actually survive this night.

Now, all we had to do was exit, lock the door, and, one way or another, these Unicorn Men would eventually face justice. Whether that justice would come from the actual police or Mr. Chang on Monday morning remained to be seen. They might get off easier with the police.

Malcolm laid a hand on the door and even in the gloom I could tell he was grinning.

"Hey," he said. "Maybe Plan B should have been Plan A all along, amirite?"

Then he yanked on the handle and nothing happened.

He turned to the door and yanked again.

"Um," he grunted. "Hold on."

More grunting. He turned to me and blinded me with his head-lamp.

"That's not good."

"What's not good?"

I grabbed the handle and pulled. Then I pushed. Then I pulled some more.

It wouldn't budge.

A clang of metal pipes echoed somewhere behind us and a scream built up in my throat.

It was locked.

"It's locked?!" hissed Marshall, reading my mind.

He grabbed the handle and pushed down.

"It can't be locked!" said Quinn, her voice too loud and echoing off the walls.

She grabbed it too. We joined together and pushed and pulled up and down. It was no use.

There was a sharp laugh from the darkness. They were moving toward us. And fast.

"What do we do now?!" said Marshall.

Malcolm switched off his headlamp.

"Plan C," he said. "Stay alive."

MALCOLM

Time for Plan C.

The problem was, there was no actual Plan C. For that, I needed time to think.

And there was no time to think. There was no time to do anything, except run.

I led them to a small room that probably served as an office back in the 1940s but was mostly storage now.

We huddled next to some cardboard boxes and shivered in the darkness.

"Is there another way out of here?" hissed Marshall.

"Maybe."

There wasn't.

"Where?"

"Let me think," I said. "I can find it."

I couldn't find it.

"What do we do next?" said Brigham.

I had no idea. I had led us to our doom.

Right now, my only plan was to avoid the Unicorns as long as possible. And, hopefully, survive.

I had nothing. No plan. No answers.

We could hear them muttering as we huddled in the dark.

From the sound of it, they were trying to open the door but had the same results as us.

"Maybe they think we locked them in?" said Quinn hopefully. "Maybe they think we're gone?"

"Ohh, kiddies," said the horrible high-pitched voice of a Unicorn. "Where are you hiding at?"

Maybe not.

QUINN

We were trapped. Trapped like rats.

Worse than that, we were trapped like rats in a maze with three hungry snakes.

I knew there was no other way out. There couldn't be. C'mon, we were underground!

There is no secret backdoor to the school. If so, Sloan would have told us. She's all about sneaking out of school.

I know panic attacks are Marshall's thing, but as we huddled in that pitch-black room, I could feel my throat closing up.

It was only a matter of time before they found us. It was only a matter of time before they dragged us back to Hell.

MARSHALL

I felt myself shaking.

I felt a panic attack coming on.

I only hoped I could gag and cough quietly enough so the Unicorn Men wouldn't find us.

But then, somehow, I kept breathing. Nice and evenly. And the attack didn't come.

Instead, something unexpected happened.

I got mad.

A wave of intense anger came over me without warning.

And it felt good.

I was sick of hiding. I was sick of cowering.

I was sick of letting these psycho-*Purge*-horror-movie rejects have so much control over me.

They could scare me, yes, but that would no longer stop me.

I didn't know exactly what I was going to do.

I just knew I was going to fight.

I also knew I was going to lose.

All of us would. But at least we'd go out on our own terms.

"I think we should turn on the headlamps," I said.

"What?!" said Malcolm. "They'll find us!"

"Yeah," I said. "But maybe we should let them . . . We need to fight."

I couldn't see a thing, but I still sensed multiple incredulous looks in the darkness.

"Look, guys, there's four of us. There's three of them. And Brigham knows karate."

"Yeah, but it's self-taught," he said. "YouTube."

"Dude," I said. "Don't doubt Master Kensei. Not now."

I felt Quinn's hand in mine, and it filled me with an unexpected sense of bravery.

She squeezed my hand.

"He's got a point," she said. "If we go down, we go down fighting."

"But," said Malcolm. "I'd rather not go down."

Brigham agreed. "I concur with not going down. But we might not have a choice in the matter if we have to—"

"WAIT," said Malcolm much too loudly.

We all shushed him.

"Sorry," he said. "Did you hear a boing?"

"What's a boing?" said Brigham.

"Just listen," he said. "It sounded like . . . like a boing."

We sat in dark silence as I held my breath. There was plenty of noise in the Underground.

The clanks of the steaming pipes.

The hisses of the boiler room.

The murmurs of the Unicorn Men piecing together a plan to capture us, their prey.

But absolutely nothing that sounded like a—

"A boing!" whispered Malcolm. "It's coming from the bomb shelter. Follow me."

We couldn't see him, so we held hands, making a chain as we tiptoed through the nothingness.

"Look!" whispered Malcolm.

"Look?" I said. "Look at what? It's literally pitch-black in—"

I stopped mid-sentence. Because the faintest of lights appeared in that nothingness.

It was a flickering glow coming from the far end of a long hall-way. And then . . . a boing. A faint but distinct boing.

"I heard it!" I whispered.

It was the tiniest of electronic sounds accompanied by a familiar eight-bit theme song.

"That's . . . *Super Mario Bros.*," said Brigham.

"No," said Malcolm. "That's *Super Mario Bros. 3.*"

We dropped down low and crept toward the flickering light and the sounds of the Mushroom Kingdom. We traveled down a hallway, through a doorway, into a small room no bigger than a walk-in closet. And it was there that a voice came from the flickering darkness.

"'Sup, my dudes."

We were not alone.

Not anymore.

Because leaning against the wall, in a battered gamer's chair, playing an old-school Nintendo on a square TV, smoking a rolled up-something, was Winky Jeff.

MARSHALL

He was bathed in the glorious eight-bit light of Bowser's Castle.

Long hair. Bright pink tank top. Neon-yellow WrestleMania headband with matching spandex. Sunglasses.

Sunglasses inside. And at night. In the dark. Vintage Winky Jeff.

"Winky Jeff!" I said much too loudly. I'd never actually called him that to his face.

Winky Jeff smiled, tilted his sunglasses down, and gave me a literal wink.

"At your service," he paused his game as Tanooki Mario froze mid-air.

Next to him was a cot with an unfurled sleeping bag, he had a jumbo bag of Cheetos in his lap, and his feet were propped up on a busted coffee table.

All in all, it was a pretty sweet set-up for Winky Jeff.

"You lost, bros?"

Malcolm, Quinn, and Brigham stood slack-jawed. They probably would have been less shocked if we had just bumped into Santa Claus.

"No, no," I glanced behind me, afraid the Unicorn Men would appear at any minute. "Well, kind of. We're trying to lose someone. Three someones, actually. We're being followed by this gang of Unicorn guys."

Winky Jeff took off his sunglasses studiously.

"We call them that because they use unicorn masks to hide their identities and they work for this super dangerous drug-dealer Jabba-the-Hut-Kingpin guy named Mister Happy who's getting people hooked on this sick drug that turns them into zombie people that he traps in his basement dungeon on the south side of town."

Winky Jeff took a long drag of whatever he was smoking and nodded. "Naturally," he said.

He rocked forward in his gamer chair and stood with the groan of a thirty-year-old dude who had already partied harder than professional hippies twice his age.

"And so, these Unicorn people . . . are they here in the Underground right now?"

"Yeah, and they're close," said Brigham.

"And they want to take us back to Mister Happy's dungeon," I added.

"And we don't want to go," said Quinn.

"I wouldn't either," said Winky Jeff.

Malcolm chimed in.

"Mr. Jeff, I messed up and got us locked in here. We're trapped. Any good ideas would be appreciated."

"My bro," he said with a grin. "I'm all good ideas."

QUINN

Creepy Jeff led us into a side passageway deeper into the bowels of the basement.

Normally, if I tell you that a man named Creepy Jeff is about to take me into basement bowels, your next step is to personally alert the police and the SWAT team, okay? But tonight, on this night, Creepy Jeff was our knight in shining armor. Or, well, yellow spandex.

Strangely enough, he seemed to be wearing the same biker shorts I was wearing beneath my skirt. I think he shops at Marshall's.

He stopped and turned, took another drag of his hand-rolled something, and then grabbed a release valve on the side of a bright red pipe. Next to it was an official-looking sign that said, DO NOT TURN.

He turned.

"So, yeah," he said. "They really need to fix the locks on the main door. Remember when that freshman Timmy Ledford had to spend the night in here a couple years back?"

I didn't but that was no surprise because I'm woefully behind on all school gossip.

"Well, it wouldn't have happened if I had been around, but I was out of town at a Molly Hatchet concert. The Take No Prisoners tour. Did you go?"

We didn't.

"Too bad, they only come around here every few years. I had to get permission from Principal Chang to use a vacation day since it was actually in Macon, and I had to take an Uber the whole way there. Worth it. Completely worth it."

He stopped and stared at one of the pipes. Creepy Jeff left us for a moment.

"So awesome."

Malcolm cleared his throat and Creepy Jeff jerked back to the present.

"Anyway, they fixed that lock but it sticks. You have to really pull up on the handle and pull back really hard to get out."

"Ahh," said Malcolm. "Sticky handle! I should have thought about that. See, Plan B is still the best plan."

"Um, I think our plan should have been 'Find Winky Jeff,'" said Marshall. "End of plan."

Creepy Jeff let out a chuckle. He walked on and stopped at another valve that appeared to be sticking.

"Yeah, well," he grunted as he tried unsuccessfully to loosen it. "But what they never fixed was the lock to the actual furnace room. And that, my bros, is where you do not want to get trapped. I know from experience because—a little help here . . ."

We all grabbed the metal wheel and turned.

"Good, good," he said as he moved it two full turns. "Anyway, I know from experience because I almost died in there once over winter break."

He turned another valve.

"Worst Christmas Eve ever."

Sweat was beginning to soak through Creepy Jeff's WrestleMania headband. He leaned against a pipe and took another smoke break.

"Want a puff?"

We shook our heads in unison.

"Good for you," he said. *"Just Say No."*

"Thanks for the offer though," said Malcolm as though he'd just turned down tea and crumpets. "So, we get the bad guys into the furnace room and then they're trapped?"

Creepy Jeff grinned and nodded.

"Like rats," he said. "Hot rats."

"So, how do we lure them in there?" said Brigham.

Creepy Jeff looked at us as though we had just failed a remedial algebra exam.

"Um, by releasing super-hot pressurized steam into the main access room on the other side of this wall of course."

He grabbed another wheel and spun.

"In other words, you do exactly what I've been doing."

He let out a low slow steady stoner's laugh.

"If my janitorial calculations are correct, your magical Unicorn friends should be just about on the other side of this wall . . . in the interior sub-chamber . . . enjoying the last pocket of fresh, breathable air."

He then stepped around the corner and, sure enough, the steamy silhouette of multiple Unicorn Men loomed a terrifying arm's length away. I gasped. Malcolm and Marshall screamed. Brigham cursed. Jeff took a step forward and grabbed a large metal door.

"Hey, horse guys!" he yelled. "Merry Christmas!"

Then he slammed the door, sealing in the startled herd of Unicorn predators.

God bless Winky Jeff.

Creepy no more.

BRIGHAM

Winky Jeff is the man.

And I told him that.

"Just doing my job," he said.

I thought about mentioning that the job of a janitor isn't necessarily to trap murderous thugs in an underground furnace room using super-heated steam, but then who am I to argue?

As we headed back to the Underground entrance, Quinn said what we were all thinking.

"Um, they're not going to die in there are they?"

"Nah," Jeff shrugged. "They'll survive. If I turn down the steam."

Then he took another drag of his joint.

"Speaking of, I should probably turn down the steam so they don't die."

MARSHALL

After a round of heartfelt hugs and fist bumps, Winky Jeff freed us from the Underground.

"Good luck my dudes," he said. "I'd come with but . . . you know—"

"Yeah," said Malcolm. "You gotta keep tabs on the Unicorn gang."

"No, not really," he said. "They'll be fine. It's just that I'm completely stoned."

We paused at the door.

"I probably won't remember this ever happened."

"Oh," I said. "Well . . . we won't forget."

"Thanks, Marsh," he said. "And wish me luck in here. Princess Peach isn't gonna rescue herself, right?!"

He let out another long lazy laugh and with one more round

of fist bumps, he sealed himself into his underground hangout. And we were on our own again. Back in the desolate C-Wing, beneath the ever-flickering fluorescents.

"Welp," said Malcolm as he clapped his hands together. "To the bikes!"

CHAPTER NINETEEN

THE BIKE FIGHT

MALCOLM

Ah yes, the bikes. It was a key component to Plan B. Or was it Plan C? Or Plan C, 2.0? Honestly, I'm not sure what plan we were on at this point. But that doesn't matter. What matters is we had four sweet rides ready and waiting, thanks to the recently formed CHS mountain bike team.

"To the gym!" I said.

"I hate the gym!" said Brigham.

I did too. But that didn't matter tonight. Our rendezvous point with Sloan was only about a mile away, but why travel on foot when you can ride in eighteen-speed style?

Of course, Marshall's key worked on the equipment closet in the gym too. Apparently, the junior star student has as much clout as the school superintendent.

"This is pretty much stealing isn't it?" he said as he flicked on the lights to reveal a row of gleaming Diamondbacks.

"Maybe technically," I said as I headed toward the handlebars of a forest green bike. "But stealing for survival isn't really stealing."

"I'm sure that'll hold up in court," said Quinn. "Dibs on green!"

And she hopped on the seat before I could.

"Red!" said Marshall.

"Blue!" said Brigham.

That left me with a neon pink ride that had been spray painted by the art club.

"Saddle up, Mrs. Lansbury," said Quinn.

I shrugged. Not a bad choice.

"Okay," said Marshall as he tested the handbrakes. "We start riding . . . and we don't stop until we get to the woods, right?"

We all nodded. And then we took off through the gym and into the long hallway of B-Wing, gliding on the smooth linoleum. I pumped hard and fast as the lockers whizzed by in a blur. The *click-click-click* of our gears echoed off the walls as we skidded to the right and headed down the steep wheelchair ramp next to the lunchroom. It felt like a victory lap. I couldn't help it. I let out a yell.

"Wahoo!"

Marshall shushed me from behind.

"Don't 'wahoo'!" he said. "There could be more of them!"

"Ah, come on, they're either trapped in the boiler room or running after the Creeper right now, right?"

Well . . . wrong.

Because as we turned the corner of A-Wing, onto the final stretch of hallway before the main exit, he was waiting.

In the center of the corridor, was another Unicorn Man. And this guy had a knife.

MARSHALL

We skidded to a halt at the sight of him.

There he was. Silhouetted against the doorway. The same stillness. The same Michael Myers stance. The same threat of cruel violence that his mere presence implied. And now the gleaming serrated knife that promised violence. He was waiting for us. He was waiting for me. He was always waiting for me.

Except, this time, I wasn't alone.

I looked at my friends.

"We don't stop 'til we get to the woods," I said. *"Right?"*

Quinn nodded and adjusted her gears. Brigham and Malcolm leaned forward on their bikes as though in a starter's position. I saw fear in their eyes, but also determination.

Sure, we were terrified. Sure, we knew we might not make it out of this alive. But whatever happened, we would do it together.

My mind flashed back to my dream. For one crazy moment, the thought of Malcolm in a chicken suit popped into my head and I actually let out a laugh. That thought alone gave me the crazy courage to pedal straight at the knife-wielding Unicorn and let out a crazy yell that came from deep within.

"FOR COACH CRAAAAIIIIG!"

MARSHALL

I don't know how to bike-fight.

I don't know if that's even a thing.

But if you were to study the security footage from Halloween night at Carter High School, you would see an actual bicycle-fight taking place in A-Wing.

Probably a CHS first.

We didn't have a plan. But we had the wheels and the momentum.

I'd like to say I kicked back on one wheel, popped a wheelie, and smacked Unicorn Man cleanly in the face with my tire. But really, I just pedaled, hard and fast. I pedaled toward my nightmare while everything inside of me was telling me to go the other way.

To flee.

To hide.

To run.

No more.

I had been fleeing and hiding and running for too long. Now I rode toward the danger.

Brigham was to my right. Quinn was to my left. Malcolm was over my shoulder. And it occurred to me for a flat second that maybe we looked as crazily unhinged as any Unicorn Gang member.

And that felt good.

At first, the Unicorn Man didn't move. He didn't even seem to flinch, until we were within striking distance. Then he stepped to the side and threw out a forearm that surely would have knocked me to the floor if it wasn't for my wingman to the right.

Brigham somehow stood up on his pedal and kicked downward, straight into Unicorn Man's shoulder.

"HIIII-YA!" he yelled like a true internet karate master.

Unicorn Man went down hard. His knife clattered across the floor, but he was still somehow able to grab Malcolm as he rolled by, pulling him to the ground.

Malcolm didn't yell. He didn't scream. He just kicked and punched and growled and fought like an ensnared wild animal. He was an angry honey badger of flailing fists and legs. But it was no use. Unicorn Man was bigger and, worse than that, he was much crueler.

From the ground, he grabbed at Malcolm's neck and closed a meaty fist around his throat.

Malcolm went silent. His eyes bulged as he clawed and squirmed. It made no difference. The Unicorn Man only squeezed tighter. It was clear he had the strength and the power and the savage inhumanity to crush my friend's windpipe right then and there. And he was going to do just that.

Looking back, I'm surprised by how much I didn't think. I just acted. I jumped off my bike as it was still rolling and it crashed into a locker. I turned and sprinted, full speed, toward a gasping Malcolm and the murderous Unicorn. At mid-stride I balled up my fist. I reared back. And I hit him square in the face.

Oh, it hurt. I'm pretty sure I nearly broke my hand. But it hurt the Unicorn Man more. His mask flew off. He let out a muffled wail and a spray of blood shot from his nose.

Septum deviated.

Under reasonable circumstances, that might have ended the fight then and there. But this guy was nowhere near reasonable. As blood poured from his face, he scrambled for his knife. He grabbed it, stood, and stared at me with dead, soulless eyes. His bearded chin was covered in thick crimson, but he didn't even seem to notice, and he had a jagged fresh cut on his forehead that no doubt came from a certain tacky stone frog ashtray. This was Conner Limehouse. This was the monster I met in C-Wing. This was the man who started the nightmares.

He looked right through me without a flicker of emotion or recognition and slashed. I felt the wind on my throat as his blade sliced millimeters from my neck.

I stumbled backward, slipping on his blood and smashing into the lockers behind me. I was cornered. And he knew it.

Unicorn Man switched the grip on his knife. Angling it downward as though he no longer wanted to slash, he wanted to stab.

He wanted to kill.

I slid down the locker and the copper smell of blood filled my nostrils as I threw my hands up in hopes of somehow deflecting his blade. And then . . . he was sideways. Conner Limehouse was in the air. He let out a startled scream as a green mountain bike blur plowed directly into his side and swept him off his feet.

There was a smack of flesh against the linoleum and a hollow thud when his skull hit the ground.

The crumpled Unicorn Man fell to the floor and stayed there as Quinn skidded to a halt and stood over him.

She looked wild and free. Like a fearsome warrior princess on a rampage.

"There's your extra credit, you psychopath!"

Quinn kind of stole my catch phrase.

I don't mind.

MARSHALL

We were out of school, and we were free.

In the distance, we heard the Creeper letting out its old-timey wail through the warm night.

We pumped hard and fast as the tidy ranch homes of Waycross Drive, all a snooze, shot by. Now the *click-click-click* of our fancy bikes boldly signaled our approach. But nobody wanted a piece of our free-wheeling biker gang.

I'd just stood up to the Unicorn nightmare.

I'd never felt more alive.

Brigham was feeling it too. He stretched his arms out and let out a "Woooo!"

Quinn laughed.

Malcolm beamed as he hunched over and pumped, his handle-bars in a death grip.

For some reason, he reminded me of Angela Lansbury on a bike and it made me laugh some more. I felt lighter than I had in months. Heck, years. I realized that there's always a steady undercurrent of fear in my life. Maybe everybody has it. School, girls, grades . . . I always feel like I'm going to mess it all up. Well, for the first time in my life, I didn't actually care. For the first time in my life, my answer was to simply not be afraid.

It made no sense that on a night when we were being pursued by a gang of murderous thugs that I would feel braver than I ever had. But I wasn't questioning it.

Meanwhile, Quinn looked even more like a warrior princess on the way to battle. Hair flowing. Eyes ablaze. Beauty on wheels.

I felt the strong urge to kiss her . . . while riding a bicycle . . . and being pursued by a demon Unicorn Gang. I'm not sure how that would work out mechanically, but I was willing to give it a shot.

We turned a sharp corner in unison and then shot down the steep hill nicknamed Stephanie's Slope, because a cute girl named Stephanie lived there once. That's the end of that backstory.

At the bottom of the hill there's an ill-placed speed bump that, when hit at full speed, has the potential to put a bike rider into orbit.

I've never had the guts to do it before, but tonight—well, to-night—I felt different. I was ready to conquer the entire world. So, I pumped harder and faster and directly toward the ramp.

Now would normally be the time for a sensible rider to apply the brakes. But I wasn't feeling sensible.

Brigham realized what was happening first.

"Hey, what are you doing, man?!"

Oh, he knew what I was doing. I was living for the yearbook.

I hit the bump, pulled back on the handlebars and took off into the night sky like Elliot and E.T. soaring past the moon.

Except, I landed much harder.

QUINN

Marshall went one way. His bike went the other.

I'll admit it was an impressive *X-Games* worthy stunt, for the first half a second. Then it became an *AFV*-worthy blooper.

His bike went higher than a bike should.

He locked eyes with me while he was about ten feet in the air and sideways. And he looked . . . happy?

Then he landed flat on his back and let out a comical "oof," as his bike dropped in front of a nearby parked Volvo.

I skidded to a halt inches from Marshall's crumpled body.

He was on his side and shaking.

As I hopped off my bike, my dress got hooked on the seat and I tripped and landed on the ground right next to him.

I realized then that he was laughing, gleefully. And kind of crazily.

"I don't think I stuck the landing," he said while wiping his eyes.

I shook my head and laughed and I looked into his eyes and could have kissed him.

So I did.

I kissed him.

Under the night sky. Under the streetlamps of Waycross Drive. I threw my arms around him and put my lips to his.

I've kissed boys before. But not like this. It's never felt so natural. So automatic. My brain thinks all the time. I think about cross-stitching. I think about Sloan drama. I think about school. I think about grades.

For this, I did not think.

I just felt.

And it felt like something I've never felt before.

I just knew I wanted to feel it more. And I definitely planned to.

But first we had to survive the night. And that was about to get much more difficult.

MARSHALL

My nose didn't bleed!

Can you believe it?!

My nose didn't bleed!

Oh, and also, I kissed Quinn.

I guess I buried the lead there.

That's kind of like Neil Armstrong landing on the moon and saying, "Hey, I didn't trip!"

But I've had a lot of things to worry about over the past few months. Homeroom heists . . . minivan stakeouts . . . Unicorn gangsters . . . you know the deal. Believe it or not, the thing that really kept me up at night and followed me around until morning, was whether I'd ever be able to kiss Quinn without my nose opening like a faucet.

But when she pressed her lips to mine, all those thoughts stopped.

There was no thinking.

Just feeling.

Keep in mind that I nearly passed out once when Quinn smiled at me from across the basement. So, to have her right there, her face so close to mine . . . it made me physically dizzy. But then she kissed me. And I kissed her back. And it was sensory overload. Like I had just been struck by lightning. In a good way.

I know what you're thinking. Now was kind of a bad time, right? Mister Happy was still at large. We were still very much in danger, and we probably should have been more focused on staying alive at this point.

And, well, you're very right.

BRIGHAM

I was happy for them. I really was.

But, um, we were kind of in the middle of something. And Marshall and Quinn were in the middle of their long awaited but completely ill-timed make out session when Waycross Drive exploded into flashing colors.

Red. Blue. Red. Blue. Red. Blue. And then an ear-splitting siren wail.

"Okay, kids, stay right where ya are," said a twangy voice over a loudspeaker.

I knew that voice.

Through the flashing lights and blinding headlights, I could make out the square, flat-topped head of the man behind the steering wheel. The man we'd been dreading.

At least one of them.

Bad Cop.

MARSHALL

It was just too tempting.

We were a few feet from the entrance to the woods. A few feet from safety.

At first we froze. I backed away from Quinn and she backed away from me. Then we turned, with our hands up as Bad Cop barked orders though the loudspeaker.

"We ride, right?" muttered Brigham.

"We ride," I said.

I glanced over at him and before I knew it, he was pedaling. Malcolm was too.

Quinn and I jumped on our bikes and fled the scene.

And we fled fast.

MALCOLM

Fleeing and attempting to elude a police officer.

That is the official charge.

And that is what we were doing.

But I prefer the term "fleeing and attempting to save our very lives by eluding an evil super-cop cyborg."

There's no police code for that, but there should be.

There was no formal decision to do this. Just instinct I guess. We looked at each other and knew. We had to run. Or rather, we had to ride.

Brigham and I were still on our bikes. Marshall and Quinn, who were suddenly a couple, had to end their PDA and pedaled frantically toward us.

"To the woods!" yelled Marshall.

All the while, an increasingly angry Bad Cop thundered through the loudspeaker.

"YOU BEST NOT MOVE AND YOU BEST SHOW ME YOUR HANDS!"

We did neither.

And, as one who respects authority, I cannot tell you how hard it was to blatantly disregard those orders.

But the bike did most of the work. So we rode on.

Marshall and Brigham were raised in these woods. Children of the Pines, I sometimes call them.

They have an eerie habit of slipping in and out of trees. Reappearing and disappearing like some kind of magic Hobbits.

Me? Not so much.

They glide through the forest. I plod and run into things.

Tonight, that wasn't an option.

Tonight, it was ride or die.

QUINN

Remember our last night-run through the forest? Think that. Mixed with podracing that required Jedi-like reflexes.

My eyes adjusted to the early morning light just as I almost ran into an oak tree.

"HARD RIGHT!" yelled Marshall.

I took a hard right.

"HARD LEFT!" yelled Brigham.

I did that too.

We pumped and pedaled. I hit a spider web. I hit a batch of vines. I hit some low-hanging limbs.

I hit everything along the way.

But I never stopped. Didn't think about it.

Into the belly of the deep forest, we went.

The deeper we went, the safer we were.

We came to a small clearing and skidded to a stop.

Marshall put a finger to his lips.

"Do you hear him?" he panted.

At that point, I mostly just heard my heart in my ears. But alongside that, the sounds of the forest surrounded us. The steady thrum of insects. The hoot of an owl. A distant dog howling. Our own huffing and puffing. But no Bad Cop.

"I think we lost him," said Brigham. "Either that or he's about to swing in from the trees and tase us all."

We started to pedal again until the ground slanted up steeply.

"We're going to have to ditch the bikes," said Marshall.

We hopped off.

"Goodbye, noble steed," said Malcolm as he shoved his bike into the woods.

I knew how he felt. I patted the seat of my trusty ride and pushed it off the trail into the undergrowth.

Then, off into the woods we went, on foot and steed-less.

MARSHALL

We stopped at Stone Pile Gap. It's a collection of stones near the center of Windham Woods that has been there since way before we first discovered it. Legend has it, that it's the final resting place of a Cherokee medicine man by the name of Soaring Eagle.

Some say it's cursed.

Others say it's lucky.

Tonight, I was really hoping for luck.

"Grab a rock," said Brigham. "Not too big but not too small."

"Oh, I get it," said Malcolm. "We're fighting Ewok style."

"Exactly," said Brigham.

"Let's hope the bad guys have Stormtrooper aim," said Quinn.
We grabbed our ammo.
"We salute you, Soaring Eagle," said Malcolm.
And we all saluted Soaring Eagle before heading deeper into the woods.

CHAPTER TWENTY

THE END CARD

SLOAN

Meanwhile, there was me.

Oh, yeah, did you forget about me?

You shouldn't. Because at this point I'm being pursued by the Unicorn Gang. A whole carload of them.

They were on me as soon as I left the school parking lot.

I swung out wide onto Warwick Street.

Then I floored it.

The Creeper may not look like much, but he's got it where it counts, kids.

I know, I know. A *Star Wars* reference. Those nerds are rubbing off on me. But I'm talking about the OG trilogy. None of this prequel or sequel nonsense.

I gunned the old engine to forty-two miles per hour and caught a glimpse of the very opposite of a Chevy Astrovan in my rearview.

It was a matte black Dodge Challenger with a steel ram-cage.

Not good.

Worse than that, Mister Happy himself was behind the wheel.

He was on me in seconds, crashing into my back bumper and whiplashing me forward into the steering wheel. A lesser minivan would have crumpled right there, but the Creeper is no dainty Sienna or Sedona. It's the steel beast of the soccer mom crowd.

279

I managed to take a sharp turn down Memorial Drive and into the nearest residential neighborhood.

The more people around, the better.

Because it was then that I fired off my weapon of choice.

My only weapon really.

AOOOOOOOOOOGGGAAAAAAAAAAAAAAAAAAAA!

The Summit 5000.

AOOOOOOOOOOGGGAAAAAAAAAAAAAAAAAAAA!

The night erupted into airhorn madness.

The Creeper's front fender rattled. A man walking his tiny dog jumped into a bush. A nearby car alarm went off.

It was my own makeshift siren.

If Mister Happy thought I was going to go quietly he had another thing coming.

I was going to go with all 150 decibels firing.

Mister Happy eased off and I laughed.

I kept the Creeper at a top speed of fifty miles per hour until I reached Lake Ivanhoe subdivision and the secret entrance to the woods.

It was exactly where beautiful Brigham said it would be.

"*As soon as you pass the gnarled oak head east,*" he said, as though we were traveling through Middle Earth.

Geez, that's my second dork-based reference in this write-up, isn't it? I may need to officially join the Nerd Squad.

As I approached the entrance, I slammed on the brakes, dove out of the car and bolted for the cover of the forest.

Mister Happy is feared. But he is not fast. His Unicorn Men, on the other hand, are both. I glanced back and three of them were headed my way.

And so, there was nothing to do but run, deeper and deeper into the dark woods, with a stampede of Unicorns right behind me.

MALCOLM

AOOOOGAAAA. AOOOOGAAAA. AOOOOGAAAA.

The old timey horn echoed through the woods.

"Run, sis, run," whispered Quinn.

By now, we were hunched on a rickety platform high above the forest floor, panting and trying to catch our breath. Technically, we were probably only a half a mile from Waycross Drive, but it felt like we were in the middle of Fanghorn Forest.

We all sat cross-legged, looking outwards, rocks at the ready.

Quinn and Marshall were holding hands and I got the weird feeling that they were treating this as a date.

Though the sun was starting to rise, the dark woods below us didn't seem to know it.

I glanced around the platform that Marshall and Brigham called "Grand Central Station."

It might have been central but it wasn't grand.

It was a rectangular platform about the size of a compact car parking space. There was a railing made of old twisted tree limbs with a dangerous unexplainable gap on one side. There was also an old broken wooden table and a gnarled walking stick that I recognized as Marshall's old "wizard staff" from the days when we'd role-play *Lord of the Rings* out here. And, well, that was about it.

If you can't tell, Brigham and Marshall were taking the lead on this portion of the plan since I've never been one for the woods life. Give me the great indoors any day.

Basically, we needed Sloan to lead the bad guys deep into the woods and then double back, hopefully before they caught her. Then, even more hopefully, we could take care of them from that point . . . with sticks . . . and rocks . . . and our knowledge of Ewok guerrilla warfare. Okay, our options were limited.

It was all we had at the moment.

It wasn't exactly cold, but I was still shivering from the adrenaline.

We looked at each other. And we knew this was it.

In the final stage of Framptonworth, before "The End Card" is drawn, there is a moment where you look into the eyes of your comrades and competitors and say the phrase *"Usque ad finem."* It's Latin for "to the bitter end."

I was about to say that very phrase when Quinn cleared her throat and looked at us. It was apparent she had something on her mind. We all did. We were all thinking the same thing. Depending on how tonight went, this could be the last time we were all together and whole. As a team. As best friends. As family. I just didn't know how to say all that. Leave it to Quinn to put those feelings into words.

"Hey, guys," she said.

She looked at me. She looked at Brigham. She looked at Marshall.

"There's something we need to talk about . . ."

She looked down at the platform and seemed to be composing herself.

"I think it's time," she said. "It's time to play . . . the Last Time I Peed My Pants."

Marshall stifled a sudden snort laugh.

I pumped my fist.

"Yes! It's the perfect ice breaker."

Brigham shook his head.

"You would think being pursued by a murderous Unicorn Gang all night would break the ice enough," he said. "But I'm a poor judge of these things."

MARSHALL

"Okay," said Malcolm. "I'll go first."

I settled in as much as I could onto my section of semi-rotten plywood.

I've heard this story many a time, but it's a classic. And it only seems to get better with age.

"There I was," he said. "In right-field at Tucker Parks and Rec. I was eight years old and on the Angels. I didn't want to be there. I never wanted to play little league. I had no desire to. Ever. But my dad made me because he still had some hope that it might awaken some kind of long-dormant athletic skill within me."

"How'd that work out?" said Brigham.

"Not good," said Malcolm. "Anyway, I really, really, really had to pee. I was nervous too, so that didn't help. But also, there was access to all the free Gatorade one could drink in the dugout. So, I pretty much drank it all."

"Uh-oh," said Quinn as she rubbed her palms together and leaned forward. "That doesn't sound good."

"The inning started out okay. We got one out. And then two outs. I had nothing to do with that because the ball never made it out of the infield. That was my survival strategy as a little league ball player. Remain uninvolved at all times. Stay away from the ball whenever possible."

"Ah, the classic ball-avoidance strategy," I said. "It's what all the Hall of Famers do."

"Right?" said Malcolm. "Anyway, the Lawrenceville Blue Jays wouldn't stop getting hits and scored fourteen points in that inning."

"Runs," said Brigham.

"Whatever. Every point and every run and every trip around the base path was torture for my bladder. I was stuck out there. Marooned. If a coach would have looked my way I would have called a time out and run to the sidelines."

"That's not a thing in baseball," said Brigham.

"Anyway. By about the seventh run, I stopped moving altogether when the ball came in my direction. I knew if I ran, I was going to lose it completely and just straight up pee in my pants."

At this, Quinn let out a loud, sharp laugh and we shushed her. With a mighty effort, she composed herself.

"But . . ." said Malcolm, "at the same time, I knew that if the ball came my way and I couldn't get an out, the inning would just keep going. The runs would never stop. And we would be out there for all eternity until my bladder quite literally exploded."

Brigham nodded sagely.

"A classic catch-22," he said. "Except bladder based."

"Exactly," said Malcolm. "So, I made up my mind then and there. The next time a ball was hit anywhere in my direction, I would do everything humanly possible to catch it and then end the inning. And also end my intense bladder pain. And that's when it happened."

"You peed your pants?!" said Quinn breathlessly.

"No, not yet," said Malcolm. "The ball was hit right in front of me. It was a shallow pop-up that I'm sure no one thought I could get to. And under normal circumstances, they would have been right. But I took off with a speed I never knew I possessed. I ran faster than I ever had in my life. It was as though I had super-powers."

"Tinkle-based superpowers," I added.

"Yes, thank you," said Malcolm. "Tinkle-based superpowers. Still, I didn't think I was going to make it in time, so I dove, I stretched out my entire body, like Superman, I threw my glove out there and somehow, someway, I made the most spectacular catch of the Angels' season. And then it happened."

Quinn clapped her hands to her mouth.

"And then what happened?"

"And then . . . I released my bladder completely."

Malcolm paused for effect. Quinn made a muffled whimpering sound. The strain of containing her laughter was obviously get-ting to her.

"This, my friends, was no ordinary peeing of the pants," he said. "This was a complete tsunami. A tidal wave . . . in my pants. There was no disguising it."

"What did you do then?" I said, though I already knew.

"I did the only thing I could. I ran to the dugout and dumped Gatorade on my head."

"Whaaat?" said Quinn.

"I gave myself a Gatorade shower. Drenched myself in order to disguise the pants peeing."

"I mean," stammered Quinn. "That's genius."

"Yeah, usually other people do the showering, but still," said Brigham. "Nice thinking."

"You would think, right? Except it was too late. That jerk,

Thomas Kirkwood, saw everything from the bench and announced my pants peeing to the entire team. So, for the rest of the season, they called me the *M-V-Pee-Pee*. And occasionally Alex Rod-Pee-Guez."

At this, the laughter could not be contained. Not by Quinn. Not by Brigham. Not by any of us. There were several minutes of convulsed snorting and chortling that shook the platform beneath us.

"Wow," said Quinn wiping her eyes. "That's a hard act to follow."

"I'll follow it," said Brigham.

BRIGHAM

Hey, might as well get it over with. I like to keep my version short and sweet.

"So, when I was in first grade, I was a big-time sleepwalker. I traveled all over the house. I never knew where I was going to wind up each morning. One time, I even woke up in the bathtub."

"I think I know where this is going," laughed Quinn.

"Yep, you probably do. But I wish you didn't," I said. "I got up one night and must've thought I was in the bathroom. Turns out, I went into the closet. My mom's closet. In my dreams, my aim was perfect and true. In real life, I didn't get proper clearance, if you know what I mean."

"No, I don't know," laughed Quinn. "But I can imagine."

"Okay, now stop imagining," I said as they all laughed. I could feel myself turning red.

I turned to Marshall. His turn to turn red.

He didn't hesitate.

"Camping," he said. "Still camping. I was six years old, there was no bathroom, of course, because we were camping. I was with my cousins in a big tent and I was spooked because we thought we heard a bear. It could have been a squirrel but, if so, it was a very bear-like squirrel. I really, really, really had to pee but we were safe in the tent. I was all cozy and zipped up in my sleeping bag. There was no way I was going out there. So, I told myself I'd just let out a little bit. Just a little bit. To relieve the pressure."

"Oh, that never works," said Quinn breathlessly.

"No," he said. "It never works."

Marshall shuddered.

"To this day, no one in my family will use that sleeping bag."

There was another round of poorly stifled giggling, and then we all looked at Quinn.

"Okay," said Malcolm. "Let's hear it."

"Um, yeah," she said. "I'll pass."

QUINN

Okay, the outrage was justified.

"What?" they blurted in unison. And much too loudly.

"Pass? There's no passing in this awful game," said Marshall. "Otherwise I'd pass all the time!"

"Yeah, you started all this!" said Brigham.

"And once the Last Time I Peed My Pants begins, there is no turning back," added Malcolm. "These are the sacred rules. I don't make them."

"Okay, okay," I said. "It's just . . . I thought your pants peeing incidents would be . . . more recent."

They looked at me all quizzically.

"Recent?" said Marshall.

"I mean, yeah, since it's called the Last Time I Peed My Pants, I figured that the pants peeing had to happen at least semi-frequently."

"Um . . . we're not toddlers," said Malcolm.

Fits of laughter erupted again.

Marshall leaned forward.

"So, this a recent pants peeing?"

"Oh, man, this sounds good," said Malcolm, also leaning forward.

"Let's hear it," said Brigham.

"Okay," I said. I took a breath. "It happened . . . October 6 . . . of this year."

There was an audible gasp, followed by much laughter, followed by everyone shushing each other unsuccessfully.

"October 6?" giggled Malcolm. "What? Where? When? Why?"

"Okay, I'll take those questions in order. What? Pants peeing. Where? The Creeper. When? Just before nine p.m. on our first stakeout. Why? Malcolm made the hilarious suggestion to play the Last Time I Peed My Pants, and I couldn't stop laughing! I'd had a lot of iced coffee and, well, nature took its course and . . ."

"No!" said Brigham.

"Nothing big!" I said. "Not like Alex Rod-Pee-Guez over here!"

"Hey!" said Malcolm. "First Thomas, now you?!"

"I just laughed so hard that a little bit kind of . . . came out."

There was a second of stunned silence.

"So, the game of Last Time I Peed My Pants itself . . . made you pee your pants," said Brigham.

"If the game didn't exist, it would have never happened," said an awestruck Malcolm.

"Wow," said Marshall. "It's like a pants-peeing paradox."

More semi-stifled laughter erupted.

I know, I know. You would have been quiet, right? At this point, we were being hunted and stalked by a murderous pack of Unicorns and perhaps corrupt law enforcement, we were stuck on a rickety platform, and we were flat-out making a scene. But, what can I say, delirium was setting in. And, to be honest, it was welcome.

Marshall shook his head and quietly clapped.

"Best round of LTIPMP ever," he said.

"I told you!" whispered Malcolm. "The perfect ice breaker!"

"Okay, so *now* is the ice officially broken?" said Brigham. "Please, please say it is because I don't think I can—"

Then we heard it.

A crack of a branch.

A crunch of undergrowth.

A soft but definite footfall just below us.

Then a voice in the dark.

"You know the great thing about teenagers? They're easy to track. Because they never shut up."

CHAPTER TWENTY-ONE

EWOK WARFARE

MALCOLM

The voice came from the darkness of the forest. Directly below us.

"I mean, seriously, I could have found you guys with my eyes closed. Do you realize how much noise you make?"

We said nothing.

The voice laughed.

"No use in being quiet now. Hold on a sec."

I could tell by his voice that this was the drug dealer from Coach Craig's video. This was Crazy Eyes. I peeked through a crack in the boards and watched as he pulled out a flip phone and punched in a number.

"Yep. I found them. On the east side of the woods. Yeah, head east. Yeah, toward the rising sun. That's east."

He hung up with a flip.

"Geez, these guys act like they've never seen an atlas before, right? I blame GPS."

We still said nothing.

"It's cute how you think being all still and quiet will make this better. It won't. You've been treed. So, here's how it'll go."

There was the distinct click of a revolver.

"Did you hear that noise? It means you can come down, one by one, on your own. Or you can come down one by one, bodies hitting the ground, if you know what I mean."

I looked into the terrified faces of my best friends. There was no plan for this. Rocks versus guns did not work.

"Just face it. You're going back to the basement. If you don't make me work hard, I'll make sure you get the good stuff right away. You'll be addicts for life, but the bright side is you won't care. In fact, you'll probably thank me once the dust hits your veins. If you're coherent enough to form a sentence that is."

I found myself shaking so much that it felt like the entire platform was going to collapse. I almost hoped it would and fall on the Unicorn Man's head. Quinn rose up and crept to the edge of the platform. Marshall grabbed for her hand, but she pulled away. Then she stood.

"This is probably the best offer you'll get tonight," said the voice from below. "My friends won't be as reasonable as me. And they're headed this way . . . So, what's it going to be? The easy way? Or the—"

There was a sickening crack of splitting skull, followed by a heavy crash of body hitting the forest floor.

Above us, Quinn stood tall and triumphant.

She had chosen her rock perfectly.

She had fired off the perfect shot.

She had taken down the Unicorn Man.

She had saved us from Hell.

"You know what the great thing is about creeps wearing bright white unicorn heads in the dark?" she said, to the forest below. "They make easy targets."

QUINN

It was very possible I killed a guy.

But there was no time to let that sink in.

Because another guy was coming.

The first Unicorn was stealthy and quiet. The second one was like a freight train in the woods.

Cracking branches and snapping twigs signaled his arrival.

We peered over the side of the platform and there he was.

Even in the darkness, the outline of his pale horned head was unmistakable.

He emerged from the forest and stood still.

It was like a scene from some kind of twisted German fairy tale, where grandmothers are wolves in disguise and children get eaten.

I still have nightmares about this very moment. I probably always will.

He stopped and looked down at his fallen Unicorn brother.

Then, he took off his mask and looked around.

This terrified me more than anything. I wanted him to cover his face. If he saw us, and we saw him, then there would be no way he'd let us out of here alive. He moved forward and picked up the rock next to the other Unicorn's head. It was dark with blood, and you could see his mind working as he pieced it together. Then he looked up. Directly into my eyes. We jumped back, but it was too late.

He knew where we were.

And he was coming for us.

MARSHALL

We heard every step up the tree. Every board. Every branch.

I silently prayed that those old rickety boards would give out.

But he kept coming.

I looked at my friends. Malcolm was wide-eyed and appeared to be frozen in place. Brigham was tensed up, his hands in fists. Quinn was clutching another rock. My rock. I handed it to her because it was clear she was our ace.

And then he was here.

His face was pock-marked. His eyes dazed.

He was younger than I imagined.

He looked scary of course. But he also looked . . . scared.

For one tense breath, I could see the person he could have been if he hadn't gone down this route.

He could have been in my classroom, sitting a few seats over from Sam Hammond in homeroom. He could have been in the AV

Club. He could have been on the yearbook committee. He could have been my friend.

I thought all of those things as I looked into his frightened eyes. And then I took my wizard's staff and cracked it directly over his head.

His mouth formed into a surprised "*o*" shape.

And then he let go of the platform.

There was a second of silence before the *crash-thump* of a solid body hitting the hard ground.

I looked down at my trusty staff, hands shaking, not really believing what I had just done.

For a moment, we were all too stunned to say anything.

"Whoa," said Malcolm, as he looked over the edge. "You shall not pass."

A very noticeable pile of Unicorn Gang members was beginning to form below us and our hidden platform was becoming much less hidden.

"We need to move," said Brigham.

Malcolm nodded and headed for the ladder, but Brigham grabbed him by the shoulder.

"Not that way," he said as he motioned toward the gap in the railing and an old metal wire. "We travel by air now. It's zip-line time, baby."

MARSHALL

Maybe now I should fill you in a little more on the layout of Windham Woods.

No one truly knows all the mysteries of this sprawling land. But you know about Terror Tree. You know about Grand Central Station. There's also the Lookout. The nearby Sarlacc Pit. There's Topsy-Turvy Bridge and the platform simply known as the Watchtower.

That's where we were headed.

Many of these platforms are connected by zip-line. But not the cushy ones you see on cruise ships and at state parks. I'm talking about a literal line, a metal wire, strung from tree to tree.

Brigham's oldest brother was a construction worker for a few summers back in our elementary school days and, because of this, we had access to all the excessively dangerous surplus building material we could dream of, including a spool of thin metal cable.

Since there's no harnesses involved, crossing the forest is not for the faint of heart.

And, at that moment, Malcolm's heart was apparently all kinds of faint.

MALCOLM

I would have screamed if I could have screamed. But you know, that would have been the lamest way to alert the bad guys.

Especially since Marshall and Quinn handled their zip-lining like pros.

One at a time, they grabbed the green plastic handle and slid into the foggy murkiness.

Once they reached the next platform, they slid the handle back.

I had gone zip-lining once before in my life at the state fair. But there were harnesses and carabiners and all of those very important safety things involved.

This was different.

"Do not look down," said Brigham as he pushed the handle into my hand.

I looked down.

Brigham rolled his eyes.

"Okay, well do not let go," he said. "That is your mission."

That I could do.

Not plummeting to my death was my top priority.

Turns out it was harder than I thought though.

Once I took a step from the platform, everything disappeared. It was just me, the foggy darkness and the steady *whirrrrrr* of the line above me.

I could have been sliding over the eternal abyss for all I knew.

It might surprise you to hear that I am not an upper body strength type of guy. I'm the guy in gym class who opts for the flex arm hang during the physical fitness test instead of the macho pull-ups.

I can't pull, but I can hang.

"Flex arm haaaaang," I whispered to myself as the forest slid beneath me.

My grip was weakening. My arms were shaking. And just when I thought I couldn't hang on any longer the platform appeared below my feet. I skidded across the boards and crashed into Marshall, then Quinn, then a large pine tree.

"Whoa, nice landing," said Marshall as I dropped down and literally kissed the old wood platform.

It was gross.

Brigham was next.

No problem there. He was the zip-line guru.

And then the line broke.

And it all went wrong.

MARSHALL

Brigham disappeared.

He was there, sliding toward us, and then with a sharp metal twang like the plucking of a giant guitar string, he was gone.

He dropped into the dark mist below us.

For one crazy second, I hoped that the fog would catch him like a fluffy pillow and set him gently on the ground.

No such luck.

You know that second of silence when the young Unicorn guy hung in the air right before he crashed into the earth?

It was like that all over again, except it seemed much longer since the person hanging in the air was my best friend.

The old metal line whip-snapped and would have caught Malcolm directly in the face if he hadn't been crouched on the ground kissing the platform.

Saved by his own theatrics.

But not Brigham.

He landed on his legs, and I heard a snap and a crack and a scream.

Brigham's been through a lot in his life. I've never seen him cry and I've never seen him show pain.

He was doing both while grabbing his leg in agony as I looked down over the platform.

But it was worse than that.

Much worse. Because he wasn't alone. Mister Happy was here.

QUINN

"Look out!" I yelled.

That was dumb.

Brigham was looking directly at Mister Happy, and it was obvious he didn't need to do more looking.

Even through the gloom, I could make out his unnaturally wide smile.

Next to him was another lumbering Unicorn Man.

Mister Happy looked at Brigham and grinned.

"Is it raining imbeciles?"

He glanced up in our direction.

"Any more in the forecast?"

He couldn't see us, but it was obvious hiding wasn't an option anymore.

"No," grunted Brigham. "Just me alone with my thoughts."

Mister Happy walked over to Brigham and stood on his leg.

I heard a crunch and then a wail from Brigham that I wish I could forget, but probably never will.

"What are your thoughts now, kiddo?"

While Brigham tried to catch his breath, we began to climb down, one by one.

"Stick close to me," murmured Marshall as we filed down the rickety nailed-on boards. "Watch where you step down there."

I had no idea what that meant since it looked like a normal flat forest floor below us.

Mister Happy seemed disturbingly overjoyed to see us.

"Ah," he said. "Here you go! Let's do a head count here. We've got Malcolm, Brigham, Marshall and Sloan's little sister, eh? I don't know which is which, but I don't really care. I just need to explain some things . . ."

Marshall moved in front of Brigham, together we formed a wall around our fallen comrade. Mister Happy stood alongside his Unicorn Man a few feet away.

"We know what needs to happen here," he said. "It just depends on how easy you're going to make it happen."

He glanced at the Unicorn Man who stood stiff and straight. He was much bigger than the other guys and I got the feeling he was kept around purely for muscle.

"Do you know how many people I've watched this dumb merciless moron beat senseless over the past week?"

I actually heard Brigham swallow.

"Is this a trick question?" he muttered.

"Four," he said.

"Oh, so it's a literal question," said Brigham.

Mister Happy let out a *heh-heh-heh* chuckle. He appreciated the sarcasm. He was having fun.

"I only say that because if you make this hard, then this big dumb meathead is about to double his weekly number."

His eyes lingered on me, and his face spread into that impossibly wide grin.

"I will make sure he knocks in your teeth for starters. That's easily fixed with a good dental surgeon. But then he'll make sure he breaks things that don't heal so nicely. Did you know a few solid punches to the kidneys can result in internal bleeding that will require emergency surgery and a lengthy hospital stay? Of course, you won't have access to medical care in my basement, so things could get dicey."

He nodded and the Unicorn Man took a step in our direction.

Mister Happy's grin grew even wider.

"We will have the finest pharmaceuticals on hand though. So do yourself, and your internal organs, a favor. And don't make this harder than it needs to be."

The Unicorn Man headed directly for Marshall.

Malcolm and I stepped in front of him instinctively.

I knew it would hurt, but we had come too far to meekly surrender.

The Unicorn Man paused and let out a disturbingly child-like laugh. He took another step toward us.

And then he was gone. With a loud snap of branches, he disappeared into the ground.

Brigham eased over the hidden chasm that had just claimed the Unicorn Man.

Then he looked up at Mister Happy with a grunt.

"Looks like he'll have to stop at four."

BRIGHAM

You know how most kids try to dig a hole to China? That's ridiculous, right? As kids, Marshall and I knew that. We knew Tucker was actually directly opposite the Indian Ocean. Any idiot with a globe could figure that out. So, that was our plan. Dig to the Indian Ocean. Most kids run out of steam within the first half an hour or so because digging is hard and it sucks. But we had two things that most kids don't. A lack of parental supervision and access to quality shovels. (My second oldest brother was working for a landscape company at the time.) So, for a good three-week stretch during the summer between fourth and fifth grade, we dug. And we dug. And we dug.

We dug so much that we eventually dug ourselves into a hole that we couldn't get out of.

We stopped digging. But the hole remained.

We deemed it the Sarlacc Pit.

When rumors of a mountain lion at large circulated at our elementary school, we covered it with branches and created the perfect trap.

Years passed and we never caught anything.

Who knew we'd eventually snag a Unicorn?

MARSHALL

Mister Happy's laugh echoed off the trees. Sharp and raw and bone-chilling. He actually thought it was funny.

"Amazing!"

He leaned forward and looked at the muddy motionless body of his Unicorn thug.

For a second, I thought about knocking him in but was far too frozen in fear.

"He fell for the old pitfall-in-the-forest-floor trick!"

He looked at us with a sense of admiration.

"Man, if you kids weren't such straight arrows I'd recruit you as my associates in a second. You could probably triple my dust sales in a week."

The Unicorn Man let out a groan from the pit. His mask was off and a shock of bloody blond hair stood out in the gloom. He looked decidedly dumb and dazed. Mister Happy shook his head and reached into his black overcoat.

"I actually want to thank you for this," he said as he motioned to our pit. "Do you know how hard it is disposing of a body? Let alone four? It's really the most difficult part of my job."

His wide grin expanded.

"I'm embarrassed to say that I'm in no shape to dig a hole like that . . ."

He pulled a black object from his pocket and held it in front of me.

"But a mass grave? This far in the woods? With no witnesses? Really . . . you shouldn't have."

CHAPTER TWENTY-TWO

THE END
OF EVERYTHING

MARSHALL

And there it was. The barrel of a gun.

Mister Happy was pointing it directly at my forehead.

Have you ever stared down the barrel of a gun before? I hope not. Because it's pretty much like looking at the end of the world.

The end of everything. Your brain speeds up and slows down all at once. And it's the questions that scare you the most. Things I had never thought about. Cold, cruel, sudden thoughts, like, if he pulled the trigger, would I hear it? Would I see it? Or would it all just end? Would it end before I could finish this very thought? No warning? Just black?

At the very same time, I thought about the people who loved me. I thought of Mom and I thought of my friends standing next to me. Who would find us? *Would* they find us? Would my funeral be a closed casket?

This is dark stuff, but I'm just trying to say that when the barrel of a gun is pointed directly at your head, you never feel a more desperate need to stay alive.

I should have done something. I should have run or hid or fought. Instead, I found myself frozen and waiting.

All of us did.

Sloan Carswell, on the other hand, had other plans.

She appeared out of nowhere from the forest, a blur of flowing hair and unbridled rage. She ran directly at an unsuspecting Mister Happy and shoved him viciously from the side. He lost his footing, slid forward, and toppled right into the pit, landing hard and directly on the dazed Unicorn Man.

"Have a nice trip, party-girl!" she yelled as she took his place at the edge of the pit.

Sloan was bloodied, bruised, and had taken a solid branch beating from the forest. But her smile was as crazy and wide as Mister Happy's on his best day.

She looked at us and grinned.

"How's that for a catchphrase?"

MALCOLM

Praise the Maker! Cue the hallelujah chorus!

Mighty Sloan was back!

And she was pissed.

Mister Happy took an embarrassing tumble into the pit but wasn't knocked out cold like his buddy.

He took a while to get to his feet.

"That was for Carrie!" shouted Sloan.

"Who's Carrie?" yelled Mister Happy.

"The girl that you let bleed to death in your basement!"

Mister Happy was caked in mud and most likely concussed but he still managed a bone-chilling smile.

"You're gonna have to be more specific, honey," he said. "Why don't you come down here and we'll talk about it?"

Sloan actually charged toward the edge of the pit, as though she would like nothing more than to duke it out with the man in a pit-battle-royale.

Quinn stepped in front of her.

"No," she said quietly.

Sloan skidded to a halt at the sight of her little sister and seemed to snap out of her She-Hulk rage.

"You don't need to fight him alone," said Quinn. "We're with you on this. "

Sloan nodded. Her fists balled up. Ready to do what needed to be done to end this.

And then—*BANG*—a chunk of the tree just over her shoulder exploded in a shower of wet pine and sawdust. Mister Happy was still armed.

Sloan hit the dirt. We all did.

BANG, BANG, BANG.

"I know your names," he growled. "I know where you live. I have an army of psychopathic thugs who will happily hurt and maim and kill everyone you know before nightfall!"

Mister Happy was trapped. He was just a voice from the pit. But that only seemed to amplify his menace, because we knew what he was saying was true. It was as though the earth itself was opening up and ready to swallow us.

BANG, BANG, BANG.

"WHEN I GET OUT OF HERE, I WILL MURDER YOU ALL!"

The very floor of the forest seemed to quake with his voice.

"We gotta fall back," hissed Brigham as Quinn and Marshall helped him to his feet.

"But we've got him cornered now!" I said. "If he gets loose, he'll be on our front doorsteps by the end of the day!"

"What are we gonna do?" said Marshall. "Bury him alive in there??"

BANG.

A bullet whizzed through a branch just a few feet above my head and brought it to the ground with a crash.

"Good point, let's get out of here!" I said. "Maybe we hire a bodyguard or call the FBI or—"

I turned to run and sprinted smack dab into a wall of a law enforcement officer.

I bounced backward and nearly toppled into the pit.

Bad Cop was here.

Bad Cop had found us.

He grinned and slowly raised a finger to his lips.

Then he pulled his gun from his holster.

He lifted it into the air, squeezed the trigger, and a clap of thunder nearly imploded my ear drums.

All the sound and fury from the pit came to a halt.

Mister Happy said nothing.

We stood rooted to the dirt, not quite believing what was happening, as Bad Cop trained his weapon on the gaping hole in the ground.

"Well, good mornin', Mister Happy!" he drawled. "That was your warning shot and your wake-up call!"

No response from the pit.

"What's the matter? Use all your ammo on the pine trees?"

Mister Happy mumbled something I couldn't quite make out.

"And what's this I hear about *murdering* my friends here? That kind of sounds like a terroristic threat charge on top of multiple counts of aggravated assault. All that murderin' is gonna be a little hard to do from a jail cell, Eugene."

Bad Cop smiled.

"Oh yeah. I do my research, Eugene Carlton Grimes III. No wonder you went with the nickname."

Bad Cop motioned for us to step back as he edged to the side of the pit.

"Now, if you don't want two to the chest and one to the head I suggest you drop your weapon, lay down on your big fat stomach, and put your hands behind your back."

Sure enough, that's just what Mister Happy—I mean Eugene—did.

"Ah ha," said Bad Cop as he spotted the Unicorn thug in the mud. "You've got company down there."

He reached for his radio clipped to his shoulder.

"All units, I've got multiple 10-99 suspects in Windham Woods. I am requesting backup to the following GPS coordinates, 33.7 -84.3," he said, looking at his smartwatch. "Looks like we'll need a med unit for four suspects . . ."

He glanced at Brigham.

"And one for the hero."

He kept his gun trained on the pit but managed a grin.

"Nice work, Scooby Gang," he said as he moved toward the opening. "Can you guys cover me?"

For a moment, I thought Bad Cop was going to deputize me.

"With what, sir?" I asked.

"Rocks and sticks are fine. That's your weapon of choice, right?" He let out a laugh that startled us and the crows in the upper reaches of the forest. "I'm kidding. These losers aren't going anywhere."

Sure enough, they weren't.

Mister Happy's transformation from Big Bad to a meek hand-cuffed suspect was sudden and supremely satisfying.

"My lawyer will have some things to say about this," he said flatly as he sat on the ground in the pit, hands behind his back.

"Oh, you have a lawyer!" said Bad Cop after he had returned to the surface, weapons secure. "Well, that's fancy."

Marshall pulled out his cell phone and hit the voice memo button.

"Maybe this could be of some use, sir. I figured this was probably worth recording . . ."

He turned on the speakerphone and Mister Happy's menacing voice rang loud and clear throughout the woods.

I want to tell you why they call me Mister Happy. It's actually a good story . . .

For the first time, Mister Happy looked flustered, flummoxed. He didn't seem to know what to say.

Bad Cop whistled through his teeth.

"Well, heeey, looks like we've got exhibit A right here don't we?"

After that, there was a flurry of cops, lights, sirens, and a stretcher for Brigham as they hauled him out of the woods.

Turns out, it was a clean break of the femur.

"Yow! Sexy calves!" shouted Sloan as he was pushed by with his leg in a splint.

Brigham instantly turned many shades of crimson.

There were also a lot of police interviews. And stern words from our parents.

Bad Cop approached my mom as she was in the middle of simultaneously hugging me and chewing me out.

"Ma'am, I understand if you want to ground your son for the next decade or so," he said. "But he and his friends just helped me nab one of the leaders of a dangerous drug trafficking ring with nothing but their own brains and wits and booby traps. That's got to get him some time off for good behavior, right?"

My mom agreed to those conditions.

Bad Cop may need a new nickname.

OFFICER HANK BRIDGES

All right, it's probably time for me to step in here.

I'm the fellow they've been calling Bad Cop in this narrative.

I like the nickname. But it's not accurate. Super Cop maybe? I would go with that.

I'm the one who's been looking for the true "Bad Cop" in this agency for months now.

I was pretty much out of ideas until I saw a frightened Marshall Fairbanks walk into the station and get absolutely no help at all from the front desk. That's when I started to piece it together.

Since this is an internal investigation that's sure to step on some toes, I figured I needed all the documentation I could get. So, I gave each of these honors students a notebook and a couple of days to fill it up with their own recollections.

Turns out, I needed more notebooks.

These kids are big on extra credit.

MALCOLM

So, yeah, who saw that coming?

Bad Cop was actually Good Cop all along! I don't think Angela herself would have figured that one out. Or, well, who am I kidding, of course she would. Turns out Coach Craig just labeled Officer Bridges as Bad Cop on his Crazy Board because, get this, he graded too harshly on the police department entrance exam! Yep, it was all just sour grapes because he flunked Coach. Which, in my opinion, makes him an even better cop.

Though Craig did detect something was amiss because as soon as he forwarded his video to a police department email address, those pesky Unicorns began to show up at his house and the school.

So, who was the actual villain all along?

Any guesses?

Get ready for the Scooby-Doo reveal.

It was . . . drum roll.

Soccer mom lady! Remember her from the police station?

Turns out, people in law enforcement aren't supposed to act that way when you come to them for help. Marshall was reporting a case of aggravated stalking and disorderly conduct at the least. Bad Cop—I mean Officer Bridges said there is a procedure for that. Usually, something involving official reports and temporary protection orders and all those things.

Debra Jane Logan just sent him away.

And then she sent word to Mister Happy and friends. She did the same thing when she received the email video from Coach Craig.

She was also wired in to dispatch from her office line and found a way to direct emergency calls involving Mister Happy and his drug house to a nonexistent police officer.

Why'd she do it? All for a steady stream of cold hard cash. And bling. Those giant shiny rings she was wearing weren't cheap after all.

All along, Bad Cop, a.k.a. Good Cop, a.k.a. Officer Bridges, was catching on. That's why he was paying attention to Marshall and mentioned it to Brigham that night at Coach Craig's house. He actually *was* concerned!

As you can guess, this is a pretty big deal.

We were on the front page of *The Tucker Times* and have caught the attention of the national media.

Turns out, news of a team of crime-solving teenagers is just the kind of scoop people like.

So, now you see why it's so important that we think of a name, right? Right?!

QUINN

Well, time to wrap it up.

How far should we go here?

For starters, Mister Happy—I mean, Mr. Grimes—isn't too happy these days. He's been charged in the death of Caroline Mae Henderson and now a laundry list of other serious Shawshank-sounding charges are in store for him and his Unicorn friends.

A few of those Unicorns, specifically our friends from the boiler room, were found at the high school later that morning, de-hydrated and delirious. Apparently, Winky Jeff had completely forgotten about his Underground prisoners. He did wind up res-cuing Princess Peach that night though.

Oh, and speaking of rescues, Coach Craig is okay! He was saved from the Hell House alongside the other poor basement dwellers. He's recovering too. We knew he'd turned the corner the other day when he mailed Marshall a package from rehab. It was a cardboard box containing nothing but his hall-pass toilet seat and an eloquent handwritten thank-you card saying: *Thanks for the rescue. You guys are #1. Now, think of me the next time you go #2 . . . Get it?!*

I know we're supposed to be covering only the crime-related stuff here. But just for the sake of closure, I feel like I should fill you in on the other stuff that's been happening since Hell Night too. I mean, we've been through a lot together, right?

First off, my relationship with my sister has never been better. Or closer. Or . . . weirder.

She's actively looking for other mysteries to solve and has even been hanging around the police station lately, looking for any-thing that might lead to the next case.

She also picked out a cross-stitch pattern of a vengeful-looking Batman beating up the Joker and asked me to stitch in "liberal amounts of blood wherever possible." I think she's doubling down on the crime-fighting vigilante vibe.

As for Marshall and me, well . . . a lady never tells.

Okay, I'll tell. We've been enjoying frequent nose-bleed-free make-out sessions. We're also planning on going on a date. An *actual* date that doesn't involve the threat of Unicorn violence!

"How do we do that exactly?" said Marshall.

I have no idea. But I guess we'll figure it out since we have a mini golf double date coming up this weekend. You heard right, I said mini golf!

I'll let Brigham fill you in on that.

BRIGHAM

I asked her out! Kind of!

Okay, maybe she asked me out more. Which I really didn't expect.

I was hobbling to study hall and Katherine stopped and asked if she could sign my cast. Of course, I said yes.

But instead of signing her name, she wrote her number with the following message:

Let's hang out sometime! Give me a call when you're free!

Next to it was a smiley face.

A *winky* smiley face, to be exact.

I don't know what came over me, but before she made it to the end of the hall I pulled out my phone and called her.

"I'm free," I said.

Too forward? Maybe. But she laughed. And, most importantly, she said yes.

I'm still pretty freaked out, but it's time to be bold, right? After all, I did come pretty close to death multiple times over the past week. Dating can't be any scarier than a drug trafficking gang, right?

Now I just need to figure out how to play mini golf on crutches.

That windmill is going to wreak havoc with my handicap.

And, oh, yeah, there's also Coach Craig.

Seems like he should get a say here, right?

CRAIG THE CONCUSSER

It's about time I get to say something here, right?

After all, I am the guy who cracked the case.

Because I'm awesome.

They also say I'm lucky.

They say Mister Happy doesn't waste bullets.

Well, he saved two specifically for my kneecaps. I'll spare you the details.

Nah, never mind. You need the details.

There was a lot of blood.

Tons of blood.

He pulled his gun out. A Glock. All business. And kind of boring. If I was a bad guy, I'd go with a Colt 45. Something big and flashy, like a cowboy. Anyway, he put it right on my knee and pulled the trigger. Then he did the same to my left. He probably would have done something even worse but one of his Unicorn bozos ran down the stairs and said something about Marshall and the kids hiding out at the high school.

Mister Happy was gone. I'd never seen a guy with so much butt move so fast.

Then it was just me and the junkies.

And a lot of blood from my kneecaps.

I don't remember much after that.

But I never talked. And I never would have. Because I protect my friends.

Because, like I said, I'm awesome.

And that's exactly why I'm now on the Tucker police force. Okay, right now I'm working the front desk while I recover and learn to stay upright for more than five minutes on my new plastic robot knees. But trust me, I'll have a badge and gun and an awesome-looking uniform in no time.

It's my dream job. And all I had to do was take a bullet for it. Twice.

Just call me Officer Coach Craig.

Reporting for duty.

MALCOLM

Look, I'd love to go on and on about our happy endings and our new careers, and everyone else's future dating plans. But first, we really need a name.

Then we need a website. Then we need a logo. Then we need business cards, a YouTube channel, an Instagram, and, yes, even a TikTok.

But before all that . . . we need a name!

So, I'm good with anything—anything really—as long as we can decide on something.

It's all about branding these days.

So c'mon, give me a brand!

QUINN

All right, all right, I think I've got it.

Ever since we helped solve the big case, we've attracted all kinds of attention.

Attention from reporters, from bloggers, from politicians, and even from the popular kids.

And it's weird.

All of a sudden we're supposed to be big-shot heroes.

But it doesn't feel like we are.

Malcolm, Brigham, Marshall, and myself. We're not the ones you'll usually find centerstage.

We have no superpowers. We have no fancy tech or real street fighting skills. (Don't tell Brigham I said that.)

We have to scrap and plan and plot for every advantage. That is our weakness, but it's also our greatest strength.

We are not the heroes here.

We are the sidekicks.

And we're good with that.

So that's it.

We are **The Sidekicks**.

High school detectives at your service.

And this is our origin story.

MALCOLM

Though, just in case that name doesn't stick, there's always **The Lansburys**.

THE END

Epilogue

(Police narratives can have epilogues, right?)

Marshall

The Nightmare is gone now.

It's been replaced by something much different.

I'm back in C-Wing. Because I always am.

And it's bustling. I know everyone there and it's bright and colorful and everybody's happy.

Tribal Ted is somehow barbecuing next to Sam Hammond's locker. Coach Craig is chatting it up with Bad Cop. Sloan is hanging out alongside Brigham and Malcolm. Winky Jeff is talking with Principal Chang and Martin.

Then I see him. Out in the crowd, Unicorn Man is back.

Everybody freezes.

Time slows down.

He does his usual thing. He puts his head down and charges.

But this time, he doesn't get far.

One by one, my friends and my family step in front of him.

Together, they form a wall around me.

Banding together to protect me.

Unicorn Man charges directly at my mom.

I want to yell, to warn her, but before I can she blasts some kind of rainbow-colored laser rays from the palms of her hands.

Unicorn Man charges directly into the light and begins to shrink until he's pretty much the size of a gerbil. By the time he reaches my mom, he's tiny.

"Aw, cute fella," says Malcolm with a grin, who's now suddenly back in his chicken suit.

My mom picks up the tiny Unicorn Man, turns around, and presents him to me. But he's the Unicorn Man no more. Now, he's

Moonstone Rainbow, her favorite rainbow-haired *My Little Pony* from when she was a kid. She gives me a wink. Then I turn and find Quinn. She's smiling and wearing that yellow sundress.

She grabs my hand and leads me out of C-wing, into B-Wing, through the main hallways, and up to the big double doors at the front of the building. The sun is shining brightly through the glass windows.

We push through the doors and, finally, we're outside.

I'm outside, in the light.

I look at her. She looks at me.

And she smiles.

Where do we go from there?

I don't know.

I always wake up.

I guess we'll just have to find out.

Acknowledgments

I would like to thank everyone for helping me write this book. Yes. Everyone.

Is that too general? It probably is, but it feels right. So many people have supported and encouraged and helped me along the way, that I'm afraid I'll leave them out.

More specifically I want to thank my wife (the love of my life who I have a crush on), my kids, my mom, my dad, my sisters, my brothers-in-law, my family, my friends, my Nugget coworkers, Nugget readers, God, and then, last but not least . . . everyone.

About the Author

Matt J. Aiken lives in Dahlonega, Georgia, with his wife Katie, kids Bowen and Theo, canine best friend Dobby, and feline acquaintances KittyBoo and Sirius. There, he works as the executive editor of *The Dahlonega Nugget* which has won multiple Georgia Press Association awards, for which he likes to take partial credit. Matt wrote most of *School of Sleuths* in his basement while using a Crazy Board to plan out all the major plot points. He thinks Malcolm would be proud.

OTHER BOOKS BY MATT AIKEN

Words to Read By: Random Ramblings of a Roving Reporter